'A novel that truly stands apart for its originality and relevance… a book about words, about language, about their power to civilise – and, in the wrong hands, to abuse and dehumanise.' – *The Irish Times*

'*The Wordsmith* is warm, original, thought-provoking, but most of all a tremendous page-turner.' – School Library Association

'There is a welter of post-apocalyptic novels out there, but *The Wordsmith* stands out for its imaginative approach and its beautiful and careful use of language.' – *The Literary Review*

'This book targets the dangers of global warming and the power of communication, love and expression. Without these words that we have, our lives would be unimaginably different.' – *The Guardian*

'With a strong cast of characters and an excellent premise this book is compelling reading. It is a salutary story, a powerful story that I highly recommend and thoroughly enjoyed.' – *Armadillo Magazine*

'An exciting adventure… a fascinating read.' – *Books for Keeps*

'In a carefully crafted and evocative story, Forde has created a world yet to come that is powerful, mesmerising and chilling.'– Mary Esther Judy, children's bookseller and reviewer

'An electric sci-fi novel with a strong ecological and moral stance.' – *The Bulletin of the Center for Children's Books*

'[A] gripping postapocalyptic thriller… it is a well-crafted page-turner, as well as a compelling commentary on censorship and the role of language, while also inviting discussion about what distinguishes humans from animals. For dystopian fiction aficionados, this well-paced entry offers plenty of food for thought.' – *School Library Journal*

'A beautifully written tale illustrating the importance of language and creativity and the power they have to change lives. With a detailed narrative and clever plot, you are instantly drawn into the post-apocalyptic world of Ark.' – *The Book Activist*

THE
WORDSMITH

PATRICIA FORDE

THE WORDSMITH

First published in 2015 by
Little Island Books
7 Kenilworth Park
Dublin 6W, Ireland

This edition published 2018

ISBN: 9781912417124

A British Library Cataloguing in Publication record for this book is available from
the British Library

Cover illustration by Sarah J Coleman
Frontispiece illustration by Steve Simpson
Insides designed and typeset by Oldtown

Printed in Poland by Drukarnia Skleniarz

Little Island receives financial assistance from the Arts Council/An Chomhairle
Ealaíon and the Arts Council of Northern Ireland

The author wishes to give special thanks to The Tyrone Guthrie Centre in
Annaghmakerrig.

10 9 8 7 6 5 4 3 2 1

In memory of my father, Tommy Forde

About the author

PATRICIA FORDE is from Galway, on the west coast of Ireland. She has previously written picture books and early readers in both Irish and English. She has also written television drama for children and young people as well as three plays. In another life she was a primary school teacher and director of Galway Arts Festival. This is her first novel.

PROLOGUE

SMITH FEARFALL was a scavenger. This beach was his territory.

He watched the canister as it danced, nibbling the waves, teasing him. He waited. He was good at waiting. Finally his quarry came within reach. He waded out. The plastic that covered his trousers snapped and cracked in the gale. The canister moved away from him. He waited, eyes on his prey, his mind fully focused.

Once more the silver glint of the metal cylinder cut through the salty water. Smith reached out and felt the hard metal beneath his fingers. The canister slipped from his grasp. He lunged and caught it once more. He wrapped both hands around it and cradled it to his body.

Back on the beach, he examined it, the sharp sand stinging his eyes. He noted the red star and the string of letters: N-I-C-E-N-E, but they meant nothing to him. He shoved the canister into his hemp bag along with the other treasures he had found that morning.

Beyond him, over the vast stretch of turbulent grey water, a gull screamed. Smith stopped and looked out to the horizon. He shivered. Then, pulling his coat closer to his bones, turned and headed for home.

CHAPTER 1

L ETTA, the wordsmith's apprentice, buried her face in her hands, exhausted. Her forehead ached and her eyes felt dry and dusty. She had transcribed hundreds of words since early morning, each one written in her own distinctive cursive style. This was their busiest time of year, the time of change. It was now that the masters took on apprentices, teachers took on new pupils and people got ready for the long winter.

She reached for another card and began to write.

Search: To explore, to look for. An investigation seeking answers

She stopped for a second, resting her pen on the edge of the table. The evening light threw shadows on the walls and added to her anxiety. She had to do something. She couldn't sit here waiting for Benjamin to tell her why a gavver had seen fit to visit them. She got up and walked to the living area, stopping outside Benjamin's study. There she hesitated. The voices from the inner room rose and fell, words slipping and sliding between the two men. Letta turned to the small round table and, with great care, filled the cups that stood waiting on the metal tray. Two cups. The boiling water released the earthy smell of burdock, its pungent depths filling the room, deep and clay-like. She picked up the tray and moved to the door. Should she go in? Through the slit in the battened door, she could just see the heavy drapes covering the window, the old green armchair standing on its three legs, the fourth corner supported by a block of timber. Beneath it, the white marble floor, smooth and cold.

She took a deep breath and shifted the tray to her left hand. With the knuckle of her index finger she tapped a dull tattoo on the door. The cups lurched. Inside, she could hear her master's voice.

'But sir,' he said. 'Five hundred words? It not … not … human.'

The gavver's answer came swiftly. 'List seven hundred words now,' he said. 'Too many. Why make work for self?'

'But … but …'

Letta flinched at the despair in her master's voice.

The gavver laughed. 'Ark need less words,' he said. 'Words no good. Words bring trouble.'

Letta stood frozen, her hand still raised, the hated beat of the gavver's speech affronting her ears. The door opened, swinging towards her. Letta jumped. The tray wobbled. The gavver stood there, his tonsured head shining as though a yellow light glistened beneath the skin. With one hand he took the tray from her. He placed his other hand on Letta's shoulder.

'No harm,' he said, his sloe-eyed stare transfixing her. 'What this?'

'Tea,' Letta said, her heart pounding. Later, she couldn't remember why she spoke, only that a feeling like a wave had subsumed her. 'Burdock tea,' she said, spitting the words at him.

The face came closer until she could feel his breath on her cheek. 'Tea,' he corrected her, his voice little more than a whisper. 'Tea. No *burdock* tea. *Burdock* not List word.'

Without taking his eyes from her face, he dropped the tray, letting it clatter to the floor. The crash echoed through the old house. Letta could feel the boiling liquid splash her bare ankle. She bit her tongue to stop herself from crying out. The gavver stepped over the tray and the cups and the puddle of tea as though nothing had happened.

At the door, he turned. 'Five hundred, wordsmith. Prepare List.'

And then he was gone. For a moment, Letta and her master stood in silence, both caught in the spell the other man had cast.

Benjamin turned to her. 'Letta,' he said, and she could see the hurt in his eyes, 'no make trouble. Not good. Fail.'

'Don't speak List to me,' she said, suddenly furious. 'We are wordsmiths. We can speak as we wish.'

'Perhaps,' Benjamin said, his eyes darting to the door, making sure they were alone. 'But we must remember that it is a privilege, child.'

Letta could feel the frustration bubbling up in her. She shook her head.

'We are the fortunate ones, Letta, the last people left on this planet.'

Letta shrugged, not able to speak.

'Five hundred words,' Benjamin said, his voice quiet. 'I must prepare a new List.'

'But master…' Letta could not keep the protest out of her voice.

Five hundred words? Could they survive on that?

'John Noa knows what he is doing,' Benjamin said. 'He always knows. You'll see.' He reached out and touched her hand, the skin on his fingers parched and cool.

'I'll clean up the mess,' she said and watched him lumber back towards the open door of his sanctuary.

She found the twig in a shadowy corner of the hall and removed the broken crockery. Through the open window, she could hear the wind moaning, and somewhere not too far away, a wolf howled as if in answer. She walked across the room and pulled the window closed, pausing for a second to look out at the bleached, wet landscape.

Across the way, the houses teetered on the side of the hill, leaning on one another for support. Small identical boxes, lime-washed, with their communal living room, two bedrooms and a toilet, all built before the Melting. In the windows, slices of faint yellow light squinted back at her, flickering giddily, as if afraid that the windmills that fed them could desert them at any minute. Further up the hill, the queue was already forming at Central Kitchen. Reluctantly, she pulled herself away from the scene outside and headed back to her work.

Through the door leading into the shop, she could see her table. The cardboard boxes nestled one inside the other, the mound of four-inch-square cards, cut the previous night, the wooden handle of her pen honed and polished until it felt smooth as glass. Beside it, the pot of ink glinted in the shadowy afternoon light. Her heart was still loud in her ears but the gavver was gone. Now, there was only herself and her words again. She moved quickly across the floor, pulled out her chair and settled down to work. She reached out and picked up a blank card.

She needed to assemble twenty List boxes for Mrs Truckle, the schoolteacher. The old lady's voice still rang in her ears from her own school days. 'Sit up straight, girl. Don't dig the paper.'

The words danced in front of her eyes just as they had when she'd been a small child. She remembered lying in bed with all the words she'd learnt in school flying about her head, fireflies from some magical place, red electric fireflies.

Sometimes, soon, sound.

All List words, of course. She hadn't known anything else then.

She turned the card over and placed it on her writing mat. The feel of the thin card calmed the turmoil inside her. She picked up her pen and dipped it in the ink, lifting it carefully lest the red dye invade the card before she could control it. She steadied her hand and pressed the nib to the vanilla-coloured paper. Slowly, the rhythm of writing and ordering the cards worked its magic, and she forgot about everything else.

School would resume in ten days and, according to John Noa's instruction, each child would be supplied with a copy of the List, five hundred words, one word per card, one box per child. Upstairs, her master muttered to himself and stamped his feet on the old weathered boards to keep warm.

He was always cold now, Letta thought. Distracted, she looked up and surveyed the familiar surroundings of the shop.

The building groaned with the weight of its years. It was unusually big in comparison to the normal houses in Ark. The large downstairs room was the shop where Benjamin conducted business and where Letta's desk stood, tucked away in the upper corner. Behind the shop was their living room and off that again Benjamin's study. Within the study was another door leading to the library. There were little nooks everywhere, small spaces hiding behind bigger ones, alcoves and cellars, sprawling over a large area. Upstairs there were three more rooms.

The house had been built in another time, when people thought nothing of wasting large pieces of glass in windows and lighting real fires indoors, not for heat but for comfort. Here, in the shop, an old fireplace stood against the outer wall with a thick black beam above it. The fireplace itself was packed with word boxes and the shelf held a bizarre array of ink pots and short sticks ready to be turned into pens, along with bits and pieces Benjamin brought back from his trips.

Outside, the walls were clad with sheets of tin, reflecting the sunlight and the faces of the people who entered. Inside, behind a counter made of solid oak, from trees from another time, Letta could see row upon row of shelves, honeycombed with cubbyholes. The cubbyholes cradled the vanilla-coloured, four-inch square cards, and the cards held the precious words. Round about her were the many relics of another world, such as the big glass eye of the holographic dome, in which Letta could see her own reflection, with her sharp green eyes and shock of red hair, looking back at her.

She sighed and went back to her work, moving on to the words that were to be taken out of circulation. Those words were stored here in the shop. From time to time, Benjamin took boxes of words to Noa's house, where Letta supposed they were held out of harm's way. She flicked through the cards in the box nearest to her.

Dream, Hope, Love, Faith

She pulled a card at random and read it. Silently first, then out loud. 'Dream, Dream.'

She didn't hear the old man come in again and jumped when he spoke.

'*Dream*: *A cherished desire*,' he said. 'Now where did I leave my bag?'

'It's here, master,' Letta said, handing the heavy leather satchel to him, not sure whether he was annoyed with her.

'I seem to lose things a lot more than I used to,' her master said, taking the box and peering at a piece of paper he held in his hands.

Letta looked at him and noticed the deep shadows under the red-veined eyes, the yellow shrivelled skin that clung to the sharp bones of his face and the chalk-white hair that he brushed across his brow.

'The new list will be ready before dark tonight.'

He didn't look at her. Five hundred words. A major edit on the orders she had already filled.

'Was there anything in the drop box today?' the old man asked her.

'Just one word,' she said, handing him a card. '*Ant*. I met the boy who dropped it off. He found this piece of paper in an old box, but he didn't know the word.'

'Ant,' Benjamin said softly. 'How quickly people forget! When I was a boy such words were commonplace but now...'

'Now they're all just insects.' Letta finished the thought for him.

He shook his head. 'There is something I need to tell you,' he said.

Letta waited, biting her lip. 'Yes, master?' she said.

'I have to go away sooner than I thought. I'm afraid I must leave at first light.'

Letta nodded. 'How long will you be away?'

The old man rubbed his hand through his hair. 'I'll be back as soon as I can,' he said. 'You keep the shop open. Take in the words and sort them. Distribute words to those who need them. Do you think you can do that, child?'

'Yes, master,' she said. 'I can do that.'

'Mrs Truckle will help you when she can. Just remember to keep your head down. Speak List. Don't draw attention to yourself.'

Letta sighed. She wasn't sure she wanted her old teacher helping her. Her master's words cut across her thoughts.

'There is a lot of unrest out there,' he said.

'Outside Ark?' Letta pressed him, fascinated and terrified all at once.

The old man shrugged. 'Maybe even inside Ark,' he said.

Benjamin turned away from her and very slowly started to climb the stairs. Not for the first time, she gave thanks that she had a home here in Ark. After the Melting so many people found themselves cast adrift, lost in a dangerous wilderness with no-one to help them, but her parents had been followers of Noa. They had come to Ark before the last days, and she had been born here. Benjamin was right when he said she was privileged. There were many who had not been so lucky.

Letta pushed her thoughts to one side and set about packing a bag for her master. She went into the living area and headed straight for the water bottles. They had still a few days' worth of water there so she took three bottles and put them carefully into the old bag. She held back only one small bottle for herself. She was sure Werber would give her more if she really needed it, but Benjamin might not come on clean water for days. His food he would collect from Central Kitchen. Mary Pepper wouldn't be happy about it, but it was another privilege of

18

the wordsmith. He had a duty to travel outside Ark in search of words and therefore the right to bring food with him.

She moved swiftly to the old cupboard that stood by the wall and pulled open a drawer. There were all his scraping and cutting tools. She picked them up and was about to deposit them in the bag when she paused. She took the little knife he used with its simple wooden handle and sharp curved blade. She closed her eyes, feeling its weight in her hand. She tried to imagine herself out in the field. Hauling some long-forgotten artefact from the loose soil. A box. Yes. A box that had once held exotic food. She would carefully clean away the mud and silt and there underneath she would find the label. Torn perhaps, but still readable. The words just sitting there, black on white. She would peel the label off with the knife and put it between two sheets of clean paper. And then, she would see what it was that she had discovered. A new word. A word long forgotten. Something from the other time, the time before the disasters. She wouldn't know what it meant at first, but she would deduce its meaning from the context, or ask an elderly person who would remember it from their youth. She sighed to herself.

She needed a walk, she thought, stretching her aching back. Fresh air, a snatched break before the night's work began in earnest. Her master didn't like her going too far from the shop but she had to have air. She pulled on her coat, the raw cotton coarse against her skin. Benjamin had clad the coat with plastic he had found on one of his trips so that it almost kept the rain out.

The street was little more than a mud track, churned up by the passing boots of the field workers as they hurried home. She pressed on, out towards the fields, moving against the flow of traffic. A man hauling pelts passed by, his eyes cast down. Behind him a cart laden with water barrels trundled by on its way to the water tower. A group of children, freed from the harvest fields, ran past her, shouting and whooping, their tally sticks beating against their chests. She sighed. Did they know that they had just lost two hundred words? Words they would never know or soon forget?

She would walk as far as the first potato fields, she told herself, and then turn back. She would still have time to pick up their evening meal from Central Kitchen. A Monday meal. Vegetable soup, parsnip cakes and green beans. She hated parsnips.

Soon, the hustle of the village was behind her and she found herself on the outskirts of the farmland. The path climbed up between the big green fields, growing steeper all the time. Letta could feel the pull at the backs of her legs. *Not enough exercise*, she thought. Her chest hurt as the path grew steeper and she tried to distract herself by looking over the great hedges to where the rows of potatoes lay. As she finally crested the hill, she stopped to get her breath. She turned and looked back at the great landscape laid bare in front of her, where curving fields scalloped the murky skies. Water lay in the lower ones after the heavy rain of the last few days. Below her, the forest glowered in the evening light, surrounding the town with its secrets and its plots, casting dark shadows on their lives. To her left, the small meadow, triangular in shape, like a wedge cut out of a pie, where a gavver had been found dead last spring. She shivered and pulled her coat closer to her body. To her right, a gap in the hedge revealed the path that led to the shoreline.

Purposefully, Letta turned and set off through the mud and the puddles. Within minutes, she could smell the salty perfume of the sea and hear the water pounding on the shore.

She remembered how afraid she had been of it as a child. How she would wake screaming in the middle of the night convinced that it was coming to swallow them up. It was always the same dream, always the same fear. Finally, Benjamin had taken her to the shore.

The path beneath her feet mutated and became more beach than field. She was sure that this was the way she had come that day with her master. Down this incline and straight on to the beach. She had cowered behind Benjamin, afraid to look up. She could smell it, though, and hear it: *Bang, swiiish, bang, swiiish.*

'Look!' Benjamin said. 'See! The tide is going out. It cannot hurt you.'

She had looked up and, holding his hand, had walked down until she was only yards from the water.

'Look!' he'd said again. 'See that line. See those rocks. Each year the sea gives back a little of what it took.'

She looked at it now. Its muddy green water suckling the earth, sucking its life force with it. Ghosts lingered in this place, the ghosts of all who had been overtaken by the sea, grey wispy ghosts who sighed on dark winter's evenings and faded a little in the light of summer. Letta could feel their presence brooding in the background as she tried to imagine the awfulness of it. The towering wall of water bearing down, the screams, the vain attempts to flee. The victims of the Melting. How strange it must have seemed to see that usually docile body of water suddenly rear up against them, swallowing houses, villages, towns and cities. Cities once brimming with life; structured, ordered days; possessions; families – all gone. Drowned in the salty beast. Letta shivered. The wind had turned and was blowing from the north. She watched as the grey wisps of ghosts were caught in its breath and pushed across the sky until they blended with the steely clouds.

She missed her parents, missed them with a terrible longing, and in that instant she could feel their presence. She closed her eyes and let the feeling flow through her until it lost its force, leaving her alone and shivering at the edge of the tide.

She looked to the far horizon. Then she raised one finger and saluted them, as she always did, just in case they were out there and could see her and would know that she hadn't forgotten them. The far horizon where they now lingered, if not in body, then at least in spirit.

CHAPTER 2

#151

Danger

Harm or hurt can happen

LEFT ALONE, Letta immersed herself in work. As well as transcribing words, she served their regular customers, the crafters and apprentices who needed specialist words that were not on the List.

And with only Letta to transcribe the words, the days were exhausting, though uneventful. The nights were long and dark and lonely.

She made up three new boxes of words, which had been ordered by a carpenter for his three apprentices. The boys came to collect the words themselves. They were giddy, their eyes bright with mischief, twelve years old and just finished school. *Anyone would think they been apprenticed to the Green Warriors,* Letta thought wryly. She had given them *saw* and *hammer* and *nails* and *tacks*, and nicer ones like *plane* and *chisel*. Twenty-five words in all, in addition to the five hundred on the main List. They'd seemed happy.

'We ready now,' the younger one had said, smiling.

She recognised him as one of the healer's boys. Daniel. Or was it Crann? No. Definitely Daniel. She'd heard about him.

She glanced at his tally stick. It had at least fifteen notches. Fifteen breaches of the language law.

Letta had handed him his box, making a silent wish that he would change his ways now that he was an apprentice.

After the boys left, she had prepared two boxes of words detailing thirty types of fruit that were to be removed. *Pineapple* had been a new word to her. List had only those fruits available in Ark: apples, strawberries, raspberries and blackberries. There were no pineapples.

Letta was about to close the shop when she heard the old wooden door rattle open.

In front of her stood a boy of her own age, but thin, the bones in his face so clear it looked as though they had been drawn there. He looked up, and Letta could see the previously hidden bright blue-grey eyes.

'No harm!' Letta greeted him, tentatively.

He looked about him, nervously. 'I need words,' he said.

'Yes,' said Letta. 'What words?'

'List words. A box of List words,' the boy replied, his right hand pressed to the left side of his chest, his eyes darting from the front door back to her face.

Letta listened, entranced. His voice was rich and fluid, not rusty like most of their customers'. He was speaking List but not in the usual way. *A* box, he'd said. Perfectly legal, but most people didn't bother with the article. Her heart quickened.

'Why?' she began. 'Why need … why you need?'

The boy frowned. 'Fail,' he said. 'Need words. No question.'

Letta took a step back and scrutinised him. He seemed nervous, his feet moving restlessly, eyes never still.

'I wait my master come,' she said, speaking carefully, only using List words. The boy's eyes clouded over.

24

'No!' The boy took a step back, looking at the door behind him again, as if expecting someone. 'I no wait. I hear you be wordsmith.'

Letta flinched, his words stinging like nettles.

'I wordsmith,' she said. 'That...that...' She could feel herself getting flustered. She tried again. 'I wordsmith apprentice, but he no here, so I wordsmith for now.'

The boy raised one eyebrow, his blue-grey eyes now studying her face. His body relaxed. 'You help me or no?' he said, with the hint of a smile.

Letta knew he was challenging her. She pulled herself up to her full height. 'Yes,' she said. 'I help.'

She turned to retrieve a box from the pigeon-hole behind her. As soon as she did, she remembered that she had given the last one to the tanner's wife earlier that day.

'Words no here. I get,' she said, cursing her own carelessness. She had meant to replenish the pigeon-holes earlier but it had slipped her mind. Now she would have to leave this strange boy alone while she went to the master's study. She could feel his eyes on her as she retreated from the shop.

In the study, she grabbed the keys from the nail and quickly inserted the smallest one in the library door. The key glided through the mechanism with a tiny metallic click. The heavy door fell open and Letta caught her breath as she always did when confronted with the master's secret library. Here were the words he kept in isolation, the words forever removed from everyday use. Shelf after shelf, from floor to ceiling, packed with boxes, the boxes packed with words that would survive, even if they could never be used in Letta's lifetime.

Nothing wasted, nothing lost. John Noa's mantra, Benjamin's mantra. *Nothing wasted, nothing lost.* If the day came that man ever needed language again, Ark would be ready.

Letta shivered. The room smelt of paper and age and a touch of mustiness. Within it lay the precious source material, the fruits of the master's many word-finding trips, where he searched painstakingly for any last remaining relic of the written word. Box upon box of tiny bits of language, waiting to be sorted, transcribed and filed. On one wall a tattered banner hung from a nail, its words faded and worn: *In the Beginning was the Word.*

Most people could read a little, but rarely saw the written word, apart from the odd poster with information from John Noa, or their little box of words from school. The sea had swallowed the written word after the Melting. The very thought caused a shiver to ripple through her. For a second, she doubted the wisdom of what she was doing. Would her master have given words to this stranger? She hesitated. What harm could it do? He was entitled to the List. Though why had he not been given the List by his master?

She picked up one of the boxes from the desk and headed back to her customer. As she passed the orderly rows of shelves, her elbow touched a box that had not been properly replaced. It tumbled from its perch and landed at her feet. She jumped as the box fell and an avalanche of cards hit the floor. She bent down and picked up the box. On the front written in her own steady hand a word looked back at her: *Colours.* She hastily stuffed the cards back into it. She would take it up to the shop and sort it later, but for now her customer was waiting.

She hurried through the door to where she could see the counter. At first she thought the boy had left, and then she saw him, or at least she saw his hand on the cold marble floor. His hand, and then his arm, and then his chest, and the crater the bullet had left, and the thick red soupy blood, and then she heard the high-pitched scream of a young girl. It took her a full five seconds to realise that it was she, Letta, who was screaming. Screaming, even as the precious box of words fell from her hands and the cards fluttered to the floor: *crimson, sienna, indigo, cobalt, ochre* and *gunmetal blue*.

Letta was about to run onto the street when she saw his hand move. He was alive. She knelt on the cold floor and put her shaking hand to the boy's throat. His skin felt warm and smelt of wild sage. He moaned.

Letta jumped back in fright. 'Quiet now,' she said, her voice trembling. 'I get help.'

She started to rise but his fingers grasped her hand. He tried to lift his head.

'No,' he said. 'Must hide. They will find me.'

'Who? Who will find you?'

The sound of a siren suddenly rent the air. Gavvers. Letta jumped up and, yanking down the cloth that covered the shop door, she slammed home the great bolts. Then she went back to the boy.

'Can you get up?' she said, abandoning all efforts to speak List.

He groaned as he bent his knees and tried to transfer his weight to his hands. Letta grabbed him, pulling him up and almost knocking herself over in the process.

'Put your arm around my neck,' she said, her breath rasping. The blood from his wound dripped onto the floor – scarlet in the beam of light that fell from the window overhead. Letta put her hands under his arms and half-dragged, half-carried him up the stairs, down the long corridor at the top of the house. At one point he stumbled and fell against the old wood-panelled wall. The wall gave, revealing an ancient hidden space where Letta had played as a child. It was known as the Monk's Room, though no-one knew why. For a second, the boy lay on the floor looking up at her, then turned towards the hidden space.

'No further. Leave me … here.'

His words were sticky, she thought, as though adhering to his lips.

'No!' Letta said, and with another heave, she got him to his feet and pulled him the last few strides, to where her own small room stood. There, she let him fall onto her bed. He groaned, a sound like air leaving a tired balloon, and lost consciousness.

The room was small, with only her bed, a chair and the old cupboard that Benjamin had made for her, leaning against the wall. She pulled the chair to the side of the bed.

It was then she heard the banging on the door. She looked from the boy to the door. The banging continued, louder and more aggressive. Letta could hear her own heart almost as loud, hammering in her ears.

A moment later she drew back the heavy bolts on the front door and found herself looking into the face of a gavver. Letta took in the dull grey uniform of John Noa's law enforcers before her eyes travelled to the face above it. The face had few if any saving graces. A bulbous nose spread across it, and above that, two small hooded eyes. His mouth was a thin wrinkle, no lips, just a fold of yellowing skin. Letta inclined her head and listened to his raspy voice.

'Wordsmith here?' he asked, his eyes fastening first on her face, then taking in the blood on the floor, the cards scattered on the white marble.

There was an air of aggression about him that frightened her. She shook her head. 'Master on word-finding –' Too late she remembered there was no list word for trip or journey. She hesitated. 'He away word finding,' she said, the clumsy words thick in her mouth. 'He no back for short time.'

She waited for his response. He took his time formulating his next question.

'Where boy?'

Letta frowned. 'No understand?' she said, creasing her brow into a puzzled mask.

The gavver snarled, pointing at the blood on the floor. 'Boy! Where he go?'

'Run away. I don't know,' Letta said.

The gavver's hand shot out and slapped her across the mouth. Letta tasted the dull, metallic blood on her tongue just before he grabbed the collar of her shirt and pulled her close. 'Where boy?'

She struggled to answer. Struggled even to breathe. 'I…I don't know. I tell you. I don't know.'

His grip tightened. Letta's eyes bulged in their cavities even as little black dots started to dance in front of them. Just then, the door burst open, and a second gavver stood there, red in the face and panting loudly.

'Carver! Come!' he said. 'Down lane! He hurt, but able run!'

Carver swung round, releasing Letta reluctantly, and started for the door.

'That way!' his colleague shouted.

As soon as Carver left, the second man turned to Letta and, with a barely perceptible nod to the stunned girl, he was gone.

Letta released a long slow breath, putting her hand to her bruised throat, feeling her lip thicken and swell. Then she

29

slammed the bolts home for the second time and stood, her knees weak, her head spinning. She looked down at the congealing blood on the floor and the word cards lying helplessly beside it. Once more the siren screamed outside. But this time Letta felt it was screaming at her, and it was only a matter of time before they would return for their quarry. Her eyes went to the door behind the counter and the boy she knew waited for her at the top of the stairs.

Letta took away the cloth that covered his wound, her fingers moving gently, her eyes darting from the bandage to her patient's face, worried lest she hurt him. It was healing already, the wound drying out and crusting over. As she watched him, his eyelids flickered, and slowly the eyes opened.

'It all right,' Letta said quickly. 'You safe.'

He tried to sit up, then fell back against the pillow, his face white and drained.

'Easy,' Letta said. 'Rest.'

'You wordsmith.' His voice was ragged, his breathing shallow.

'Yes,' Letta said. 'Wordsmith. Letta. What your name?'

'Marlo,' he said and closed his eyes again.

'Marlo,' Letta repeated softly. 'Marlo.'

She let him sleep then. She had closed the shop and brought her work upstairs with her so that she could fill the school boxes for Mrs Truckle, but she found it difficult to concentrate. The night had fallen quickly and outside rain lashed the street and beat on the window.

She shivered. What had she done? She had no idea who the strange boy was. He wore a tally stick, but, when she examined it, there was something not quite right about it. Normal tally sticks had a mark burnt on the base. The mark was an individual one, no two the same. This tally stick had no such mark. It was illegal to interfere with the tally stick. She looked at it again. It had three notches on it, showing he had broken the language law three times. Twenty breaches meant expulsion from Ark. There were other things too. When she had removed his shirt she found old scars on his back. Large black shadows where the skin bloomed, black as night. She had heard of the Black Angel. Hurts and heals at the same time. She had asked the master about it once but he had brushed her questions aside.

'Not something you need to worry about,' he'd said. 'Do your work. Keep your head down and the law will have no truck with you.'

Yet she couldn't erase from her memory the face of the gavver who had slapped her. Instinctively, she put her hand to her swollen lip. He had treated her like a criminal. Criminals had always been shadowy creatures to her, people bent on the destruction of the new world; bandits who roamed the forest; or the surly inhabitants of Tintown. Yet here she was, harbouring someone who could be a felon, maybe even a Desecrator. She pushed that thought away, but the question still nagged her. Who was he? She picked up a card and started to write.

Plough: Break and turn over earth

He was no farm boy, she was sure of that. His hands were clean and soft. A healer? Perhaps. She looked at him again. A sheen of sweat glistened on his forehead. He moved his head restlessly.

'Finn!'

Letta went to him.

'Shh,' she said. 'Relax.'

'Finn!' he cried out again. His eyes shot open, bright with fever.

Letta stepped back.

'Don't tell them about the pump house,' he said. 'Don't tell anyone. North of the river. We mustn't betray them. The gavvers…'

He started to climb out of bed. Letta moved quickly.

'No, Marlo,' she said firmly. 'Lie down. No gavvers. Rest now.'

She pushed him back onto his pillow and was relieved when he closed his eyes again. It was the fever, of course. She knew that, but it still frightened her. And he was speaking the old tongue, not List, throwing words about in an easy, fluid way, not thinking about where to find them, confident that they would come.

Betray, he'd said. It was such a rare word. She had only recently learned it herself. *Deliver to an enemy by treachery.*

Who was he? Excitement filled her body, little bubbles bursting in her brain. A wordsmith? Was it possible? But Benjamin was the last wordsmith. That is what they had always believed.

Over the course of the night, Marlo grew stronger. He still muttered in his sleep about Finn and the pump house. He mentioned other names too, Carmina and George, but he was growing calmer. Letta bathed his head with cool water just as the first rays of the morning sun peeped through the window. She pushed the long strands of red hair out of her eyes and wondered what her master would think. The boy opened his eyes. She noticed how beautiful they were, blue with flecks of grey, like the sea on a calm day. She smiled.

'What you thinking?' Marlo asked.

Letta hesitated, then decided to tell him part of the truth. 'I was wondering what my master would think if he saw you here. That's all.'

Marlo frowned.

'No speak List?' he said, and she could see the watchfulness in him.

'I know you speak the old tongue,' she said. 'You've been talking in your sleep.'

'Oh,' he said, looking sheepish. 'Did I say anything interesting?'

'No,' Letta said. 'Mostly nonsense. But, tell me, where did you learn to speak like that?'

She waited. He said nothing. Then she asked him the question that had been buzzing in her head during her long vigil. 'Are you a wordsmith?'

Marlo laughed. 'No,' he said. 'Lol! I am not a wordsmith. The people who reared me – many of them have good language. That's all.'

She stopped, taken aback. 'Lol?'

'Sorry,' he said. 'It means "laugh out loud". L.O.L. See? My uncle Finn taught it to me. It's an ancient expression that was handed down through his family.'

'Laugh out loud,' Letta said, mentally promising to write it down as soon as she could. 'Isn't it funny that they said it instead of doing it! I wonder did they say "cry bitterly" when they were sad?'

She took up her twig and began to sweep the worn wooden boards.

'They probably hadn't time,' Marlo said. 'They'd just have said CB.'

'Lol,' Letta retorted, and they both laughed.

He sobered first.

'So what would your master have done with me?' he asked.

'I don't think he would have allowed you to die on the shop floor,' Letta answered. 'You might have bled on the words.'

He smiled.

'Feeling better?' Letta said.

Marlo reached out his hand and pulled her towards him. She felt his finger on her lip.

'What happened to you?' he said, looking at her, his head on one side, a frown tightening his forehead.

Letta was caught off guard by the sudden question. 'Nothing,' she said, pulling away from him. 'Just a small accident. Nothing important.'

He lay back on the pillow again and she saw a cloud descend on his eyes.

'I had a dream last night,' he said. 'I dreamt I was a hare, a small brown hare, and when I looked up, I saw eyes in the undergrowth, red eyes, watching me.'

'It was just a dream,' Letta said. 'It may be the fever.'

Marlo shook his head. 'There's always truth in dreams. Don't you know that? We have to learn what they mean, that's all.' He paused for a second.

Letta waited, fascinated. He knew the word *dream*. An abstract.

'Do you dream, Letta?' he asked so softly that she had to lean in to hear him.

'Dream?' she said. 'Sometimes I dream of words. Especially if I've been working hard.'

'What words do you dream of?' he asked.

Letta shrugged, suddenly self-conscious. 'I don't remember,' she said, though she did. She had always dreamt of words. Beautiful words, haunting words and, last night, terrifying words.

He lay down and a few minutes later Letta heard the now familiar sound of his breathing as sleep once more overtook him. She rubbed a hand across her eyes.

In the shop, their stock of regular words was running low. Mrs Truckle had already called twice. Letta would need to stay up all night just to fill the orders she had.

Even so, she couldn't resist sitting on the small armchair beside his bed and watching him. His face, so well formed, like something that had been sculpted out of a piece of rock. The curly black hair, damp with perspiration, the long lashes lying casually on the sallow skin and the smell, always the faint smell of sage. She breathed it in and resisted the impulse to trace the shape of his face with her finger. She had never seen anyone so exotic. She ached to know what his story was. What was the pump house he talked about? Who were his friends? She longed to talk to him, to know everything he knew. Why were the gavvers chasing him? Was he a criminal? A thief? A murderer? He didn't look like one, she thought, but then what did thieves and murderers look like? Benjamin had met plenty of both in the early days, after the Melting. Gangs who roamed the earth, killing for food, killing for shelter, killing for the sake of it. Remnants of them still lived deep in the forest and were a constant threat to Ark.

She should never have taken him in, she knew that. She had brought danger right to their door. But there was something about him, a spark of energy like she'd never encountered before.

Excitement.

She got up and, with one last look at his sleeping face, left the room, pulling the door behind her.

CHAPTER 3

Food

#189

What we eat

IT WAS BUSY in Central Kitchen. The line snaked around the walls and tailed out the door, past the two burly gavvers, and on to the damp street. The gavvers were there every morning, stout and hatchet-faced, a grey cloud at the door, observing the workers as they collected their food. Letta had never paid them any heed, but this morning she felt as though their eyes were boring into the back of her head.

She had left Marlo alone in the house. She'd had no choice – she had to get food. She shuffled along about ten people away from the head of the line, her eyes taking everything in.

The room was long and low, painted a hueless mouse colour, with no windows and a rough stone floor. At the far end, a long counter, slightly elevated, cut across the width of the building, and behind that stood the ovens and cooking paraphernalia that produced meals three times a day for the southern end of Ark. The queue was three deep, a rolling wave of hungry people, grim-faced but determined. Some of the women had young children attached to their hips and occasionally the infants cried out, only to be quickly hushed by their vigilant mothers.

The air was foetid with morning breath and the smell of dank clothes, undercut by the cooking smells emanating from the kitchen at the top of the room.

Letta shifted restlessly, wanting to get back to the shop.

Up ahead, Mary Pepper was dishing out food and instruction in equal measure:

'Lift bowl! Take bread! Stand back! Next!'

Letta shuffled forward. She kept her head down, not wanting to talk to anyone, while all around her was a wall of noise.

'Rain bad last night,' a man beside her shouted to his friend further back the line.

'Yes,' the man replied. 'Rain bad.'

'Gavvers about,' the first man said, dropping his voice slightly.

Letta stiffened.

'Looking for boy,' the second one said. 'Came to house. Looked. Nothing.'

The first man chuckled, a rich, deep sound that spread out and seemed to fill the room.

'No look in my house,' he said. 'My mate only have girls.'

The second man leant over and slapped him on the back, clearly enjoying the joke, then they went on to talk about the state of the harvest. Letta willed them to say something else about the boy, but they didn't.

'One or two?'

Letta jumped and, looking up, found Mary Pepper glaring down at her. The older woman's hair was as grey as her skin and it hung down in greasy waves against her sharp cheekbones.

'Eh … one breakfast. Two lunch,' Letta managed to say, proffering her tokens.

Mary Pepper's rat-like eyes narrowed. 'Two? Benjamin not away?'

'Yes,' Letta stammered. 'Two. He back lunchtime.'

The other woman muttered something under her breath but handed over one portion of boiled egg and two small carrot and parsley pies.

'Take bread!' she growled, and Letta grabbed the three portions she was entitled to.

'Next!' Mary Pepper roared, and Letta scurried away, grateful to leave the cook and her mean stare behind her. She walked quickly down the left side of the room. Past the waiting queue, through the door and on to the street. She was about to cross back towards the shop when she felt a heavy hand on her shoulder. She stopped. It was one of the gavvers from the doorway. His companion had also abandoned his post and stood looking down at her.

'Wordsmith?'

'Apprentice,' she said.

'See boy?'

Letta thought quickly. She could not lie to them. They would know he had been in the shop. She nodded.

'Yesterday. In shop.'

The man looked at her thoughtfully. *He doesn't believe me*, Letta thought. *If he searches the house now...*

The gavver turned to his companion.

'See!' he said. 'Found in wordsmith's shop yesterday, not potter's shop.'

The other man shrugged, and then both gavvers strolled back to their positions either side of the door, ignoring Letta.

Letta stood for a moment, her knees shaking, then turned and sprinted towards home.

They shared the food. She gave Marlo some water, though she knew they could ill-afford it. She would have to go to the water station and try to get an extra helping. She could tell them she had a fever. Marlo was quiet. Letta felt his forehead: it was warm and clammy.

'I think the gavvers are looking for you,' she said.

His eyes widened.

She told him what she had heard.

'I should leave.' Marlo went to get up, pushing the blankets away.

'No,' Letta said. 'You are too weak. They won't come here. My master is too well respected. They wouldn't dare.'

She paused for a moment. She could see him watching her, waiting.

'They shot you? The gavvers?'

He nodded.

'Black Angel. It cuts through you, then burns the vein closed so that you don't bleed to death. Hurts and heals.'

Letta nodded.

'I have to go home,' Marlo said, looking away from her. 'They'll be worried.'

'Where's home?' Letta asked.

He shook his head.

Letta felt a flash of resentment. Did he not trust her? A sudden banging on the door distracted her. Gavvers. Letta was sure of it.

'You have to hide,' she hissed at Marlo.

Another bang on the door. Would they kick it in? She looked around desperately. The cupboard. She flew across the room and threw open the door. It was empty but for an old box and Benjamin's father's cloak hanging from a single nail.

'In here,' she said to Marlo. 'Don't make a sound.'

He struggled from the bed and Letta ran to help him.

She could feel his arm around her neck, his skin hot and dry. He climbed in awkwardly, sinking to the floor of the cupboard at once. She slammed the door and dropped the latch with shaking fingers. Another bang on the front door, three short raps. She raced down the stairs. Stay calm, she told herself. Stay calm. Taking a deep breath she pulled back the bolts and opened the door.

'What you doing?' the voice outside admonished. 'Door closed? No shop?'

It was Mrs Truckle. She charged past Letta.

'Tally sticks?'

Letta spun around.

'Tally sticks?' she said back to her old teacher, her mind a total blank.

Mrs Truckle fixed her with a quizzical stare.

'You sick?' she said, head on one side, her eyebrows knitted in a tight frown. She was a small woman, strongly built though not stout with wide-set lively eyes and a short sharp nose. They had called her Bird in school because of her habit of putting her head to one side to look at you. There was a lovely rhythm to her words even though she only spoke List.

Letta smiled. 'No,' she said. 'Not sick.'

Mrs Truckle nodded, examining her carefully. 'Tired?' she said.

'Yes,' Letta said. 'Tired.'

The little woman smiled back. 'Sleep early,' she said, wagging her finger at Letta, in mock severity.

Please go, Letta willed her. The image of Marlo sitting in the cupboard, his skin grey and lifeless, tormented her. She had to get back to him.

'Now,' Mrs Truckle went on. 'Tally sticks?'

'Yes,' said Letta. 'Tally sticks come yesterday.'

There were forty-two of them, carved by the woodmen and branded by the gavvers. Letta had entered each one in the old red ledger. The child's name and the brand mark on his or her tally stick. The book was old and delicate and recorded the tally sticks since the foundation of Ark.

'I get them,' she said to Mrs Truckle and ducked down under the counter to pull out the large box the sticks had come in.

She handed them to the teacher, who sighed when she saw them. Everyone knew Mrs Truckle hated the sticks. She was required by law to put a notch on the stick each time a child failed to use List. Mrs Truckle blamed the parents for exposing their children to words that were not List. If they didn't teach the children the old words, they wouldn't be able to use them.

'Word boxes?' Mrs Truckle said, picking up the box of tally sticks.

'Soon,' Letta said.

Mrs Truckle looked surprised but said nothing.

Please go, Letta begged silently again.

'Eyes like your father,' the old woman said softly, before turning around and walking out the front door.

The words stuck in Letta's heart. She wanted to call Mrs Truckle back to find out more about her eyes, about her father.

Instead, she turned and raced up the stairs, down the corridor and into the little room. She couldn't hear anything. She yanked open the door and with a small thud Marlo's body fell out and lay at her feet.

'Marlo!' she cried, the word almost strangling her. She knelt beside him and put her ear to his mouth. She was rewarded with a gentle breeze and she knew he was still alive. She half-lifted, half-dragged him back to the bed.

He was worse, she knew immediately. She ran downstairs and got her small wooden bowl and the flannel. She grabbed the sea-water bottle and tipped some into the bowl. Finally, she picked up their bottle of drinking water. It was almost empty. She would have to go to the water station and convince Werber to give her a fill without a token. She couldn't think about that now.

Upstairs, she placed the wet flannel gently on his forehead. He didn't move. She sat there tending to him as the day wore on, moistening his lips, fanning his head and running up and down from the shop as people called. By afternoon, he had opened his eyes and was sitting up again, though she could see how weak he was.

'Should I call the healer?' Letta asked him, noting the unnatural brightness in his eyes.

He shook his head.

'Sometimes people react to the drug in the bullet,' he said softly. 'It will pass.'

'I have to go and get water for us,' Letta said. 'Will you be all right till I get back?'

He nodded again. 'I'll sleep,' he said and his eyes closed even as he spoke the words.

She didn't want to leave him, but they had to have water. She took an empty bottle and closed the shop. She put her head down and headed north to the water station. The farm workers were still in the fields and the streets were quiet. There was no sign of the gavvers. She relaxed a bit, though she could still feel ripples of tension in her shoulders.

She went on, past the potter's shop and down the hill to where the grassy track ran level at first, then curved and dipped sharply before emerging into a small square. The water station stood on a little rise in front of a tall, lichen-bleached building.

42

An old mill. The windows, which had once boasted real glass, were now roughly patched with wooden planks. Its roof was made of tin, well bitten by orange rust, which flaked onto its gables like dandruff. Old women huddled outside chatting, their weather-beaten faces turned away from the wind.

Werber Downes was distributing the water with two gavvers watching from the opposite side of the square. Werber smiled as she approached. He was the same age as Letta, tall and good-looking, with blond hair plastered to his head. His cheekbones were high and he had a perfect bow-shaped mouth, though Letta thought it would have been better suited to a girl. She had never warmed to Werber. He had always been so sure of himself and his obvious good looks. But she needed the water. She steeled herself and went up to him.

'Letta! No harm!' he said, beaming at her, his white teeth flashing against his brown skin.

'No harm,' Letta responded politely.

Werber raised an eyebrow, waiting for her to speak.

'Water, please,' Letta said. 'No token. Need extra. Fever.'

He frowned.

'You sick?'

'No,' Letta said. 'Better now, but no water.'

She held up the empty bottle. He put his hand on her forehead, and it was all she could do not to pull away. One of the old women caught her eye and sniggered. It was well known that Werber wanted to mate with Letta. She waited, willing herself to be patient.

'Please, Werber,' she said with her nicest smile.

He took the bottle. 'I call see you later?'

His too-handsome face leaned in close to her, too close, his eyes consuming her.

43

I will make sure to be out, she thought belligerently, but she nodded her head and said nothing. He handed her the bottle. She wanted to snatch it and run but instead she took it from him gently, letting his soft fingers touch hers. Then she walked away with all the dignity she could muster.

She knew her attitude to Werber was wrong but she couldn't help herself. She knew there were far too few people available for her to mate with, and Werber was young. Still, she thought, kicking a stone out of her way, she didn't need to worry till she was eighteen. Eighteen. It might as well be a century away.

Crossing the square, she dismissed Werber and let her mind focus on Marlo. She decided to call the healer if he was no better. What if he died? She quickened her pace. She would give him a drink, then set about queuing for dinner. If she could make him eat he would grow stronger. With that thought, she went around to the back of the shop, hope once more flickering in her heart. The light had already begun to dip as she opened the back door. She put her hand out to switch on the light.

It was then she heard the noise of someone breathing, slowly, heavily. She held her own breath, barely daring to turn around. Then, she saw him, leaning nonchalantly on the counter, a sneer fixed on his face. The gavver, Carver.

'Ah!' he said. 'Wordsmith.'

'How you get in here?'

She tried, in vain, to keep her voice steady.

'You think me fool?' he said.

The voice grated on her ear, even more ugly than she had remembered it.

'What … what you want?' Letta faltered, her eyes riveted on the face of the gavver, her hand clenched on the water bottle.

44

He leant on the counter, staring at her, and Letta could see the provocation in his eyes, daring her to give him an excuse to hurt her.

'I know … boy … was here,' he said, stumbling over the words. Letta shook her head. 'Told you. Boy ran away.'

Was here. At least he hadn't found him yet.

The gavver grunted and pushed past her through the door to the living quarters. He went straight to the master's study. Letta stood helplessly at the door, as the gavver pulled open drawers and swept clean the old desk cluttered with the research of years. He didn't seem to notice the door to the library, but she knew it was only a matter of time. She tried not to let her eyes wander to the stairs. Maybe he wouldn't go up there. She had no way to alert Marlo. The gavver would find him in the bed, helpless as a lamb.

The man grunted and turned towards her.

'What upstairs?' he said.

'Nothing,' she said and knew at once that she had said it too quickly. 'I make tea for you?' she said in desperation.

He didn't answer, just walked past her and headed for the stairs. Letta's mind was racing. She had to warn Marlo. At least give him a chance to escape.

'Stop!' she cried. 'No go up there! No go!'

The gavver glanced back at her and laughed, a cold mirthless affair, then continued on up the stairs. Letta followed him. Down the corridor, all the way to her own room. Then he disappeared through the door. She squeezed her eyes closed waiting for the rumpus, but nothing happened. She opened them again and ran to her room. The gavver was standing over an empty bed. Marlo was gone. She almost cried out. Then her eyes went to the cupboard.

The gavver ignored her, pulling the mattress from the bed, knocking over the chair. Then he walked across the room and leant on the old press.

'You do what with him?' he said. 'Tell me.'

'I know nothing,' Letta insisted, keeping her voice steady.

'Ha!' the man said and went to the window.

'He out there?' he said. 'He out there make trouble?'

Letta said nothing.

'Desecrator he is. You know that? Master know that?'

Letta knew how Desecrator was defined: *Rebel. Creator of art. Enemy of New World.*

The gavver turned and, in one swift movement, crossed the room, grabbed the latch on the cupboard and let the door fall open. Letta stifled a scream. Her eyes widened. It was empty. Empty! She could scarcely believe it. Empty except for her old box and Benjamin's coat.

Carver picked up the box. Letta breathed a sigh of relief. She had locked it after the last time she'd opened it. She watched as he picked it up. Watched as his hands caressed the smooth wood, then, holding it high over his head, he let it fall to the ground. The lid flew open, the hinges sundered. Letta gasped involuntarily. She didn't want him to know it mattered to her. He picked up the box and began to paw through the contents, those things Letta owned that were private to her, these things no other hand had ever touched. She saw him take the little lock of her mother's hair, blond hair tied with a faded crimson ribbon that Benjamin had given her on her twelfth birthday. On the ribbon, the letter F. F for Freya, her mother's name. She knew he was watching her for a reaction and Letta tried not to show how much she cared. He took the little wisps of hair and sniffed them like a bloodhound might, then threw them away from him.

46

Letta could no longer deal with the rage that was building in her. She turned and walked away. At least she wouldn't give him the satisfaction of seeing her distress.

As she stood in the corridor outside her room, she listened to him searching, grunting as he worked and felt sick to her stomach.

Where was Marlo? She could hear the gavver growling as he threw stuff around her room. He would move off soon, checking the other rooms. She rushed down to the other doors and flung them open. Nothing. Then, down the stairs again. She searched the master's study, the living area, though she knew he wasn't there. She even looked under the counter. He couldn't have gone far. Was he on the street? She stood at the door and looked out but there was no sign of him. She turned to see the gavver watching her. She jumped.

'I be back,' he said, his small eyes pinched and mean. 'I be back.'

And then he was gone. Letta banged the door behind him and threw the bolts. Then she leaned her back on the warm wood and tried to slow her racing heart. She went up the stairs again, down the corridor and then she heard it, the smallest sound of something shifting. She raced back and ran her hands along the panelling till she found the door to the hidden Monk's Room. She pressed and it sprang open.

Marlo sat slumped against the wall. He turned towards her and gave the smallest smile, but it was enough to bring life to his blue-grey eyes.

John Noa moved slowly towards the window. Old age had not been kind to him and, though he could still sit a horse, his rigid joints grew more painful by the day.

47

Looking down from his lofty vantage point, he could see the town below, on the cusp of waking. A lone wolf stood in the square, his head tilted to one side. The old man smiled. He had always loved animals and none more than the grey wolf. Before the Melting they had been almost eradicated, hunted to extinction. 'Extinction': the saddest word of all. Using science, and with great care and attention, they had bred five pairs of wolves in captivity, producing fifteen new cubs, and then released them into the wild. Since then, the wolves had thrived. Amidst all the destruction, it had seemed like a miracle to him.

He loved the view from the high window at this time of day. The workers not yet awake and only the comforting sound of the water bubbling in the great tank. He sighed. Sadly, he couldn't stay. He had work to do. Work! Always work. Problems to be solved, plans to be made. He had never expected it to be this difficult. On his bad days he wondered if it had been worth it at all. Another glance at the wolf brought a smile to his lips. Yes. It was all worth it. He firmly believed that it was his passion for Ark that had kept him alive when so many had been lost.

The images of death and destruction were always with him. Floods, earthquakes, famine, as livid in daylight as they were in his nightmares.

Images of the past.

But there were nightmares in the present too. Bandits. Desecrators. Tintown.

People intent on destroying what he had built. People intent on going their own way regardless of the price. He felt the old rage stir in his heart.

They would be dealt with. They would find that they were no different to the beetle or the rat in the end. Their arrogance would not survive his determination.

He noticed that his hands were shaking. He took a deep breath. He would focus on the positive. He was alive. Amelia was alive. The planet was crippled but not dead.

And, most importantly, he had a plan. A plan that would change the course of history. A plan that would save Earth. He could live with the casualties, he told himself.

He shivered and withdrew to the safety of the tower.

CHAPTER 4

Betray #66

(1) Tell about friend
(2) Work against Ark

MARLO had been asleep for hours. Letta felt his forehead and knew his temperature still raged. Through the window, she could see a sliver of yellow moon, lying on its back in a cloudless sky. On her knee, she held her box, where she had carefully re-instated all that she could find of her mother's hair. Carefully, she placed the broken lid on top. They had been gone for such a long time. She could still smell her mother's scent when she closed her eyes. Still feel her own small hand in her father's strong one.

'Be brave, little one,' he had said. 'We'll come for you soon.'

Her parents had been so sure that there was more to the planet than Ark. John Noa had given up all explorations by then, but her parents were stubborn. They had disobeyed Noa and gone on one last trip.

She stroked the warm wood of the box and looked at the boy asleep in the bed. He was a Desecrator. She had checked the red ledger. There was no tally stick registered to a Marlo. Nothing.

Was Marlo even his name? Names were closely controlled in Ark. Babies were presented one week after birth and the wordsmith proffered the approved list of names to parents.

She couldn't remember seeing Marlo on that list. People born before the foundation of Ark retained their given names, but Marlo was young. A Desecrator.

Even the word terrified her. Would his people come looking for him? People said that the Desecrators lived in the forest or outside the walls, in Tintown. She had often stood at the gates of Ark and wondered what it would be like to live out there. No proper houses, no electricity. The people of Tintown were those who hadn't made it into Ark, Benjamin said. They had set up home as near as they could get to John Noa's safe harbour and lived off the scraps of Ark. They were scavengers in the main, though some of them got work in Ark during harvest time, or doing the jobs no-one else wanted to do. In return they got a limited supply of clean water. Tintown was also where the Wordless lived, strange troubled souls who wandered aimlessly, silent and half-mad. She looked at Marlo again. Maybe they had forced him to join them. Maybe he'd had no choice. Her mind flew back to that first evening in the shop.

She was so stupid. He had already been shot when he came in, she now realised. He hadn't been looking for words: he'd been looking for somewhere to hide. She gritted her teeth. She would go to the gavvers in the morning. Turn him in. Explain that she didn't know.

Didn't know what? She had known the gavvers wanted him. She had known they shot him. She nodded grimly in the darkening room. She would have to turn him in, and she would have to tell the truth.

He stirred. She had managed to get some ginger root and onion and had made it into a tea. She took a spoon, and with it, poured some of the liquid between his lips. His breath was warm on her fingers.

'Letta?' he said, his voice hoarse and high-pitched.

'Yes,' she said. 'I'm here. Rest now.'

The night seemed to go on for ever. She picked up a card and wrote carefully, but her mind refused to focus. She had to have Mrs Truckle's work finished. School started on Thursday. The day after tomorrow. They had never been this late before. If the words weren't ready it would draw even more attention to her. She gripped the pen firmly:

Word 473 Water: Clear, colourless, odourl–

The nib snapped. Red ink splattered the card. Letta threw the offending pen at the far wall. She got up and ran downstairs to the shop and went straight to the old fireplace. She reached up and took a pen from the shelf above, then felt around in the dust for a nib. She was just shoving it onto the pen handle when she heard a ruckus outside.

She went to the door and opened it as quietly as she could. Through the narrow slit, she saw the cause of the commotion. Gavvers. Four of them dragging a struggling boy between them. With a sickening feeling, she realised that she knew him. It was Daniel, the healer's son. Across the street she could see the healer himself trying to restrain the boy's mother. He had wrapped his arms about her in a bear-like embrace but Letta could see her struggling and hear her screams. At first, she couldn't make out the words, but gradually her ear attuned, and she understood what the distraught woman was saying.

'My boy! Give me back my boy!'

Daniel was also struggling, kicking, shouting at the gavvers, as they loaded him onto the horse-drawn cart. One of the gavvers was carrying a stout wooden bat and, as Letta watched, he hit the boy with it, striking his lower back and causing the lad to double up in pain. This time, the mother managed to escape from her husband. She ran towards the boy; he turned and saw her and screamed in a voice Letta would never forget.

'Maaama!'

And then the horse moved. The cart jolted. The healer caught his wife and pulled her back, the horse's feet tapped out a staccato rhythm on the old stones, punctuated by the sobs of the mother, and then the street was quiet again, as though nothing had happened. Letta waited a moment then slipped outside.

'Help?' she said to the couple. 'Help you?'

The mother was still weeping, her voice high and shrill, her face pressed to her mate's chest. The healer was a tall man but to Letta he seemed to have grown smaller in the last minutes. He looked at her with pink-veined watery eyes.

'Boy steal potatoes,' he said. 'Gavvers search. Find.'

'What they do with him?' Letta asked, her voice shaking.

'Banish,' the man said. 'Banish.'

Letta shook her head. She knew that banishment meant death. 'No!' she said. 'Only boy.'

The healer turned away from her and, half-carrying his wife, went back towards his house.

Letta felt anger building in her. They couldn't do that. He was only a boy. She walked faster and faster in the direction the cart had gone till she was no longer walking but running. Down through the town, past the sleeping houses and on to the West Gate. The gavvers on duty looked up lazily as she passed among them. She stopped and stood like a young colt, unsure what to do next. This was the place known as Limbo. An in-between place. Nothing but scrub and dusty pine trees, dark skeletons, stripped of their leaves, black and ominous, in the washed-out

53

light of the morning. Nothing grew here and it was always quiet, as though even the birds didn't want to be around this kind of gloom.

To John Noa and the Green Warriors, the trees were sacred things, responsible for the air they breathed, habitat to animals and birds, and as a result they were guarded and protected in Ark, but Letta had always found them menacing and mysterious. She took a few steps forward, kicking loose clinker and flinty shale as she went. The wind gusted, blowing her hair into her eyes. She pushed it away and squinted at the forest. There was no sign of the cart. No sign of the boy. Her heart sank. She couldn't dispel the image of his mother's face. She kicked a lump of clinker angrily. This wasn't what Ark was supposed to be about. This wasn't what she had been taught. She turned quickly and went back through the gates. The gavvers stopped talking as she approached, staring at her silently. She ignored them and walked on.

She didn't go straight home. She took the road north, where there were fewer houses. She needed to walk. She needed to think. If she told the gavvers about Marlo they would expel him or execute him. She was sure of that. He was a Desecrator. A rebel. If they expelled Daniel over a few stolen potatoes, what would they do to Marlo? Ahead of her the road climbed steeply. She pushed on, welcoming the pain in her legs, the tightness in her chest. At the top of the hill, the Goddess loomed.

She stopped in front of her. The Goddess was cut from a single block of white marble, her complexion the pure white of hoar frost, her face radiant with fine features. Her almond shaped eyes were open, staring at the sky. Her dress fell in generous ripples about her shapely body. Her hands held a bunch of drooping bluebells. On her feet were brocade sandals

54

etched with exotic birds. Letta reached out and touched the white hands.

The Goddess had been here for ever. Since before the Melting. They said she was the last prophetess, a messenger from God, who came to warn the people that the end was nigh. Some people said that she was the first human clone before it all went wrong, when people thought cloning was something to celebrate. They grew her in a laboratory, and her first words were that she had come from God. Benjamin said they made the first one divine so that people would accept the whole idea of cloning. Mrs Truckle said all religion was evil and that the new world should believe in John Noa. The clones were long gone, along with the rest of the new technology. But the Goddess remained.

Poor Goddess! She had come to warn them but they hadn't listened, of course.

And then came the Melting. The ice that turned to water and flooded the planet, the sea devouring everything in its path. Towns and villages swallowed whole. The old technology destroyed. Animals extinct. And all of the written word gone. Letta stood back and looked at the Goddess.

'Why do we call you that?' she said aloud. 'You were a prophet not a god.'

The Goddess said nothing.

Walking back down the hill, Letta made her decision. She would have to tell Marlo this morning, but first she had to get food for both of them.

Mary Pepper looked at her and narrowed her eyes. 'Benjamin not home,' she said.

Letta blushed. She'd forgotten all about their conversation the previous day.

'No,' she stammered. 'Not come home.'

The older woman nodded grimly. 'Breakfast only,' she said, handing Letta an egg. 'Still have yesterday lunch. Take bread.'

Letta took the piece of bread she was entitled to and hurried out. They would have to live on one egg between them until the evening meal. She daren't use Benjamin's tokens to feed Marlo. Her stomach was already protesting. Marlo drank the tea she gave him but refused to eat. Letta felt guilty but she ate the food gratefully.

'Have you been shot before?'

He nodded.

Letta dipped her bread in the hot tea and lifted it to her mouth.

'We can't go on like this,' she said finally. 'Can we contact your uncle?'

Marlo hesitated. Letta watched him closely.

'Maybe,' he said.

'Maybe?' Letta repeated. 'Where does he live? What does he do?'

She could feel herself getting angry. He wouldn't tell her the truth. He was trying to concoct some story to keep her happy. She raised one eyebrow. He nodded.

'There is something I should tell you,' he said.

'Yes,' said Letta, finishing her tea. She was enjoying this, she realised. Let him make up a lie. It would be interesting to see him try to hoodwink her.

'My uncle is a Creator. I am his apprentice.'

Letta almost stopped breathing.

'Desecrator, you mean,' she said.

'That is Noa's word, not ours. We call ourselves Creators. I'm sorry I didn't tell you.'

'I knew already,' she said.

Marlo's eyes widened. 'You knew?'

'The gavver told me.'

'And you didn't betray me?' Marlo said softly.

'I was going to, I know I should, but now … now … I think we should contact your uncle and let him take you away.' The words poured out before she had time to think about it. 'I cannot keep a Desecrator here. My master and I are loyal to John Noa.'

'I know you have been told terrible things about us.'

'Yes,' said Letta, blood rushing to her face. 'I know you are thieves and murderers. I know you want to destroy the new world.'

'Do you?' said Marlo, lying back on the pillow. 'Or do you just believe whatever Noa says?'

Letta stood up, her knees shaking. 'You should be ashamed.'

He closed his eyes. 'I am sorry,' he said. 'I will think of a way of contacting my uncle.'

Letta turned and walked away. Outside the room door she stopped to get her breath. His words rang in her ears.

Do you just believe whatever Noa says?

She remembered the scene on the street earlier and Daniel's face as they threw him on the cart. That wasn't right. She was sure of it. But she did know what the Desecrators did. She knew how they stole food and water. She had seen their posters, inciting people to rise up against John Noa. She knew they staged shows from time to time, using banned arts to distract the workers. She shook her head. They might not be as vicious as the bandits that roamed the forest but they were equally destructive. She hadn't time to think about it now. She had to be at the schoolhouse at twelve bells with words for Mrs Truckle. Words that weren't written yet. She hurried to her desk and started to work.

She arrived at the school as the bell struck the hour. Letta opened the door and walked in. The small classroom was exactly as she remembered it. Here she had sat, day after day, and learnt the List words; memorised the definitions; learned to form letters. Children in Ark were taught the bare minimum when it came to reading. Enough to allow John Noa to communicate with them using the written word, but no more. Letta had learnt to read and write properly from Benjamin.

'Letta,' Mrs Truckle said, walking across the floor to her. Letta smiled at her. The old woman seemed more stooped than usual.

'Words ready,' Letta said, proffering the boxes, but Mrs Truckle didn't smile. She didn't even look at the neat array of boxes now sitting on her table.

Letta frowned. 'You good?' she said stiltedly, wishing she could free her tongue and speak properly.

Mrs Truckle shook her head, and Letta could see the tears welling in her eyes. Letta went to her.

'Sit,' she said, pulling out a stool for the older woman.

Mrs Truckle sat down, her shoulders heaving as she struggled to control her sobs.

'What's the matter?' Letta said softly, abandoning List in her worry about the schoolteacher.

'Daniel.' Mrs Truckle coughed out the word.

'I know,' Letta said, taking her hand.

'Good boy,' Mrs Truckle said, turning her eyes to Letta. 'Good boy.'

'I know,' Letta said.

'Not first time,' the woman went on. 'Always in trouble. Always, but good heart.'

Neither of them noticed the door open. The click of it closing made Letta look up in time to see Werber Downes standing there, his round face wreathed in smiles. In his hand he held a bottle of water for the teacher.

'Mrs Truckle!' he said and then stopped, noticing Letta.

'No harm to all here,' he said. 'Mrs Truckle sick?'

The old woman stood up quickly, wiping her tears away.

'No,' she said. 'No sick.'

'Healer boy taken,' Werber said, drumming his fingers on the table. 'Daniel. Criminal.'

Letta felt her face flush.

'No criminal,' she spat at him. 'Daniel no criminal.'

Werber smiled.

'Yes,' he said. 'Criminal. Steal food. Bad boy.'

He smiled again, wiggling his eyebrows, mocking the boy who had been banished, and Letta had an overwhelming desire to punch his stupid face. She raised her hand, blood rushing to her face, but Mrs Truckle caught the hand and held it firmly.

'Help carry words, Werber,' Mrs Truckle said swiftly, never taking her eyes off Letta. 'Help carry words to back room.'

Werber's face fell, but he knew better than to disobey his old teacher. He put down the water and started to pick up the word boxes. Mrs Truckle's eyes met Letta's and they nodded to one another. Letta felt the weight of unspoken words, frozen in the air between them.

As soon as she got home, she sank down on to the floor behind the counter. What would Mrs Truckle think if she knew a Desecrator was upstairs in Letta's bedroom? He had to go. Somehow, she had to get him out of the house. But how?

Much later, worn out from going over the problem from every angle and finding no answer, Letta climbed the stairs slowly and went to see Marlo. He was awake.

'How do you feel?'

'Thirsty,' he replied and smiled sheepishly. She took the cup that sat on the table beside the bed and held it for him as he drank. His hands under hers shook badly.

'I had another dream,' he said.

Letta said nothing.

'I dreamt I was a fox. I was living in the forest and being hunted by dogs.'

'Stop,' Letta said, unable to listen to any more.

Marlo looked up at her, one eyebrow raised.

'I don't want to hear about the forest,' she said curtly. 'The gavvers banished a boy there today.'

'Someone you knew?'

Letta nodded.

'Do you know where they entered the forest?'

Letta shook her head. 'No,' she said. 'I followed them towards the West Gate but then I lost them.'

Marlo nodded.

'My friends might be able to help, if ...'

'If?'

Letta felt her heart fill with hope.

'If they knew where to look. If the wild animals don't find him first. I don't want to raise your hopes.'

'How can we let them know?'

'There might be a way,' he said.

'Go on,' Letta said urgently. 'Tell me.'

'Maybe you could contact Finn, but –'

'But?'

'But – I have to be able to trust you,' he went on, not meeting her eye.

'You don't trust me?' Letta snapped at him. 'I'm risking everything for you and you don't trust me?'

'That's not what I meant,' Marlo said. 'It's just … it's not my secret to tell.'

Letta waited, her mouth set in a hard line.

'There's going to be a show on Friday.'

'A show?'

'Finn and some friends are going to perform and then talk to the workers. You can find him there.'

Talk to the workers. Letta knew the Desecrators didn't just talk to people. They incited them. Tried to lead them to revolt against John Noa. She felt sick.

'Where?' she managed to ask. 'When?'

'The main wheat field, at midday. There's a shed there, with a flat roof.'

'They'll be on the roof?'

'Yes,' Marlo said.

'Maybe by then you would be well enough to go and meet them?' Letta said. 'And tell him about Daniel?'

He nodded again, but didn't say anything.

'And if you are not well enough …'

His beautiful blue-grey eyes looked up at her and she could see the fragility in them.

'I will go,' he said. 'I will be ready.'

The words hung there in the air between them, sparking with electricity. Finally, Letta nodded.

'So be it,' she said.

CHAPTER 5

Non-List

Music

Agreeable, harmonious sounds

LETTA didn't sleep well that night. Her dreams were full of panic, and more than once she shot up in bed, convinced there was someone in the room. By the time morning came, she was relieved to be able to get up.

She tiptoed out of the house, going by the back door, pulling it quietly behind her, careful not to wake Marlo. The streets were quiet. A shrew crossed her path, darting by only a stride from her ankle. She hated shrews. If they were bigger, Benjamin had once told Letta, they would be one of the most feared animals on the planet. She watched it go, its tapering snout investigating every stone on the road. Like all animals, it was protected in Ark. It reminded her of Marlo's dream. Her stomach tightened every time she thought of Daniel. Was there a wolf out there following his scent even now? How long could he last without food and water?

Her feet seemed to find the path to the beach all on their own. Fifteen minutes later she was standing on the sand, watching the waves break on the rocks. She turned and walked into the wind, feeling it lap her face and pull her hair back so that it streamed behind her. The sea mist settled on her warm skin. *It feels like I've been crying,* she thought, wiping the moisture away.

What would Benjamin do? she wondered. Would he help Marlo? Would he talk to Desecrators? What would her parents do? She knew so little about them.

Both her parents were experienced sailors. They had been in the leading team John Noa had put together to explore the ocean and see if they could find land. When Noa called off the exploration, convinced that they were the last humans to survive, her parents had gone out one last time, against John Noa's express orders. Benjamin had always said that they weren't rebels just romantics, idealists. They had set off like innocent children, sure they would find other places.

'They had it all mapped out,' Benjamin had told her sadly. 'Charts and compasses and who knows what else. Thirty days, your mother told me. They would sail for thirty days and if they found nothing turn around and come home. Sixty days in all. They had taken enough food and water to last that long.'

Benjamin still didn't like to talk about them and had warned Letta not to mention them outside the house.

'John Noa was very disappointed,' he told her once. 'Disappointed that they had not listened to him.'

And Letta had taken his words to heart. She didn't ask about them, much as she longed to know more.

The sound of male voices jolted her out of her reverie. She jumped, her pulse quickening. But it was only the water workers coming to start filling the barrels of salt water, destined for the water tower on the far side of town where it would be cleaned and purified for drinking.

She turned and looked out to the horizon. Why hadn't her

63

parents come back? They had left her with such emptiness inside, an enormous crater that wouldn't be filled.

She tried to imagine what it would be like to see a small sailboat suddenly appear on that blue-grey canvas. She'd always imagined their boat as having silver sails. How fanciful was that? And yet she couldn't picture it any other way. Silver sails, a tall dark man hauling on the main sail, beside him a smaller woman with golden hair and an upturned nose, just like her own. They'd sail right in and then suddenly he would see her. The rope would fall from his hands. Her mother would turn to see what had distracted him and...

She shook her head. She was getting too old for these daydreams. She had real things to worry about. Reluctantly, she let the imagined boat go and turned her mind to the fugitive living under her roof.

He wasn't getting any better, she was sure of that. If she did go on Friday, if she did meet the Desecrators, at least they could come and take him. And maybe they could help Daniel. She tried to persuade herself that if she did go, it would be for Daniel. Marlo was a Desecrator. She should feel no need to help him, and yet...

He wasn't what she imagined a Desecrator would be like. He was just ordinary. Ordinary and nice. She had enjoyed talking to him when he was well and able to joke with her. She wasn't used to talking to people her own age and to someone who didn't talk List. His language was amazing. She knew, of course, that older people had good language, though they were forbidden to use it. She tried to imagine how he had been reared, in hiding obviously, surrounded by people who spoke whatever way they wanted to. She felt a twinge of envy. She loved Ark but she hated List. She had never really admitted that before, she thought, bending to pick up a shell. Not even to herself.

She raised her arm and threw the shell hard, towards the sea, but it fell short, surfing the sand and coming to rest in a small hollow, safe from the waves. No. She couldn't imagine it. Besides, she had always been taught that words were the root of evil. Before the Melting, people had used all the words there were, and it did nothing to save them. John Noa would say that they talked themselves into the disasters that they created. The animals lived peacefully on the planet, doing no harm, living in harmony with nature. Man was the one who spoiled everything. Man and his words.

She dragged her toe in the sand making a narrow trench. Tomorrow she would go to the wheat field. She couldn't see any other way forward. She looked out to the horizon again. Sometimes people didn't have any choice about which road they took. She knew that now. She raised her hand and saluted them, as she always did, and turned for home.

Marlo was worse, much worse. She found him tangled in a damp sheet, raving incoherently. His lips were caked and dry, so dry she could see the tiny fissures in them. His eyes rolled in his head and he kept trying to sit up. His words were slurred and delivered in that strange, half-pitched whine.

Tea, she thought. *I'll make him tea and sponge him down. That will help.* She rushed out of the room. She wasn't a healer. What if he died?

In the living area, she found the bowl she needed and half-filled it from her precious water supply. Bowl. Water. Flannel. She was beginning to feel feverish herself. What else? The tea. She still had some ginger. She hunted around furiously. Not in the cupboard where she kept such things. Where else could it be? Her breath caught in her throat. There was no ginger. The tea was no good without it. The healer – she would go and talk to him. He might help her. She raced out through the shop, pulling the heavy front door behind her. The healer's shop was on the other side of the road. She hurtled across and was just about to bang on the door when it opened. The healer, John Lurt, stood there, his long face drawn and grey.

'Yes?' he said, raising one eyebrow.

'Help,' Letta said. 'I need help.'

'Come,' he said and stood back to let her through.

The healer's shop was one of the houses designed by the Green Warriors just before the Melting. A perfect square, thirty strides on each side, made from a plastic resin invented in the last decade before the Melting. It was warm in winter and cool in summer, requiring almost no energy to run, unlike Benjamin's porous house across the road. The herbs and other remedies hung from the ceiling in great clumps, and shelves covered the walls, displaying the familiar brown paper twists the healer used to package his wares. The place smelt dry and medicinal, Letta thought, as she went to stand at the counter. The healer followed her, and then resting one hand on the counter, he turned to face her. His eyes were steely, Letta thought, the pupils small and wary. He leaned his head towards her.

'Yes?' he said.

'Fever,' Letta said.

'You?' the man replied, scrutinising her face.

'No,' Letta said. 'Boy.'

The man turned and pulled down his coat from a hook near by.

'I go,' he said.

'No,' Letta said, as firmly as she could. 'No go.'

The man sighed.

'Must see,' he said. 'Who sick?'

Letta swallowed hard. 'Please help,' she said again.

There was silence for a minute. John Lurt was waiting for an explanation.

'Who sick?' he said again, and for the first time she noticed the hardness in his words, the way he dropped them sparingly, as though they were too heavy to carry any more.

This had been a mistake, she thought. A mistake. The word bounced in the space between her and the healer.

'Nobody,' she said, backing out. 'Nobody.'

Then she went through the door as quickly as she could, feeling his eyes following her. She ran across the street, her mind racing. She would go back in and lock up the shop. Then she could concentrate on taking care of Marlo.

She pushed open the front door, berating herself for having been so careless in leaving it open in the first instance.

Mrs Truckle was standing at the counter. 'Letta!' she said. 'Need two more boxes.' Then, seeing Letta's expression, she continued apologetically, 'Door open. Walked in.'

'Yes,' Letta said quickly. 'Two more. Have here.' She had forgotten to add them to the order Mrs Truckle had asked for. She reached under the counter and pulled them out.

'You good?' Mrs Truckle said gently.

'Yes,' Letta lied, 'good.'

The word wasn't out of her mouth when she heard an almighty crash overhead. Letta jumped. The two women looked at one another. Mrs Truckle turned her head slowly and looked up towards the stairs.

'Box,' Letta said, the words tumbling out. 'Box fall. Upstairs. I go.'

Mrs Truckle looked anxiously towards the room behind Letta.

'Be careful, child,' she said, taking her word boxes. 'Very careful.'

The old woman touched her hand and Letta, feeling the warmth of that small embrace, wanted to tell Mrs Truckle everything, to hold her and keep her with her. But she knew she couldn't. She walked to the door with the older woman.

'Lock now,' Mrs Truckle said before disappearing into the outside world. Letta did as she said, throwing the bolts as quickly as she could, then tearing through the shop and up the stairs.

He was lying on the floor. She knelt beside him and took his head in her hands. The skin was dry and hot. She jumped up and quickly fixed the bed then kneeling behind him, and gripping him under the arms, she hauled him up. It took all her strength, and even then she felt her back would break from the strain and that her arms would be wrenched from their sockets, but she got him on to the bed. She knelt on the floor to get her breath. Kneeling there on the hard floor she knew that he would not be going to that wheat field the following day.

For the rest of the day, and through the night, she cared for him as the fever raged in his body. She bathed his face, squeezing the little water that she had from the flannel, and wet his lips. She struggled to keep him lying down, tried to stop him shouting in his ravings and was terrified that someone on the street would hear him despite her efforts. Towards dawn, the fever broke, and he opened his eyes.

'Oh, Marlo,' she said, relief flowing through her.

'I'm sorry,' he said. 'Have you been there all night?'

She smiled at him.

'How do you feel?' she said.

'Good,' he said. 'What day is it?'

'Friday,' she said softly.

He went to stand up.

'I should go,' he said. 'Finn will be there and –'

She pushed him back. 'You can't go,' she said. 'You can hardly stand.'

He turned his face away from her and she could feel his frustration.

'It's all right,' she said. 'I'm going to go.'

He turned his head slowly and looked at her.

'No!' he said. 'It's too risky.'

'It's risky having you here,' she said, straightening the bed cover.

He caught her hand. 'Why are you doing all this?

His question stumped her. Why was she doing it? Because she didn't want him banished. No matter what he had done. She knew that was the truth.

'Never mind that now,' she said, pulling away from him. 'We need to get food and water. What will happen you when I'm gone? If the fever comes back.'

'It won't,' Marlo said. 'I will stay in the Monk's Room.'

She nodded, though she could feel the anxiety building in her. She didn't want to imagine him cowering in the Monk's Room burning with fever.

She spent the rest of the morning getting food and drink to leave with him, taking almost nothing for herself. He was still not inclined to eat but she coaxed him to swallow a little bread and a thin vegetable broth. She heard the bells ring eleven times and got ready to leave.

'I'll help you to the Monk's Room,' she said. 'And I'll lock up the shop. You'll have water and I shouldn't be more than an hour or so.'

69

'I'll be fine,' Marlo said. 'You need to look out for yourself. Once the show is over, our people will scatter really quickly, heading off in different directions. Try to find Finn. He's a big bear with jet-black hair and a beard. Tell him Marlo needs him, but be careful.'

'I will,' Letta cut across him impatiently. All this talk was making her even more nervous. 'It's time I went,' she said.

Marlo nodded and put his arm about her neck.

Fifteen minutes later she closed the door on the Monk's Room. It had taken that long for him to walk with her help the few strides it took to get him there. He collapsed onto the floor and Letta thought his skin was the greyest she had ever seen it.

'Good luck,' he'd managed to whisper, before shutting the small door.

Letta walked carefully through the town, eyes downcast, trying not to draw any attention to herself. She turned north at the tailor's shop and started the long climb to the wheat fields. The day had been cloudy till this, but now the autumn sun erupted from between the clouds, warming her hair. They might not even be there, she told herself. Anything could have happened to make them change their plans. Anything. She kicked a stone out of her way and almost slid on the wet mud. She stopped to get her breath. The potato fields came into focus first, with the potato pickers bent over like lines of crane birds. Letta ignored them and hurried on. She still had no plan. What would she say when she got to the wheat fields? What business had she there?

They would know at once that she was up to no good. She must have been mad to think she could pull this off. Her feet seemed to move of their own volition as her brain screamed at her to stop and change course. She came around the corner and realised she had reached her destination. The wheat fields stretched out on either side of her. The field nearest the road was where the Desecrators planned to be. The long low shed with its innocent flat roof ran along the west side just as Marlo had described within fifty strides from where she stood. From that lofty perch a row of magpies watched the scene unfolding in the field below, their black and white plumage lit bright by the sun. Amongst the waving sea of golden wheat, the men were stripped to the waist, each one carrying a scythe. Letta watched, hypnotised, as they moved through the yellow grain, their scythes swinging in unison, the swish of their razor-sharp blades alongside the tinkling of the shorn stems.

She couldn't see the supervisor, but he was there somewhere, she knew. She looked at the shed roof again. Marlo's friends weren't there. She could go home.

She looked again at the reapers as they swayed from side to side, leaving ribbons of yellow behind them. The feeling of foreboding was everywhere, bearing down on her, making the very air she breathed smell rancid. She turned to leave, glancing one last time at the shed as she did so. One minute the birds were on the roof, the next they had taken to the air with loud screeches, and when Letta refocused her eyes she could see a woman. Letta held her breath. An alien sound filled her ears. Music. Music swirling around her. Dah, dah, dah, dah, *daah*.

Letta stood shivering in her excitement, her fists clenched, her eyes never straying from the source of the exquisite sound. A tiny, delicate woman playing a saxophone. Her hair billowed about her face in blue-black waves and the sharp edge of her collarbone jutted out from beneath porcelain skin. She wore a black skirt on which were printed enormous old roses, dusky pink, surrounded by soft green leaves. She was in her middle years or older, Letta thought. The instrument itself was a relic from another time and Letta couldn't take her eyes off it. She had never seen one but she knew the word *saxophone*.

Shrill, wailing notes filled the air, dark and intense, followed by light trilling passages. The woman's body moved in time to the music, urgent, determined, and Letta's own heart quickened at the sound. Memories came flooding back. Her mother's scent, soft arms around her, twirling, spinning, laughing.

Dah, dah, dah, dah, *daah*. The men in the field stopped. They stood facing the shed, their weapons hanging impotently at their sides. Letta forced herself to move, climbing over the rough ditch into the field. The ground was rough and uneven, the stumps of severed wheat blocking her path. She skirted the field, keeping as close to the ditch as she could, walking past the workers, who had stopped where they stood, all eyes on the shed roof. She tried to block the pain from her mind as the wheat stubs cut her legs. She could see him now. Finn. He was tall and well built, his shoulders broad and his head covered in a forest of unkempt black hair on the top of his head and a wild straggly beard covering most of his face. He stood beside the shed but his eyes were on the field, his large head moving slowly from side to side, missing nothing, waiting to spring into action. Letta hurried on. She had to get to him before they finished playing. No-one looked at her, though she heard one man humming along to the music and could feel the heat emanating from his body as she stalked past him. Finally, she was so close to Finn that she could have touched him. She stopped. He was looking away from her towards the far end of the field.

'Finn!' Her voice emerged as little more than a whisper. She tried again. 'Finn!'

This time he turned, startled. She held his gaze. He moved a stride towards her.

72

'Who are you?' he said, his voice deep and rich.

'Marlo sent me.'

In a heartbeat, he was beside her, gripping her arms in his rough hands. 'Marlo!' he said. 'You have seen Marlo?'

She nodded. In the background, the music was swelling to a climax.

'He's sick. In my house,' she stammered.

'Where?' Finn asked, his eyes boring into her. He shook her ever so slightly. 'Where?'

'The wordsmith's shop.' She got the words out, and pulled away from him. And then she was running. Running and stumbling, sweat trickling down her back, her mouth dry. She thought she heard someone shout, but she didn't stop to look back. Just as she neared the road, she tripped on a small stone, and went sprawling head first into the clay. The music stopped, to be replaced by an eerie silence for a moment, and then somewhere behind her, she could hear feet pounding the ground, voices calling, sharp whistles. *Get up!* The words roared in her head, and then she was on her feet again, and running onto the road. Only then did she risk looking over her shoulder. Back in the field, there was chaos, with people running in all directions. She couldn't see Finn, but the roof of the shed was empty.

CHAPTER 6

#299

Name

~❦~

Word to call person

AS LETTA opened her front door, the music of the saxophone was still in her ears. She could barely wait to tell Marlo all about it. Even remembering it stirred powerful emotions and memories. Was it always like that with music?

She sprinted up the stairs, not stopping to take off her coat. She stopped at the Monk's Room. The door was open.

'Marlo?'

There was no-one there. No sign that anyone had ever been there. Had he recovered enough to go down to the bedroom? She couldn't imagine that. He had been so weak earlier. She hurried down there regardless, an uneasy feeling gnawing the pit of her stomach. She threw open the bedroom door. Everything was exactly as she left it. Where could he be? She hurried back downstairs, her mind racing. Could the gavvers have found him? If they had, wouldn't they be here waiting for her? A sudden draught of cold air hit her. She walked towards the back door. It was ajar. Had he left? She ran to the door and out into the lane. He was lying there, not moving.

'Marlo!'

He groaned but didn't open his eyes. She looked up in alarm. She could see the street but mercifully no people. She had to get him inside before someone noticed. Grabbing him under the arms she dragged him, stride by stride, to the door and then over the threshold. As soon as he was inside she slammed the door and leant against it trying to get her breath, her arms aching. He moaned again. Had she hurt him? She knelt down and took his cold hand in hers. He opened his eyes.

'Letta!' He squeezed her hand.

'What were you doing?' Letta said. 'Why didn't you stay in the Monk's Room?'

'I thought I could get to the field. I felt better and…'

'And?'

'I shouldn't stay here. I'm putting you in danger.'

'Can you stand?' Letta looked at him anxiously.

'I think so,' he said.

It took a long time for Letta to get him to his feet and even longer to make the long journey up the stairs, Marlo's arm around her shoulder, their feet keeping time with one another. Finally, he was back in bed. As soon as he lay down, his eyes closed again.

Letta sank into the chair in the corner of the room and breathed a long sigh of relief. She could hear him breathing, moaning slightly. After an hour or so she got up and walked over to the bed. A stray wisp of hair covered his eye. Gently, she swept it away and then left her hand for a moment on his forehead. A shiver ran through her.

He sighed and opened his eyes. She pulled away from him, pretending to straighten the covers. He turned to her, his eyes full of questions.

'I gave Finn the message,' Letta said. 'Now we have to wait.'

'You saw the show?' he asked.

Letta nodded. 'A beautiful woman played music, a saxophone.'

Marlo smiled. 'Leyla,' he said.

'It was amazing,' Letta said. 'The music. It is so long since I heard it.'

Marlo nodded again. 'She plays beautifully,' he said. 'She used to work with Noa, until he banned music.'

She found it hard to believe that the woman would have left John Noa to go and live with Desecrators because of something like music. Did people never understand that they had to make sacrifices for Ark?

Silence filled the space between them but Letta felt that it was a comfortable silence with each one lost in their own thoughts. Outside, the rain was pelting down, hopping off the tin roof and interspersed with low grumbles of thunder.

She wondered where Benjamin was. Was he out in that weather? It was hard to believe that he had only been gone a few days. She lay back in her chair and gave herself over to the melody of the rain. She jumped when Marlo spoke.

'Thank you,' he said. 'You are very brave.'

'Am I?' she said softly.

'What do you want to do with your life, Letta?' Marlo asked.

Letta shrugged. 'I want to be a wordsmith. I want to be part of the new world. I don't think about it much.'

Marlo nodded. 'You think we can build a new world, here, in Ark?'

'Of course,' Letta said. 'Don't you?'

He shook his head slowly. 'Not like this. Not without freedom.'

Letta frowned. 'I don't understand you,' she said. 'John Noa wants what's best for all of us. For humans and animals and the planet itself. You know what happened before. How could you risk everything again?'

Marlo shrugged. 'Everything is a risk. Life is a risk. We have to be what we are. Our souls are not like the soul of a fox. Our hearts are not like the heart of a sparrow.'

She could see he was getting more passionate, his eyes bright, his cheeks flushed. She leaned in towards him, concentrating on his every word.

'We are full of … full of … feelings. And yet …'

'And yet?' Letta prompted him.

'Feeling isn't even a List word.'

'But … but …' Letta struggled to put words on her thoughts. 'If we give ourselves up to our feelings aren't we destined to make the same mistakes all over again? There are so few of us left, Marlo. If we are to survive we have to compromise. Change. Not be like we were before. Not waste our time on abstract things, things that only lead us off the path.'

'Things like music?' Marlo cut across her.

She nodded, though her heart felt heavy.

'Yes,' she said. 'Even music.'

Marlo sighed. 'I envy you, Letta. I envy your ability to believe in Noa without question. I just know I can't do it.'

He sank back on his pillow again and closed his eyes, leaving Letta alone with only the sound of the rain for company. His words stayed in the atmosphere, bright fireflies like she remembered from her childhood. Words darting all over the room.

Freedom. Music. Feelings.

Were they things they could live without? Images of Daniel taunted her. His mother's face as they took him away.

It wasn't sadness that assailed her now but anger, her old nemesis, her temper. She got up and started to pace the room. Didn't Daniel have a right to live here too? She had always been taught that it was John Noa who had built Ark, that it was to Noa that they owed their very survival. And yet, hadn't they a right to live on the planet? She shook her head. There was no sense to her thoughts. She should go downstairs and get back to her work. Marlo and his rebellious thoughts had no place here in the wordsmith's shop. She turned and looked at him sleeping quietly, a thin line of sweat on his upper lip. He looked so peaceful, she thought. So innocent.

In the shop, Letta settled down to her work. She looked in the drop box and found a little notebook with fifty words carefully written down with a slight explanation with each one. Her eye scanned them thoughtfully, delight flooding her heart as she went through them. This is what it was all about. New words. Words they didn't know. Words that could be saved.

Smith: A person who works metal
Anvil: A block of iron on which metals are shaped

She had heard rumours that old Manus Burkked the black-smith was unwell. He was an old man, maybe eighty or even more. He had lived through the age of technology, fought in the last war, and now he was going to die in a world very far removed from all of that.

A lot of old people left them their words before they died. She closed the little book carefully and took it to her desk. She pulled a card towards her, dipped her nib in the familiar red ink and started to write. Soon, she was lost in the world of the blacksmith. She barely noticed the noise from outside, the

78

creaking of a cart as it passed the door, the barking of a dog, the pitter-patter of the rain.

As she wrote, her left calf began to cramp, sending spasms of pain through her leg. She stood up to try to ease it and walked across the floor. The door was open and outside she could see the cat collector's cart and two of his men walking alongside it. She smiled. When she was a little girl she had believed they were literally cat collectors. One evening, when she saw them passing the shop she had taken Benjamin's old cat, Fidget, and hidden him in a cupboard under the stairs.

She looked at the men again. They weren't really collecting cats, of course. They were collecting any kind of rubbish they found on the streets, including dead animals. That was how they'd got their name. She was about to go back to her desk, when one of the men turned to her. For a second she couldn't place him, but then she realised who he was.

'Finn,' she whispered.

He nodded. He had shaved his face, and was wearing a hat with a broad brim, pulled down over his eyes. His partner beside him had a similar hat and an old pair of dungarees. As Letta watched, he picked up a dead pigeon and threw it in the cart.

'Back door?' Finn asked quietly.

Letta nodded. 'Lane alongside,' she said, just as she saw the healer crossing the street to the cart.

He frowned in Letta's direction then addressed Finn. 'Dead dog near water station,' he said gruffly.

Finn nodded but said nothing. The healer seemed satisfied, and crossed back to his own shop.

Letta went inside, pulling the heavy door behind her. Once out of public view, she flung the bolts across and stood leaning against the wall, waiting. She knew the back door was open and, sure enough, she soon heard their steps in the hall.

Finn seemed even bigger indoors than he had in the wheat field. Behind him, his companion was small and lean, with a sharp face that reminded her of a stoat.

Finn smiled. 'We don't even know your name,' he said, speaking the old tongue fluently but with a slight accent.

'Letta,' she said, noticing how brown his eyes were.

'Letta,' he repeated. 'And where is Marlo?'

She nodded towards the stairs.

'The room at the end,' she managed to say. 'But he won't be able to walk far.'

'We'll put him in the cart,' Finn said and nodded at the other man. Together, they thundered up the stairs, while Letta waited in the shop, tension making her bones ache. She strained to hear something from upstairs, and in a few minutes was rewarded with the sound of their feet on the steps.

They came through the door supporting Marlo between them. His face looked white and thin beside the ruddy complexion of his friends and Letta's heart ached for him.

'So,' Marlo said with a smile. 'This is goodbye.'

She nodded.

'Thank you, more than I can say.'

She nodded again. She didn't seem to have words for any of this.

'We have to go,' Finn's companion said, his voice deep and gruff.

'Don't forget Daniel,' Letta said to Marlo.

'I won't, but don't get your hopes up,' he said, his hand warm on her arm. 'I don't want you to be disappointed.'

Finn caught Letta's eye and smiled. 'Thank you again,' he said. 'You're a brave girl.'

The banging on the front door caught them all unawares. No-one moved. Letta felt as though they were all in a picture, caught forever, exactly as they were.

'Gavvers! Open!' The voice outside was firm, full of authority.

Letta felt weak. What was she to do? They would break the door down. She had to say something but what?

'Gavvers! Open!'

Finn nodded to her, willing her on with his gaze. This time, she found her voice.

'Minute!' she called. 'Find key!'

Her eyes sought Finn again. He took his arm away from Marlo, and signalled to the other man to take the boy through to the back door.

As they moved away to obey him, he pulled a knife from his pocket, and with the elegance of a deer, vaulted the counter and hid beneath it.

Letta stared at the place where his head had been but there was now no sign of him. The banging started on the door again. She took a deep breath, turned, and pulled back the great bolts.

Please don't let them notice that there is no key, she thought as she did so.

Slowly, the door opened.

Two gavvers. She recognised one of them as Carver.

'Come,' he said.

'Where?' Letta answered, trying to imbue her voice with confidence.

'John Noa,' the gavver replied.

John Noa? Why would John Noa want her? Could he know about Marlo? The gavver was trying to look past her into the shop. She had to stop him coming in, somehow.

'Why?' she asked. 'Why John Noa want me?'

'Not for you to ask,' Carver snarled. 'Come.'

Letta moved forward but the second gavver put up his hand, stopping her.

'Coat!' he said.

Letta looked at him blankly. What had he said? Why couldn't she understand him?

'Coat!' he said again.

He wanted her to get her coat.

'Yes,' she stammered. 'Coat.'

She turned, her mind gripped with panic. Where was her coat? By the back door. What if they followed her? She went to close the front door but Carver got his hand to it, preventing her. Were they going to come in? She walked across the floor, her knees weak. She looked over her shoulder. The gavvers hadn't moved.

'Hurry!' Carver said, his eyes boring into her. She continued on. Don't look at the counter, she warned herself. Don't look. Through the door into the hall. She could see her coat on the peg beside Benjamin's old winter scarf. She reached up her hand to take it down and almost screamed. The Desecrator and Marlo were standing under the garments, completely hidden from view. Marlo's blue-grey eyes stared out at her.

'Go,' Marlo whispered.

Letta took her coat and moved quickly back to the shop.

Carver was standing inside the door looking out at the rain. She glanced at the counter. Nothing. Not a sign that a man was there holding a knife.

'Ready,' she said.

Carver moved onto the street. Without a backward glance, Letta pulled the door behind her and followed him.

The room was large and airy. Shelves lined the walls on three sides, shelves that stretched way above his head, bending under the weight of the hundreds of books stored there. The fourth wall was covered in old newspaper, yellowed and faded, but still readable. The room had become a shrine of sorts, he supposed. The books he had saved before the last days. He ran his finger along the spines: Shakespeare, Dickens, Keats, the ancients, all there alongside books from the last century. Nothing wasted, nothing lost. His private collection. He would find it difficult to let them go when the time came, but he would let them go. He couldn't risk them being found at a later date.

There were few incidents where people managed to decode words after Nicene, very few. None the less, he wouldn't take that chance. They would be destroyed along with everything the wordsmith had managed to salvage.

For a second, images of the wordsmith filled his head, but he pushed them away. He turned his back on the books and walked across to the wall of newsprint.

Here was a potted history of the past hundred years.

The warnings.

The signs.

Global warming.

Water levels rising.

It was incomprehensible even now that man had just ignored it all. Young people talked about the Melting as if it were a single event, but it hadn't been like that. The Earth had been heating up for years. His finger touched one of the news sheets. Scientists were warning of an alarming acceleration in the melting of the Polar ice caps. They predicted a dramatic rise in sea levels. That was back in the twenty-first century! He shook his head.

He chose another article, from around the same time. The writer was warning about the disappearing ice caps.

'Until recently, the Arctic ice cap covered two per cent of the Earth's surface. Enormous amounts of solar energy are bounced back into space from those luminous white ice fields. Replacing that mass of ice with dark open ocean will induce a catastrophic tipping point in the balance of planetary energy.'

Torrents of words had followed. Words from politicians assuring people that there was no such thing as global warming. Words from industrialists who justified their emissions of CO_2 into the atmosphere. Words to hide behind. Words to deceive. Useless, dangerous, destructive words...

He drew back his hand and punched the wall, hurting his knuckles and leaving a trail of blood on the yellowing paper.

CHAPTER 7

THE CLIMB was not an easy one. They had just passed The Round House, the gavvers' base, when the path started to rise steeply. John Noa's building was right at the summit of the mountain, a half-circle cut into the rock. Its back was made of stone, but the curved front piece was almost all synthetic glass. At night, when it was lit, it looked like an old fashioned spaceship. Letta looked up at it, to where it broke out of the mountain, towering above her. Her feet struggled to find purchase on the stony path, the pebbles and shale shifting as she walked. The higher they climbed, the stronger the wind became until Letta was struggling to push against it. The gavvers walked behind her, giving her a none too gentle push each time she slowed. Her mind was racing. What could Noa want? If he knew about Marlo, he would have had the gavvers arrest her. It couldn't be that.

The rain had stopped, and Letta could hear the men breathing heavily behind her and the sound of a bird somewhere far above them, screeching as he flew, as though warning of some great misfortune. Letta realised that they had arrived at the bottom of a long flight of stone steps. Carver shoved her, his hand rough on the small of her back. She stumbled, then righted herself and started up the steps. She looked up. They were approaching the house from the western side. She could smell the sharp tang of salt air. The ground levelled out. In front of her was a door set into the gable. To her left, a low hedge. And below her, far below her, the sea. She averted her eyes. *Breathe*, she told herself. *Breathe*. A gavver leaned in past her and knocked on the door. They waited. Behind her, the gavvers mumbled something she didn't catch.

The door opened abruptly. A woman stood there. She was tall and thin, vampire-pale, with a sharp angled face. Her hair was a grey bleached colour and Letta suspected that released from its tight bun it would reach her waist. Amelia Deer. Everyone knew her. She worked for Noa and people said she was the second most powerful person in Ark. She was also known as the woman with the breathing problem, and now that Letta was up close to her, she could see why. Amelia's breathing was like the sound of a punctured bellows. Her lungs had been damaged in a chemical explosion before the Melting, or so Letta had heard the women at the water station say. Up close, Letta could see that each breath was an effort for her, a slow sucking noise that made Letta shiver. Letta went through the door and Amelia closed it, leaving the gavvers outside. A long corridor stretched out in front of her.

'Come,' the older woman said, and Letta followed her. Half-way down the corridor, Amelia stopped and opened a door. The room they entered was large and comfortable. A seat hung from a chain in the middle of the ceiling and all around were soft chairs and tall, elegant candles that would supplement the modest electric light. The far wall was entirely made of glass, or what looked like glass. Up close, Letta could see that there was a door embedded in the glass. Amelia opened it and gestured to Letta to step outside.

Letta moved forward tentatively. She was standing on an enormous platform, a half-circle bordered by a low wall of glass. As she stepped onto it, it felt as though it were swaying in the wind. She clenched her fists and looked up. A man stood against the wall looking out beyond the house. John Noa. Letta registered that it must be he, but she couldn't concentrate on that. The wind was howling around her ears and she felt dizzy.

The man turned. 'Come,' he said in a high, sharp voice that she could just hear above the din of the wind.

She wanted to turn and flee to the safety of the house, but she had to do as he said. She felt as though she were on a tightrope, sure the gusts of wind would pick her up and throw her over the edge. The floor was transparent, and through it she could see the teeth of the cliff. She wanted to lie on the ground, to close her eyes. She took two more steps forward. As she neared John Noa she almost stopped breathing. The platform stretched out over the edge of the cliff and looked down on an angry sea. She could hear the waves below, feel the salt spit on her face. She felt the dizziness return.

'Are you all right?'

She could hear Noa, as though he were miles away, his voice echoing through a tunnel. Her legs grew weak and then his arms were around her.

'What's the matter?' he said, and she could feel his breath on her cheek.

'I don't like heights,' she managed to say. The truth was she was terrified of heights. She always had been.

Noa took her arm. 'You poor child.'

He led her back to the safety of the room. She almost collapsed as he closed the door, shutting out the wind and the terrible vista outside. He lowered her on to a chair.

'I am so sorry,' he said. 'I thought you would enjoy the view. I even asked them to be sure you brought your coat.'

He filled a glass of water from a jug that stood on the table. 'Here,' he murmured. 'Drink.'

She swallowed the cold liquid gratefully and felt better.

'Th... thank you,' she stuttered.

John Noa looked down at her. A tall, gangly man, he had deep-set dark eyes and curly hair, brown streaked with grey.

He smiled at her. 'Better?'

She nodded. Was he talking List now? As though he could read her mind, he spoke.

'So,' he said sitting on the chair opposite her. 'You are a wordsmith. No need for us to speak List then, is there?'

'No,' she said.

'I don't often get the opportunity to speak in the old tongue. I find it quite enjoyable.' He picked up the jug and poured himself a glass of water.

She noticed his long, tapered nails. He was Benjamin's age but looked twenty years younger, she thought.

'You must be wondering why I sent for you?'

'Yes,' she said.

He frowned. 'I'm afraid I have some bad news.'

Letta's thoughts raced. Bad news? Was he going to shorten the List again? Or something worse? Why was he telling her and not Benjamin?

'It concerns your master, Benjamin Lazlo.'

Letta felt as though the world had stopped spinning. Her body went cold all over. Time had slowed down.

'Has … something happened to him?'

She could hear her own words but didn't recognise her voice. He looked up and she knew she didn't want him to speak. She didn't want to hear the next thing he said. She pulled back in the chair trying to put more distance between them, but there was no stopping him now. In slow motion she watched his lips part.

'I'm afraid he is dead, Letta.'

Dead. Deprived of life. No longer living.

The word fell from his lips like a grenade, and then exploded in the air between them. *Dead.* Had he really said it? John Noa was on his feet. His lips were still moving.

'A terrible shock … a great man … we go back a long way.'

Not Benjamin. Please not Benjamin.

Noa took her hand, helping her out of the chair.

'Listen now, Letta,' he said. 'Listen child.'

She forced herself to look at him, to concentrate on the words that were still pouring from his mouth.

'You are the wordsmith now. The only wordsmith we have. Do you understand?'

She nodded and looked away, but he took her chin between his thumb and finger and turned her face back to him.

'You have a grave responsibility. Are you ready for this challenge?'

She nodded again. He seemed satisfied.

'I am sorry for your loss,' he said, and left the room.

She stood there for a few minutes feeling the heaviness that had descended on her. Never had she felt so alone. Benjamin was gone. The pain in her heart forced her to sit again. *Benjamin.*

89

She barely noticed Amelia walking into the room.

'I'm sorry about your master.' Her soft voice broke the terrible silence, speaking the old tongue, like Noa. 'He was a great man and a great friend, and he played an important part in building Ark. You can be proud.'

'Where? How?' Letta tried to say the words, but it felt like they were lodged too tightly in her throat.

'Smith Fearfall, the scavenger, found him. Found his body. He had been savaged by wild animals, but Fearfall recognised him.'

Savaged by wild animals.

'Where?' Letta said, not looking at Amelia.

'South of the river, in the forest. He was working there. We have some of his things, if you'd like to have them?'

Letta nodded and heard the woman slip quietly out of the room.

Savaged by wild animals.

Her head was beginning to throb. Could it be true? Was Benjamin really gone for ever? She didn't think she could bear it. She tried to picture his face, his eyes, but there was nothing there. She almost panicked then. Why could she not picture him? She walked towards the window. Outside, it had started to rain again, the repetitive tapping of the rain on the glass, the whistle of the wind outside. She couldn't bear any of it.

She turned and found Amelia standing watching her. In her hand was Benjamin's familiar old satchel. She almost ran across the room, banging her shin on the low table as she passed it. She grabbed the satchel, holding it close to her face. His smell filled her head, the smell of paper and wool and warmth.

'I'll see you out.' The woman's voice cut through her thoughts.

Letta nodded and followed her to the door.

'John Noa will want to see you soon, to talk about your new work,' Amelia said, and then the door was closed and Letta found herself once more in the rain and wind. She turned slowly and walked back down the stone stairs.

By the time she reached the shop, it had grown dark. The night-light had just come on, its quiet glow bathing the room in shadow. She sat down on the soft chair in the living area, Benjamin's bag on her lap. The leather felt warm despite the glaze of rain. She opened it, the clasp cold beneath her fingers. Inside was a half-empty water bottle, his tools and a collection of odds and ends. She pulled out a label. It was made of some sort of plastic and on it was written *Sunshine Replacement Therapy*. She knew it was old, though she had no idea how old. She thought they had all those words already, but maybe not. She would ask him later. Or, no, she couldn't. Even as the thought flitted by she was overcome by loneliness.

Finally, worn out, she lay in the big chair and fell asleep. In her dreams, she was in the middle of the ocean in a boat with silver sails. A warm summer breeze ruffled her hair and she could feel the sun on her face. The waves beside her were small and flecked with white foam. Deep in the body of the wave, words tumbled, one over the other.

Mother. Fish. Step. Summer.

Tiny red words, bobbing and weaving. A cold breeze rushed by, and the sun dodged behind a cloud. She shivered. Something was wrong. The waves were getting bigger. She struggled with the sail, which had changed from silver to black. The rope cut her hands. She couldn't lose the boat. Her father's boat. The wind was roaring and the waves towered above her. She turned

91

just in time to see a giant word rise from the foam. It was as big as a building and for a second it hovered above her.

Dead.

She managed to read it just before it crashed down on her, sending her to the very bottom of the ocean. She woke screaming.

The new day brought only more misery. She went to Central Kitchen, opened the shop, transcribed words – all in a kind of numbness. Nobody mentioned Benjamin. Letta knew that people had been told but it wasn't done to discuss the death of a loved one. Too many people had died in the disasters, nobody acknowledged death any more. But there were little kindnesses, smiles of sympathy, warm glances. She knew they felt for her, she didn't need their words. Werber called with her water allowance and for once she was almost glad to see him. Mrs Truckle came and brought her an apple. She said nothing about Benjamin but Letta knew the older woman understood, none the less.

'You wordsmith now,' she said to her before she left. 'Not child. Wordsmith.'

When she wasn't grappling with her grief over Benjamin, Letta wondered about Marlo. She still hoped they might find Daniel. The healer's wife had called in the afternoon to order words for their new apprentice, her face a mask of grief. Letta longed to tell her that Marlo's friends were going to look for Daniel but she knew she couldn't. So instead, she sat and transcribed the words that were needed.

Feverfew, lilac, rosemary, thyme.

It was one of the longest lists that had to be prepared and one of the most difficult. Letta worked on it all afternoon, glad of the distraction. The day dragged on. She couldn't eat, couldn't bear to think any more. She went into Benjamin's study and looked through the things on his desk. The words he was working on, his maps, drawn in his own hand. The forest was a strange place and very few people knew anything of its geography.

She pulled one of the maps closer to her and examined it. She could see the official path along which the water pipe ran from the lake buried in the centre of the forest. That was the road Benjamin took. It was patrolled regularly because of the water and was therefore considered reasonably safe. Beyond the path was the dense, dark forest, haunted by wild animals and, some believed, bandits. Benjamin had often told her that the greatest danger was the lack of food and water and the possibility of getting lost in there. She was about to put the map away when something caught her eye. A river. Benjamin had written the word clearly and underlined it.

THE RIVER.

She realised it meant something to her. Hadn't Amelia said that they had found his body south of the river? But the river was miles from the official track. What had Benjamin been doing there? She looked at the map again. The river was nowhere near the main path. She knew Benjamin wandered off path a little on his trips. If he found something interesting he might expand the dig in any direction, but he would never lose sight of the main road. So what had he been doing at the river? She felt that there was more she knew about the river, some other context, but it wouldn't come to her. They said a scavenger had found him. Fearfall. She was sure that was what they had said. She picked up a card and wrote it down. *Fearfall.*

If he was a scavenger he probably lived in Tintown. She had never gone down there – Benjamin wouldn't hear of it. It was a lawless place, a place people avoided. And yet, she wanted to talk to this man. He had found him – surely he could tell her why Benjamin had been there. Then another thought struck her. What had Fearfall been doing there? She frowned. None of it made any sense. Not for the first time, she wished she had someone to talk to, someone like Marlo.

It hit her like a thunderbolt. That was it! Marlo. It was Marlo who had mentioned the river. In the throws of his fever, he had talked about the Desecrators and the pump house and the river. She wondered what Marlo was doing. Had they found Daniel? Did he think of her at all? She sighed.

All she had was questions. Benjamin had gone to a part of the forest that was both dangerous and off his normal route. A scavenger had happened on his body. A scavenger who had no business in the forest. Was the scavenger lying? Had he murdered Benjamin and taken his bag? Why then would he go to Noa and tell him everything?

She stood up and walked to the window. Where was his body now? She couldn't bear to think of Benjamin thrown to the animals. Was he cold? With all her heart she wanted to hold him in her arms, to wrap a warm blanket about him, to let him know that he was not forgotten. Her dream came back to haunt her and she shivered. She remembered what Marlo had said.

There's always truth in dreams. Don't you know that? We have to learn what they mean, that's all.

CHAPTER 8

#326

Outcast

Person who is not part of Ark

THE rest of the day passed in a blur. Letta busied herself with her normal jobs, but her thoughts were in turmoil. She had to talk to the scavenger. She would go to Tintown. She pulled her coat from the nail and put it on, her hands shaking. Then, she picked up Benjamin's old satchel and thrust a bottle of water into it. As she left the shop, she locked the door behind her and looked around. The streets were quiet. The children were still at school, their parents in the fields. She could see Mrs Pepper sweeping the path in front of Central Kitchen. A woman and her baby were coming out of the healer's, the mother clutching a remedy in her hand.

As Letta turned to head south, she could hear the baby crying. Yesterday's rain had disappeared and a weak sun shone in the sky. She walked quickly, nerves bubbling in her stomach. Would the gavvers stop her at the gate? She reminded herself that she was the wordsmith now. She had to appear confident.

It took her very little time to get to the southern wall. Through the open gates she could just glimpse the flashes of light glinting on the roofs of the ramshackle town. She pressed on.

Two gavvers guarded the gate. As she approached, one of them stood up.

'Where go?'

His accent was rough, and Letta was sure that this was not his mother tongue. She pulled herself up to her full height and looked him in the eye.

'Tintown,' she answered.

'Why?' The man glared at her.

'Collect words,' she said firmly. 'Wordsmith.'

The man looked her up and down, then went to confer with his colleague. Letta tried to look mature and professional, but inside she was deeply uneasy. After what seemed like an age, the man returned.

'Pass,' he said, and instantly Letta found herself on the far side of the gate. She stood and looked down. Stretching on all sides were layer upon layer of flimsy dwellings, built from scrap of all sorts. Every roof seemed to be made of tin and the metal glinted even in this weak winter sun. But it wasn't the image of the town that most shocked Letta but the smell. Rising like a black cloud from the hovels below her came the stink of rotting vegetation and possibly rotting flesh too, she thought. It was a heavy, pungent aroma and already Letta could feel it soaking into her hair, into her skin, into her very bones.

The first hovels she passed were quiet enough. No sign of life, apart from clothes strewn on bushes, drying in the sun. There was only one water source here and no tokens for it. A communal pipe opened once a week and people fought for their supply of water. Benjamin had told her that a human could survive for one hundred hours without water, and sometimes, in Tintown, they had to.

Under Letta's feet animals scurried out of her way. Rats, mice, shrews, cats and dogs. Layer upon layer of humanity. Then a small gang of children appeared, like rabbits, jumping up in front of her. They were sparsely clad and barefoot. Three boys and two girls all under the age of ten, she reckoned. The tallest of them was a thin boy with long greasy blond hair, a sharp chin and bright slanting eyes. He took a step away from the others and sidled up to her. Letta kept walking, forcing him to jog alongside her.

'Who you?' he shouted.

Letta ignored him.

'Who you?' he said again. A sharp sting on her cheek brought her to a sudden stop. Her hand flew to the spot and she felt the warm wetness of her own blood. She looked around sharply just in time to see the boy shove a catapult into his pocket, his lips twisted in a sneer. Letta didn't stop to think. In two strides she was beside him. She caught him by the shoulders and shook him as hard as she was able.

'Bad boy,' she yelled.

She didn't expect the first kick and it caught her just below her left knee. She stumbled. Instantly, the other children were upon her. Small fists rained down on her back. Hands searched her pockets. She knew she hadn't brought any tokens with her or anything else of value. Another kick in the small of her back sent her sprawling into the mud. She struggled to get up, hitting out at bare legs, but the children threw themselves on her, punching and kicking as they went. Someone tugged at Benjamin's bag. She felt the strap dig into her flesh. She hit out as hard as she could but she was outnumbered. Just as Letta felt exhaustion claim her she heard an adult voice somewhere over her head.

97

'Stop!'

Instantly, the children scattered. Letta raised her head. The woman who stood there was tiny. Letta reckoned she was only four strides high. Pitch black hair was piled on top of her head, tendrils falling into her hooded eyes. Her hands were on her hips and her eyebrows were drawn together in a solid black line.

'Thank you,' Letta managed to say, pulling herself up from the ground, every muscle aching.

'What you want?' the woman growled.

Letta was about to answer when she saw a tall child approach her from the left. Without a second glance, the woman picked up a small sharp stone and threw it in the boy's direction. The stone caught him on the side of the head. Letta saw his face wince in pain, blood running down his cheek. This time he fled with the others.

'Rat.' The woman spat the word after him. Then her gaze returned to Letta.

'What you want?' she said.

'Look for man,' Letta said.

'What man?'

'Scavenger.'

The woman laughed, a short bitter sound.

'Many scavengers here,' she said.

'Fearfall,' Letta said and she thought she saw recognition flash in the woman's eyes. 'You know him?' Letta pressed on.

'No,' the woman said and turned and walked away.

'Wait,' Letta cried. 'Please.'

The woman turned. 'No know him,' she said.

'Know where find him?'

The woman shrugged. 'Try water hole.'

Letta followed the woman's gaze and could see in the distance a pool of some sort at the bottom of the hill. She started to walk in that direction. Her body ached from the attack by the children, and she could feel a sharp pain in her lower back getting more intense with every step she took. The shantytown was busier now with people standing outside their homes watching her as she passed. There were children everywhere, playing on the road, crying in their mothers' arms. The further into the town she went, the worse the smell became. The bodies around her were half-dressed and all seemed to be without shoes. The smell of sweat and dirt assailed her nostrils and made her feel queasy. She passed an old man sitting on the ground, one leg stretched in front of him, the shin cut right through. Letta glimpsed white bone under the torn flesh. She thought he might be the oldest person she had ever seen. He was small and painfully thin – it seemed like his cheekbones could slice through his face at any moment. He had pale, watery eyes and the surface of his face was lined with deep ridges of yellow skin. Flies buzzed about the open wound and the man did nothing to stop them. Letta took her water bottle from her satchel and knelt beside him. He didn't look up.

'Drink,' she said gently, holding the bottle to his lips. He looked surprised, but his lips parted and he drank deeply.

'Good,' he said, handing it back to her.

'Leg bad?' she said.

He nodded.

'Been worse,' he said.

I'm sure you have, Letta thought.

'Fought flood and worse to get here.'

Letta noticed the strange cadence of his speech. He obviously had a lot of language. It was harder for people to speak List when their heads were teeming with words.

'You come here after Melting?' she said gently.

He nodded.

'Bad times. Scientists not welcome.'

Benjamin had told her about these scientists who had arrived at Ark. They were seen as the enemy, the people who had opposed the Green Warriors before the Melting. There was no place for them in Ark. The miracle was that he survived all those years here in Tintown. She smiled at him.

'You very strong,' she said. 'Survivor.'

He nodded.

Letta pushed the bottle into his hand.

'Keep,' she said, and got up. A young man suddenly appeared.

'Father not well,' he said.

Letta nodded.

'Where you go?' the young man asked.

'Look for scavenger,' Letta said. 'Fearfall.'

The young man bit his lip. 'Smith Fearfall?'

Letta's heart leapt. 'You know him?'

The man nodded. 'Come,' he said.

Letta followed him. He was walking towards the pool she had seen earlier.

'Your name?' Letta asked.

'Kirch,' he said. 'Kirch Tellon.'

They walked on in silence then, Letta almost running to keep up with him.

She found it hard to believe that people lived in these conditions. No water, no power except what they could get for working in Ark. These were the people who had been too late, the unbelievers. Benjamin had told her about the hordes who had descended on Ark after the Melting, only to find the gates closed against them. Thousands had died. The ones who now lived in Tintown were the survivors.

Kirch stopped when they reached the pool. Up close, Letta could see it was just a hole full of stagnant, stinking water. A group of men and one small boy stood at the edge of the water, talking. They stopped when they saw Letta. It was then she realised that the pool was obviously the preserve of the men. She shifted awkwardly. Kirch stepped forward.

'Smith?' he said addressing a dark-skinned man in the centre of the group.

The man looked up.

'Girl want talk,' he said.

The men laughed and the one next to him nudged the dark man in the ribs. Letta lifted her chin and glared across at them. The dark-skinned man looked straight at her.

'Talk with me?' he said.

'Yes,' Kirch said. 'Talk with you.'

At first Letta thought that he was just going to ignore their request. He stood staring at Letta, making no move to join her. She felt herself blush under his gaze.

'Why?'

Letta took a deep breath. She wasn't going to let him see how intimidated she felt. 'Benjamin Lazlo,' she said. 'Wordsmith. You found him.'

Again the man waited, not moving. Letta could almost see the wheels in his brain turning. He bent down to the boy at his knee, who was playing with a mound of small stones.

'Allove!' he said.

The boy looked up.

'Stay!'

The boy went back to his game. The scavenger walked towards her. Up close, he had black eyes and the whitest teeth she had ever seen.

'Walk,' he said, and headed off away from the pool.

Letta took time only to turn to Kirch and mutter a hurried thank you before following him.

The man walked as far as the big oak tree that dominated the outskirts of Tintown before stopping and looking at Letta.

'Who you, who?' he asked, and Letta noticed that he had a strange dialect, one she hadn't heard before.

'Letta,' she said. 'Wordsmith.'

He nodded.

'Smith Fearfall,' he said. 'Scavenger.'

'You found my master?'

He nodded again.

'Lazlo. Yes. Find.'

'Where?'

'Forest. Near river.'

'His things?'

He looked surprised at the question.

'Bag,' Fearfall said. 'Gave to Noa.'

Letta moved the satchel on her shoulder. She saw the man glance at it but he showed no reaction. *Strange*, Letta thought. *The bag is right here in front of you but you don't recognise it?*

'What you do at river?' She knew as soon as she asked that it was a mistake.

A veil descended over his eyes. He turned away from her abruptly.

'No question now,' he said. 'No more.'

Before Letta could think what to do, he was walking away from her. She ran after him and caught his arm.

'Please!' she said, but he pushed her away and lengthened his stride.

She had to run to keep pace.

102

'Please,' she said again. 'Need to talk.'

He turned and glared at her, his eyes shining with menace. 'No talk,' he said. 'Go home.'

Then he broke into a run, his long legs eating up the road.

Letta stood helpless, watching him go, until he was lost in a blur of people and houses. She looked down at the old satchel around her neck. Why had he not recognised it?

Her journey out of Tintown was tense and stressful. People eyed her slyly as she passed, nudging one another and pointing. A man shouted something after her but she couldn't catch what he said. She hurried on, keeping her head down.

And then she saw the soft glow of fire away to her right, off the beaten path. She hesitated. John Noa had banned all open fires in a bid to save what was left of the ozone layer. The light from the fire flickered in the encroaching darkness, throwing sinister shadows about at will. Letta walked on, resolute. Who would dare light a fire here? And then she saw it.

A tight knot of people, standing around a brazier. As she approached them they turned to stare at her. They were the Wordless; people who had no language at all. She could hear them grunting at one another and pointing at her. Her mouth felt suddenly dry and her legs slowed despite herself. No-one knew exactly how they had become wordless. After the Melting, many children had been separated from their parents and had wandered for months or even years with no-one to teach them the rudiments of language. Some people believed the Wordless came from there. Others believed they were evil spirits wandering the planet looking for mischief. An old woman had told Letta that when they lost their words they also lost some of their humanity. Now, they were as unpredictable as wild animals and just as dangerous. Letta watched them dancing around the fire, arms and legs fluid, as if being blown by the wind. The gavvers had tried to put them to work in the fields but they caused so much unrest amongst the workers that the plan had to be abandoned. No-one wanted to be near them, watching them struggle to speak, making animal noises that could not be understood. Now they lived in the wild, like animals, encroaching on Ark from time to time, but mostly staying in Tintown or at the edge of the forest.

As Letta watched, mesmerised, a man broke from the group and smiled at her, a big toothless grin. He was tall, over six foot and very thin. The skin on his face was pocked and raw. His hair, long and matted, clung to his face. Rough red stubble covered his chin. For a moment Letta couldn't move at all. She could feel the heat of the fire on her cheek. The man stretched his hand out towards her. Letta didn't know if the hand was there in friendship or as a threat. She didn't wait to find out. She turned and ran as fast as she was able, not looking back. Her heart thumped in her chest, her lungs gasped for air, but she didn't stop till she reached the gate.

She looked down at the ground and hurried through. The workers were coming home from the fields, filling the town with their voices, and giving everywhere an air of business. Letta tried to calm her beating heart, the images of the Wordless still haunting her. She remonstrated with herself as she walked. There was nothing to be afraid of. They were just people who had never learned to talk. Why, then, did they fill her with such horror?

She walked down the hill towards the water station. As she turned the corner into the square she stood stock-still.

There on the wall of the old mill was an enormous painting of a forest, dense lines of green trees under an orange sky. Letta stood staring up at it, unable to comprehend what she was seeing.

All around her the workers were stopping too, all chatter ceased, all eyes directed at the mill.

The scene had been painted on a giant canvas, the cloth stretched across the old mill wall so that it took out every other vista. Letta's eyes devoured it. At first she thought it was all green but now she could see it was layers of colour, sea green, grass green, intercut with bands of daffodil yellow and deepest gold. And if she screwed up her eyes, she could see faint shadows of lilac with their hint of summer. It was beautiful. All thoughts of the Wordless and Tintown vanished and she lost herself in its loveliness.

Around about her, people had no choice but to stop and stare. In the midst of it all, an old man walked out from behind the mill. He had long grey hair flowing free and a thin wispy beard that fluttered in the breeze. On his head was a woollen hat, and he wore no coat. In his hand he held a paintbrush.

'Look!' he said. 'This is art! Look at it! This is what John Noa is afraid of! You have a right to express yourselves. You are human not animal! Feast your eyes. Don't be afraid!'

Letta never saw where the gavvers came from. One minute the old man was still talking, waving his hands about, the next he was lying on the ground, blood flowing from his head into the drain beside the path.

Letta's instinct was to run to him, to help him, but in a single heartbeat, gavvers surrounded his prone form. All around her people were gasping and exclaiming. It seemed they were as shocked as she was. A voice rose, a man to the right of Letta, shouting at the gavvers.

'Hey! Easy there! Back off.'

There were more mutterings of agreement, and then suddenly the gavvers were reaching for their truncheons and running at the crowd. At the same time whistles were being blown to summon help. A woman screamed. As if in slow motion, the people started to move, glancing back all the time even as they ran further and further away, as though afraid there was more action to come. Letta found herself carried along by them, moving inexorably away.

Inside the shop, she stopped to get her breath. The old man had been a Desecrator. She was sure of it. Had Marlo been there? Was the world gone mad? It hadn't been a week since Benjamin had left but she had totally lost her bearings. She looked at her desk and even that looked unfamiliar to her. She could feel Benjamin's presence. He was in the very air here. She wanted to reach out and touch him. *Where are you? Are you dead? Talk to me!* Anger bubbled up, making her head ache. She wouldn't rest until she knew what had really happened. That scavenger, Fearfall, had not found Benjamin. She gritted her teeth. Why had he lied to John Noa? Was he still lying?

She sat at her desk and rested her chin on her hand. She wanted to go to this river, to see where Smith Fearfall said he'd found Benjamin. But how could she do that? She knew nothing about the forest. And then an image slipped into her mind, unbidden.

Marlo. The Desecrators knew the forest. Would they help her? She clenched her fists in desperation. They would have to. She would have to convince them. Somehow.

CHAPTER 9

Hope _Non-List_

Expect to get something
intensely wished for

AS LETTA left Central Kitchen the following morning, Carver
the gavver suddenly appeared beside her. Despite herself, her
heart quickened.

What did he want? Had he found out something?

'Yes?' she said, doing her best to pretend that it was normal
for a gavver to approach her, though a pulse was pounding in
her neck.

'Words,' he said, pushing past her and walking towards the
open door.

'Words?' Letta echoed.

'Words for gavvers. Apprentices.'

She almost laughed out loud.

'How many boxes?' she asked.

'Ten,' Carver replied, throwing the word over his shoulder
but not bothering to look at her.

Letta nodded.

'You collect?'

'You bring.'

Without another word, he was gone. She'd never done words

107

for the gavvers before. That had always been Benjamin's job. It wouldn't do if these particular words fell into the wrong hands. Like every trade, they had their codes and mysterious modes of communication.

She walked through the living area and into Benjamin's study. There, she unlocked the door into his private library. She breathed in the smell of books and age and suddenly grief overcame her like an unexpected shower in summer. She hadn't been in here since she'd got the news. She sank to her knees, overcome with emotion. Where was he? A tear burned its way down her cheek and she wiped it away impatiently. There was no time to waste on crying, she told herself. She headed over to the shelves. Her eyes scanned the rows of boxes.

G. Gavver

There it was. She took the box and hurried out of the room, carefully locking the door behind her. Back in the living room, she put on a large pot filled with seawater to boil. The beetroots would arrive later and she would have to start the long process of making ink. She had gone out earlier and carried the two tin buckets full of brine back from the beach. Soon a man would come from the fields with the beetroot, and she could begin. It was always the same on the first day of the harvest moon. For as long as she could remember, on that day, the house was filled with the earthy smell of beetroot. Benjamin had used different plants at different times of the year to make ink but autumn ink was always beetroot.

Letta had taken some pleasure the previous evening when Mrs Pepper had arrived with the little stove that Letta would be permitted to use in order to make the ink. It was well known in Ark that Mrs Pepper had no use for words or wordsmiths. She and Benjamin had always had a testy relationship, and her sour countenance had been very much in evidence when she handed Letta the little stove. Letta smiled at the memory.

Up at her desk, she took out the cards carefully. There were about thirty in all, each one in Benjamin's clear script.

Artist: Creator of art, enemy of New World, Desecrator

Letta knew that the word had had another meaning in the time before the Melting. Benjamin had told her how artists had been revered when he was a boy, but that they had become arrogant and led people astray. They were not tolerated in Ark, and even their work was banned. They had become a secret organisation, known as the Desecrators. She picked up another card:

Report: Make known to the authorities

Letta dipped her pen in the ink, drew out a fresh card and started to write. She was so engrossed in what she was doing that she didn't hear the door open and someone walk in.

'Letta!'

Letta jumped, sending ink splashing across the words she had just written. She looked up. Werber. Now what did he want?

'Yes?' she said, not managing to keep the impatience out of her voice.

'How you?' Werber smiled at her, revealing his large white teeth.

'Good,' she said. 'Work.'

He nodded.

'Work later,' he said.

She walked to the counter and stood waiting to see what he wanted.

'See Desecrator?' he said suddenly.

Letta drew in a fast breath. What did he mean?

'Desecrator?'

'Yesterday, at mill?'

Letta calmed down. 'Yes,' she said. 'Saw him.'

'Saw him today,' Werber said smugly.

'Today?'

'Down at gavver base. Underground.'

Now she understood. She had seen the grating on the outside wall of the gavver base. They kept the prisoners underground, and sometimes you could see a hand begging for food through the grating. She realised Werber was still talking.

'Kicked sand in his eyes!'

'You did?'

He was obviously very proud of himself, Letta thought. His chest swelled and the smile grew even bigger.

'Desecrator,' he said again and spat on the floor.

Letta couldn't take any more. 'Want something?' she said. 'Work.' She nodded towards her desk.

'No,' Werber said, shifting from one foot to the other. 'You come walk with me?'

Letta's heart sank. That was the last thing she wanted to do. She shook her head. 'Work,' she said again, indicating her desk.

He scowled. 'Later?'

She shrugged her shoulders and went back to her desk, hoping he would get the message and leave. He stood for another minute.

'I ask Helen,' he said and, like a sulky child, he turned and left. Letta almost laughed. Werber really was foolish. He had been the same in school, always taking umbrage when the children teased him, running to Mrs Truckle over every small slight.

He had always made it known that he would like to mate with Letta. She had found that out when she was ten years old. Benjamin had advised her to be friendly with him, but not to make any commitment until she was eighteen. At eighteen, girls were expected to settle down with a man and produce children. No more than two children. It was a fine balance. Noa needed to repopulate the planet, but resources were limited, thus the two-child rule. Occasionally, people had a third child. Those children were taken and given to families who had no children or only a single child. A fourth child would have seen the parents banished.

There were few accidental pregnancies in Ark, and when they did happen, there were herbs from the healer to make sure the child didn't grow to term. Werber was a third child. He had been born to the Diamond family, whose mother was a tailor and whose father worked in the fields. The herbs hadn't worked, in that case, obviously. It happened. He had been taken from his mother and given to the Downes family. Third children were a rarity, and Benjamin always said that they became difficult, never really feeling part of the adopted family and living too near their family of birth. It was true in Werber's case.

Letta went back to her desk, but she couldn't concentrate. How would she contact Marlo? No-one had any idea where their hiding place was and even though she knew it was in the forest, she also knew she would never find it.

She sat lost in her own thoughts and, just as she was about to give up she heard Werber's voice in her head: 'Saw him today.'

Of course! Werber had seen a Desecrator. She could see the same man and talk to him. He could tell her how to contact Marlo. She tried not to think too much about the detail of her plan. There was no guarantee the prisoner would still be there or that he would talk to her. If he did talk to her, why would he trust her?

She would finish the word boxes, ten of them, and that would give her an excuse to go to the gavvers' base. At least she could try. If it meant she found out the truth about Benjamin nothing else would matter.

She went into the living room and tried to eat her lunch. A hunk of dry bread, a bowl of tomato soup made from the recent glut and an apple all stared up at her, but she had no appetite. She picked up the apple and took a bite. The smell reminded her of every autumn in Ark, the wagons loaded with apples fresh from the orchard, the sweet smell of fruit permeating every breath of air. For weeks Central Kitchen would produce jugs of apple juice and mounds of stewed apples with every meal. It didn't bother Letta. She liked apples. She took another bite. As her teeth sank into the firm flesh the door opened again and a young man came in with a large box. He placed the box on the counter.

'Beetroot,' he said, and before Letta could thank him he was gone. Letta took the box and brought it back to the living room. Then, taking the small sharp knife she had seen Benjamin use so many times before, she started to cut the beetroots into small chunks. The juice immediately covered her fingers, turning her skin bright red.

She looked at her hands and thought about all the wordsmiths who had gone before her. Not all of them had been required to make their own ink but maybe some of them had. She continued to chop the tough beetroots, throwing them into the pot to be covered by the boiling water. Finally, when all the roots were in the water, she reduced the temperature and left them to cook.

Then she went to finish the gavvers' word boxes.

By mid-afternoon, her hand ached but the ten boxes were finished and the shop was filled with the heavy smell of the beetroot. She walked over to the stove and turned off the heat. Then, carefully, she strained the crimson juices into a large bowl. She picked up one of the bigger chunks and pushed it through the old wire strainer to thicken the liquid. She stirred it, watching the blood-red soup swirl and wave. She knew there was no more to do but to let it cool.

Outside, the bell chimed four o'clock. It was time to go. Letta went and got her coat. Butterflies danced in her stomach and her hands had begun to sweat. She would play it by ear, she thought. One step at a time.

The gavvers' base was below John Noa's house to the south of the town. It was nestled at the bottom of the hill and Letta always thought it looked as though John Noa was looking down on it, keeping an eye on the criminals that were held there. She took the long way around, passing the mill, eager to see if there was any sign of yesterday's painting but there was nothing. The mill stood unadorned as though nothing unusual had ever happened there. Letta couldn't help feeling a little disappointed. She had never seen anything like it and she knew she would never forget it. The old man's words lingered in her memory too.

You have a right to express yourselves. You are human!

He was wrong, of course. Before the Melting, people had expressed themselves as they wished, and look at where that got them.

She turned the corner on to Mill Street itself. On the opposite side of the road, two Green Warriors were standing, talking. Letta bowed her head in their direction but they didn't

113

seen to see her or take any notice of her greeting. She pressed on, the face of the cliff visible in front of her, beyond that the silhouette of Noa's house perched near its summit. In front of her, she could see the Round House, the gavvers' base, its round stone walls broken only by narrow slits for windows, its high metal gates guarding the perimeter, and its massive front door painted black.

She shifted the satchel from her shoulder where it had started to eat into her flesh and held it awkwardly in the crook of her elbow. She took a deep breath and marched on through the gates up to the front door. She pushed on the door and it opened. Inside was a small entrance hall with a short desk, behind which sat a gavver. He looked up when Letta came in. He was young with bright eyes, full of curiosity. He stretched his neck forward when he saw her.

'Yes?' he said.

Letta put her bag on the desk and started to take out her boxes.

'Words,' she said. 'Carver.'

He nodded, taking up a box and examining it.

'Good,' he answered, and smiled at her, showing two rows of white teeth.

Letta nodded towards the boxes.

'Apprentices,' she said, by way of explanation, but really just to keep him talking.

'Yes,' he said. 'You wordsmith?'

Letta nodded. 'Wordsmith,' she agreed.

There was an awkward silence then till Letta realised there was nothing else of value she could get from the young gavver. She couldn't very well ask him about his prisoners. Could she?

Letta smiled at him. 'Many prisoners?' She angled her head to one side, hoping she looked alluring.

114

It seemed to work. He smiled again. 'Yes,' he said. 'Many.'

'Good,' Letta said. 'Desecrators?'

He nodded. 'Some.'

'Saw one,' Letta said, feigning excitement. 'At mill.'

The gavver nodded barely concealing his pride. 'Hugo.'

'Still here?' Letta asked.

The young man glanced nervously behind him. 'Yes,' he said. 'In prison.'

'Any others?'

'Why you ask?'

The voice made Letta jump, her heart started to pound. She turned around slowly. Carver stood there watching her, his mouth curled in a sneer.

'I...I bring words,' Letta stammered.

'Go now.' Carver spat the words at her.

The young gavver put his head down and seemed afraid to look at her. Letta grabbed her bag and walked out, trying not to let the older man see her fear. She could feel his eyes burning into her as she passed him in the doorway and then she heard it bang behind her and felt the cool air on her face. She sighed with relief. What should she do now? Hugo the Desecrator was still here. She knew where the grating was. She had to try to talk to him. But what if Carver came back out? What possible reason could she have to talk to a prisoner? She hesitated. She had to try. They could move the prisoner or expel him at any time and then she would have no way of finding Marlo.

She turned right, walking close to the building, around the corner to the gable. She had seen the grating before. She looked down. No hands stretched out in supplication. She went to the first grate and hunkered down beside it.

'Hello?'

The word sounded foolish hanging there in the open air. It wasn't even a List word. She waited, glancing nervously behind her. Nothing. She tried again.

'Hello?'

Out on the street, through the railings, she saw a cart go by. She jumped up quickly, but the driver didn't even glance in her direction. She moved swiftly to the next grating. Again she hunkered down.

'Hello? Hugo?'

She waited. *This is pointless*, she thought. *There's no-one there.* She would try one more time and then go home.

'Hugo?' she said again.

A hand appeared at the grating. Letta almost screamed.

'Yes?' the voice sounded eager.

'Are you Hugo?' Letta said, never taking her eyes off the gnarled old hand at the grate.

'Yes,' the old man said. 'I am Hugo. Who are you?'

Letta looked around nervously. He wasn't speaking List so she answered him in kind.

'I am Letta,' she said. 'The wordsmith.'

'Letta,' he said, with a deep sigh. 'What a lovely name!'

He sounded so calm, so confident, as though he were chatting to someone in Central Kitchen. Letta took a deep breath.

'I need to get a message to Marlo,' she blurted out.

Letta squinted through the grating and could just see the shape of the old man. He was manacled to the wall just beneath the grating. The first band of steel was about his upper arm and the second nearer his wrist. The manacles made sure that he couldn't sit or lie down, couldn't move away from the open grating.

'Ah,' said the old man. 'I see.'

Suddenly the air was rent by the screams of another prisoner from inside the jail.

'What's happening?' Letta said, afraid of the answer.

'Torture,' the old man said grimly. 'They are torturing someone.'

Letta shuddered. 'Why?' She could barely say the word as the screams grew more intense. She tried not to imagine what was happening back there in the darkness.

The old man's voice broke into her thoughts. 'Why do you want Marlo?'

'I helped him,' she managed to say. 'Now I need him to help me,' she said.

'I know who you are now,' the old man said. 'I heard about you.'

'Will you help me?' Letta persisted.

'Leave a message under the stone behind the Goddess.' The old man had to raise his voice to be heard now. 'Before dawn tomorrow.'

Letta nodded. 'Can I...can I do anything to help you?' she said.

The man laughed. 'I think I am beyond help,' he said.

Letta rummaged in her bag and found a small bottle of water. She put it into his hand. 'Take that,' she said.

The old hand grasped the bottle and coaxed it through the bars of the vent.

'Thank you,' he said.

'Good luck,' Letta managed to say, hauling herself to her feet.

Just as she did, the young gavver appeared at the corner and walked towards her. Letta's heart sank. What was she to say?

'Gate?' she said and, even as she did, she knew she sounded like an imbecile. He stared at her for a moment then laughed. He pointed to where the gate was.

'That way,' he said and she could see the amusement in his eyes.

117

'Thank you,' she said and scurried past him.

At the corner, she looked back. The gavver wasn't looking at her. He was urinating into the grate, a steady stream of yellow waste pouring into the cell below.

Letta ran to the gate, rage burning in her gut. This was the man she had joked with, smiled at, only minutes earlier. Why would anyone do that? Her temper flared, sending hot blood into her cheeks. She leant against the railings, teeth clenched, her hands balled into fists. She wanted to go back there and push him away, to hurt him in any way she could. She took deep breaths. He was a pig. If only she could say that to him. A pig.

And then her pulse slowed and her heart sank, a feeling of helplessness flooded her body. She couldn't challenge him. She couldn't attack him. He was a gavver and she was nothing. Nothing at all. In her mind, she could hear the man in the cell screaming again. She didn't think she would ever forget that sound and the image of Hugo's weathered old hand clutching the grate. She walked away only stopping once to look up at John Noa's house. Did he know what was going on in the building beneath him? Did he know? Had he ordered it?

She hurried along the street. She couldn't think about any of that now. She had succeeded in what she set out to do, she reminded herself. She knew how to contact Marlo. In the morning, she would go to the Goddess and leave a message.

As she reached the door of the shop, she realised she was thirsty. She reached for her bag and remembered that she had given the last of the water to Hugo. There would be no more till the morning. She couldn't ask Werber, not after the way she had treated him. She swallowed hard. She couldn't think about any of that now. She had to compose her message to the Desecrators.

Even as she formed the thought, she shuddered. What had she become? She looked down at her blood-red hands and shivered. It didn't matter. None of it mattered. She had to find out what had happened to Benjamin, and she would talk to anyone who could help her. With new determination she opened the door of the shop and stepped inside. She went straight to the drop box. There was only a single card there. A card like the ones they used in the shop. She pulled it out and examined it. The words were written in block capitals. Letta read them. A small cry escaped her lips. She read them again to make sure she had understood.

BENJAMIN NOT DEAD

The card fluttered to the floor. The words flew about the room. Benjamin. Not. Dead.

CHAPTER 10

THE HOUR before the dawn was dark and unpromising, Letta thought, looking out her bedroom window. Her thoughts were racing. Questions had kept her awake through the long night. Who had dropped the card there? And most pressing of all: was it true? Could Benjamin be alive?

She tried to suppress the excitement she felt. *Please let it be true. Let him be alive.* Another part of her brain shouted even louder, calling her a fool. John Noa had told her that Benjamin was dead. He wouldn't have said it if it weren't true. But what if the scavenger had lied to him?

On the street below, there was no sound. The full moon was hidden behind brooding clouds and the morning electricity hadn't yet kicked in. Letta looked at the note in her hand, the red ink on the white page.

Need help. Letta

Three words. Two List and a name. And yet it had taken her half the night to compose that message. She had spent hours debating whether or not she should sign her name. If the note fell into the wrong hands there would be no escape. But if she didn't sign her name, how could they know it was she? She was beyond caring. She would leave the message under the stone just as she had written it. Hugo had said to leave it there before dawn. She blew out the candle beside her bed and got dressed in the grey light.

She walked through the quiet town as though in a dream, trying not to think about the danger, trying not to think about her thirst, which was now a raging beast. The moon had come back out and lit her path and she was grateful to it. She headed towards the West Gate, turning right before she came to it, and climbed up the steep hill to the Goddess. As she walked she could hear the whirr of the tumbling windmills at the top of the hill. They were there from the time before the Melting when John Noa had started to prepare for the disaster he saw coming. Now they provided power to Ark, about the only technology they had. Power was of course strictly rationed. It would come on just after dawn for three hours and again in the evening for two hours during the winter months. This was when Central Kitchen cooked the food and other essential services were carried out. Only John Noa and the Green Warriors had power all day, as befitted their standing.

Letta trudged on. She could just see the shape of the Goddess silhouetted against the sky. She was almost upon the statue when she realised there was someone there. Letta stopped. She could hear a voice. She crouched there for a moment totally still. A female voice. But who would be up here at this hour? A gavver? There were some female gavvers. She had to get nearer. She crept along the edge of the path, the dry stalks of grass scratching her bare legs. She could make out words now.

'Goddess! Please. Daniel is good boy. Please!'

Letta peered at her, as the early morning sun climbed into the sky momentarily blinding her. It was the healer's wife, Rose, kneeling in front of the statue and rocking over and back, keening softly. Letta stayed there, transfixed. The wind was starting to build and the noise of the windmills was getting stronger. Letta edged forward.

'Rose!'

She tried to keep her voice low so as not to startle the woman but she got no reaction. The keening continued interspersed with the odd word.

'Please! Not for me. For Daniel.'

Letta came out of the long grass and stood on the path within three strides of Rose, but it was clear that the other woman was too far gone to even notice. Very gently, Letta walked up to her and touched her shoulder. The face that turned and confronted her was alive with naked fear. Rose opened her mouth to scream but no sound came.

'It's all right, Rose,' Letta said. 'Me. Letta. No harm.'

Rose's eyes opened wide and she stood immobile looking at Letta. Letta stroked the older woman's arm and whispered reassurance to her until finally the hunted look left her eyes and large tears rolled down her face.

'You poor thing,' Letta said. 'You miss your boy.'

The woman nodded, and Letta could see that she was unable to speak.

'There might be someone,' Letta said.

The woman stared at her uncomprehending. Letta took her arm.

'Listen' she said. 'I'm going to ask someone … if they could help you.'

The woman collapsed into Letta's arms, great sobs racking

122

her body. Letta held her, feeling the warm tears through the thin fabric on her shoulder.

Rose looked up. 'How?' she said, searching Letta's face as though she could find the answer there.

Letta put her finger on the other woman's lips. 'Sh!' she said. 'Go home now. Wait.'

The woman nodded, then turned and fell on her knees before the Goddess. 'Thank you. Thank you. Thank you.'

Then she got up and took off down the hill.

Her stomach in a knot, Letta watched her go. Why had she promised to help Rose? She couldn't even help herself. And yet she couldn't bear to see her pain and say nothing. If there was any chance, didn't she deserve hope? But still feelings of guilt lay heavily on Letta. What if the Desecrators couldn't help? Or wouldn't help? She went behind the statue and found a big flat stone. She lifted it at one corner and shoved the note underneath. Now all she could do was wait.

Before she left, she stood in front of the Goddess and looked into her cold, empty eyes. How wonderful to believe there was a power greater than yourself! Someone who could sort things out for you.

'I'm sorry, Goddess,' she said aloud. 'I don't think I can believe in you.'

She took a deep breath. The air already had a hint of winter in it, sharp and cold. Beneath her, under the weak rays of the new sunrise, the town sprawled, guileless, an infant waking to a new day. The weak electric lights came on strung like stars across the landscape.

Letta hurried down the rough path, noticing dark clouds scurrying across the sky and joining the broody bank that had already settled over Tintown. Below her, the fields were orange in the

123

early morning light, with a gentle breeze riffling through them.

Her stomach grumbled and she quickened her step, making her way to the line that had already started outside Central Kitchen. Her tongue cleaved to the roof of her mouth with thirst. As soon as she walked in, she could smell apples and was rewarded with a glass of juice alongside her piece of bread and the two eggs Mrs Pepper handed her. She drank the juice before moving out of the line. The cold, bitter liquid drenched her tongue. She held it in her mouth for a moment before swallowing.

Mrs Pepper glared at her.

'Go!' she said, but for once Letta didn't care. Her thirst had been abated and soon she would be able to go to the water station for her water allowance.

Her thoughts went back to the Goddess and Rose's behaviour in front of the statue. Praying. That's what Benjamin called it. Was it any worse than her leaving the note? Who was to say that Hugo had told her the truth? Even if he had, and Marlo's friends got the note, why should they trust her?

By the time she got back to the shop, her head ached and she couldn't think clearly any more. When the bells rang for the eleventh hour, the door opened and Mrs Truckle came in. Letta knew that the old woman was keeping an eye on her. She knew her old teacher would not let Benjamin be disgraced. She should be grateful for that.

'Mrs Truckle!' Letta said, giving no hint of the way she was thinking. 'No harm.'

Mrs Truckle smiled. 'Where ink?' she said, her bright eyes darting about the room, as if Letta might have hidden it there.

Oh no, Letta thought. She had totally forgotten about it.

'Nearly ready,' she said, hoping the teacher hadn't noticed her alarm. 'Many bottles?'

'Twenty,' Mrs Truckle said, and Letta's heart sank. She had better tell the truth.

'Not filled yet,' she said, trying to apologise through the tone of her voice. There was no word for sorry on the List. Mrs Truckle shrugged.

'Come,' she said. 'I help.'

Before Letta could say anything, the small woman had gone through to the living room and was standing over the full bowl of ink. She tutted to herself as she removed the wire strainer with its mashed-up beetroot and peered into the bowl.

'Good colour,' she muttered, and Letta rushed to get the small bottles they used for the ink. She handed the bottles to Mrs Truckle, who filled each one carefully using Benjamin's old iron funnel.

'Busy?' she said to Letta, never taking her eyes from the task.

Letta nodded. 'Busy,' she agreed.

They both turned as the door into the shop opened.

'One minute,' Letta said, putting down the bottle in her hand.

She ran out to the shop only to find Rose standing there.

'Rose!' Letta said, unable to hide her surprise.

Rose was holding a bottle of water, a bottle big enough to be an allowance for two people. She pressed it into Letta's hands.

'For you,' she said. 'For you.'

'No,' Letta said, trying to give it back to her. 'I do nothing.'

'You help Daniel.'

And before Letta could say another word, Rose was gone. Letta stood looking at the water. This was crazy. She couldn't take it. She had done nothing to deserve it. But there was something else bothering her. She hadn't liked the way Rose had looked at her. It reminded Letta of the look Rose had had on her face as she knelt before the Goddess. She turned to find

Mrs Truckle framed in the doorway behind her, a worried frown creasing her old face.

'Why she give water?' she said, and Letta was back again in the classroom with a woman who always demanded an answer.

Letta shook her head. 'Nothing,' she said. 'Nothing.'

Mrs Truckle nodded to the bottle of water in Letta's hands. 'Water not nothing. She say you help Daniel?'

Letta paused. Now what could she say? 'Day they took him,' she managed finally. 'Helped her, day they took Daniel.'

Mrs Truckle looked at her without speaking, and Letta knew she didn't believe her. After what seemed like a very long time, Mrs Truckle reached out and took Letta's hand.

'Be careful, Letta,' she said, with steel in her voice. 'Be careful.'

Afterwards, when Mrs Truckle was gone, Letta sat at her desk, lost in thought.

The sound of the door opening startled her. She looked up. A man stood there. He was wearing a long black overcoat with a hood. The hood almost covered his face, wreathing it in shadow and making it impossible to see him properly. Letta opened her mouth to speak to him, just as he removed the hood. The morning light hit off his curly black hair and Letta gasped. Marlo!

He turned and saw her, a big smile spreading across his face.

Letta looked up at him. 'You came,' she said.

'You sent for me.' He smiled back at her. 'How did you know about the stone?'

'Hugo,' she said.

He nodded. 'Of course.'

'Maybe I should close the shop?' She looked nervously towards the door.

'Might look suspicious,' Marlo said. 'The gavvers are on full alert at the moment since Hugo's show.'

Hugo's gnarled old hand flashed through Letta's brain.

'What will happen to him?' she said.

Marlo looked away from her. 'They banished him this morning.'

Letta felt the room sway. She clutched the counter behind her.

'We've been out all night looking for him, but we didn't find him. He's an old man. He wouldn't have survived long out there.'

Marlo's voice seemed to be coming from within a long tunnel.

They had banished him. She couldn't process it. He had been alive and well yesterday.

Letta. What a lovely name!

'It's all right,' Marlo said putting his arm around her shoulder. 'They can't hurt him any more.'

Marlo pressed a bottle of water into her hands and she gratefully sipped from it, leaning her head on his shoulder.

'What's happened, Letta?' Marlo's voice was gentle, but there was tension there too. She could hear it, and see it, in the way he kept glancing at the door. She tried to marshal her thoughts.

'John Noa told me Benjamin was dead, but I don't believe him.'

It sounded bizarre now that she had said it to someone else. Why would Noa lie?

But Marlo didn't look like he thought it was bizarre. He frowned and said, 'So you think he's alive?'

Letta nodded and told him about the note and her conversation with the scavenger.

'We need to find out what he knows,' Marlo said and Letta's heart lifted at the use of the word 'we'. She had begun to feel

127

so alone, surrounded by things she couldn't figure out. It was good to have someone to discuss it with. Though she wasn't sure about talking to the scavenger.

'I don't think he'll say any more,' she said. 'Smith Fearfall is not the easiest man to talk to.'

Marlo smiled a small secret smile. 'We have ways of talking to people like that,' he said.

'Maybe I had better close the shop,' Letta said. 'We can't risk a gavver wandering in.'

Marlo nodded. Letta walked to the door and was just about to slide the heavy bolts across when someone pushed it open. Letta stumbled under the pressure. When she looked up, John Noa was standing looking down at her. For a second, Letta couldn't quite take it in. She recognised John Noa, she saw the two gavvers standing outside the door, but she couldn't put it all together. She opened her mouth to speak but no words came.

'May I come in, wordsmith?'

Noa's voice brought her back to reality. What was she to do? She stood back and he swept in past her. Marlo was still standing where she'd left him at the counter. Letta saw his eyes widen, then he bowed his head, staring at the floor.

Noa looked at Marlo, eyes narrowed.

'What your name, boy?'

For a second there was silence, and Letta could hear the beating of her own heart.

'Leo,' Marlo said, still without looking up. 'Name Leo.'

John Noa's eyes swept over him like a radar.

'Why you no work?'

Letta felt the blood drain from her face.

'Tintown,' Marlo said, still not looking at John Noa.

Noa frowned. 'Tintown. I see.'

128

Suddenly, Letta couldn't take it any more. She had to say something. She had to finish this. She turned to Marlo and took his arm roughly.

'Go now!' she said sternly. 'No food for you here. Need talk to John Noa.'

Marlo scurried out past her, the very vision of a shy peasant. Letta prayed the gavvers didn't recognise him. She held her breath as he walked past the two guarding the door.

John Noa laughed. Letta turned to him.

'You like your new power, Letta. I can see that.'

Letta glanced at the door. Marlo was gone. She started to breathe normally again, but her legs were still shaking, and her head felt light.

'Are you not going to invite me in?' John Noa said, and Letta could see the amusement in his eyes.

'Of course,' she stammered. 'Please.'

He followed her into the living area, and she gave him Benjamin's chair.

'Can I make you tea?' she asked.

He shook his head. 'I wanted to talk to you, Letta,' he said.

'Yes?' Letta answered, hoping he couldn't hear the shake in her voice.

'About Smith Fearfall.'

Letta felt the room tip. Fearfall. He knew. He knew she had been to Tintown.

'I…I…' Letta stammered.

'You spoke to him about Benjamin,' Noa said softly.

'Yes,' Letta whispered.

'You went to Tintown and questioned him.'

'I…I didn't mean any harm,' Letta said. 'I hoped he could tell me…'

'Could tell you what?' Noa said in the same gentle voice.

'Could tell me ... could tell me more ... about Benjamin.'

'Yes.' Noa nodded. 'You wanted to know what Smith was doing there?'

Letta was afraid to answer now. The atmosphere in the room had become oppressive. Noa hardly moved and didn't raise his voice but there was an air of menace about him.

'Well, let me tell you why he was there.'

Letta held her breath.

'I sent him to look for Benjamin.'

For a second, Letta forgot to be afraid.

'You sent him?' she said, blood rushing to her face. 'Why would you send him?'

Noa sat back in his chair and Letta felt his eyes sweep over her, examining her from head to toe. She shifted uncomfortably. Could he see through her?

'I was worried about your master. We were old friends, Benjamin and I. I knew him from before the Melting. Benjamin served our cause well.'

Letta could see that the old man was lost in thought, all the tension gone out of him.

'Benjamin wrote stirring articles on the web of the world, telling people about the cause, warning them that the end was nigh. Of course they didn't take him seriously. A conspiracy theorist. That's what they called him. Even as the water was rising on all sides of us, they challenged our every word.'

He stopped talking, looking down at his hands, twirling his thumbs. She noticed how white the skin on his hands was and saw again the long nails.

Then he looked up at her. 'I was worried about him. The Desecrators have been busy of late, and they have no respect for the likes of your master, so I sent Fearfall to track him down. You know the rest.'

Letta nodded. Guilt came in waves. Had she been so wrong about Fearfall? About the Desecrators? About John Noa?

'In future, come to me with your questions, child. I don't like people snooping around behind my back.'

He stood up. Even in old age, he was a forbidding figure, Letta thought as he towered above her.

'I'm sorry he died, Letta, but he is dead. You should accept it, and move on. Ark needs people like you. You are our wordsmith now. Don't get stuck in the past. Your place is in the future.'

When she looked up from the floor he was gone, but his words hung in the room as real as the table beneath her fingers. She heard the door bang and she sank to the floor, feeling the cold of the marble seeping into her bones.

Talking to the girl had awoken old memories. 'Don't get stuck in the past,' he had told her, and yet here he was revisiting it yet again. He remembered the end so distinctly, beat by beat, image by image.

It had started with rain. Three weeks of unrelenting rain. People had laughingly started to talk about building an ark. He had been way ahead of them. He had built Ark from nothing and with nothing. The Green Warriors had inputted all the available data and had come up with the ideal place to be when the end came. They knew, as others did not, that it had to be a place that could sustain them when all technology had been taken from them. They had built a new city incorporating some of the old buildings, inventing new ones. Most importantly, they had designed and made filters embedded with natural water channels extracted from green plants that could remove salt from sea-water. Water was the key to life and John Noa and the Wariors held that key.

From the safety of Ark, he had watched the end unfold. The rain. Three weeks of the heaviest rain the world had ever seen. In the cities, the force of the water in the drains propelled the manhole covers from their moorings. He remembered pictures of a car with a manhole cover embedded in the windscreen. There was water everywhere but still the politicians reassured people with soothing words, fraudulent, empty words.

And then as the rain still pounded the Earth, the storms came – storms that gathered in the oceans like wild horses, huge storms with waves one hundred feet high lashing the coast mercilessly. The earth shuddered under the attack. The electricity had to be cut for fear of fires. The world was plunged into a terrifying darkness. And still Nature roared.

Gales of four hundred miles an hour had no respect for that fine line between sea and coast. The wind chased the water in, over the man-made barriers; through the streets; over the buildings; drowning everything in its wake.

Millions of people died. Millions of animals, millions of birds. All lost.

He remembered one of the last speeches given by John Hardy, Prime Minister of England, Ireland and Wales.

'I have nothing left to give you,' he'd said, tears streaming down his face. 'Nothing but my words.'

Noa wiped away his own tears and stared into the middle distance. Soon, there would be no more words. None at all.

CHAPTER 11

Admit #11

(1) Tell hard truth
(2) Let in

AFTER John Noa left, Letta found it hard to concentrate on anything. Benjamin was dead. John Noa's words trickled down her spine like icy water.

But none of it made sense to Letta. Why had the scavenger not recognised the bag? How had he known where Benjamin was? Or maybe she didn't want to believe that Benjamin was gone for ever? *I have to stop this and do my work,* she told herself sternly. *Benjamin is dead. Noa would not lie to me.*

She sat at her desk and pulled a sheet of paper towards her. The new List needed to be transcribed. Her hand trembled as she picked up her pen. The words on the List looked back at her.

Above

Accept

She wrote carefully, trying to stop the letters from shaking. This was familiar territory, but she couldn't concentrate. Her mind kept replaying the conversation with Noa, and she knew she couldn't settle to anything. Noa wouldn't lie, but maybe the scavenger would? If Benjamin was alive, didn't she owe it to him to investigate things further? What if Noa wasn't telling the truth? She shook her head. How could she even think that? She had to be careful. Ever since she had crossed the line and taken Marlo in, she had strayed further from everything she believed in. She had to accept what Noa said. Accept it. But she couldn't. She knew she couldn't rest until she talked to Noa again. She would find an excuse to engage him in conversation and then casually ask him.

She got up and grabbed her coat. She opened the back door. A gust of wind hit her in the face and she gasped. The temperature had dropped and there was a distinct feeling of winter in the air. She pulled her coat closer to her and set off towards the hill to Noa's house.

As she walked, her mind was racing. So much had happened in a few days. She had hidden a Desecrator. She had spoken to them. She had heard the music, seen the painting. If John Noa found out, she would be banished. And yet, in her heart she could not believe that the Desecrators were the enemy. Surely there was a way that they could all live together? But there was such a chasm between the world they saw, and the one John Noa had seen before the Melting. Could the two ever come together? There was no word on the list for *hope* or *love*. Her heart quickened. Maybe that was where she could start with Noa. She was the wordsmith. She would suggest to him, with respect, that he put some abstracts on the list. Maybe only one at first. *Hope*. Hope could never be a bad thing, could it? Her own heart flooded with it, as she hurried through the streets.

Come and see me any time.

That was what he had said. She could smell the evening meal cooking as she passed Central Kitchen. Wednesday. Onion tart.

134

The sweet smell of the onions made her stomach rumble. She hurried her step. Past the tailor, and on past the tinsmith's shop, where a battalion of tin buckets stood to attention on the path outside. As she passed the Round House, a group of gavvers was standing as though waiting for something. Their eyes followed her as she headed up Noa's hill, but they said nothing.

The climb seemed longer this time, her mind racing with ideas, rehearsing the conversation she would have with Noa when she met him. *Hope*. Just one word. Then, over time, they could add others. Excitement coursed through her. This is what she was meant to do. All through history, wordsmiths had helped form the world. They were called other things – writers, journalists – but they had all worked with words and knew the power of words.

At the gate, she stopped to catch her breath. Overhead a gull screeched as she walked up to the door. She knocked twice and waited. Amelia Deer opened it.

'Come in,' she said, as though Letta's appearance was the most normal thing in the world. Letta stood and looked up at the tall woman.

'I want to see John Noa, please,' she said.

Amelia nodded. 'Of course,' she said. 'John is at a meeting, but if you would like to wait?'

Letta nodded. 'Thank you,' she said.

Amelia turned and started down the long corridor. Letta followed her. As soon as Amelia started to walk, Letta could hear the wheeze from her lungs, sucking the air in and delivering it back under pressure. Amelia stopped at a door halfway along the passage. She opened it and Letta stepped into a small room. There was a window at one end and a bench against the wall. Opposite the bench was a chair. The place felt cold and inhospitable. Letta shivered.

'Sit,' Amelia said, pointing to the bench.

Letta sat.

Amelia stood for a second, the husky wheeze getting stronger, and then she started to cough, a terrible hacking noise. Letta looked up, alarmed.

Letta didn't know what to do. Should she help her? Gradually the coughing subsided, but Letta noticed the muscles in the other woman's neck working hard to draw in air.

'Are you all right?' Letta said.

'Yes,' Amelia said, gasping out the word between great sucking breaths. And then she swayed.

At first Letta thought she was imagining it. Then Amelia did it again, and this time Letta noticed how grey and pinched her face was.

Amelia put her hand on the wall to steady herself. Her breathing was becoming more laboured, a wet, tortured sound coming from her lungs. Letta thought she could see fear in her eyes. She jumped up and took her by the arm.

'Sit down,' she said, pushing her into the chair. Amelia sat, great gasps coming from her mouth as she searched for oxygen, her hand like a claw at her breast. There was a tint of blue about her mouth. Letta's own heart was beating so fast she could feel its pulse in her throat.

'I'll go and get help,' Letta said, looking into Amelia's eyes and trying to sound composed, though her thoughts were in chaos. 'Try to relax,' she said. 'I'll find someone.'

Amelia managed to nod, and Letta could see that speech was beyond her. She turned and ran from the room. Down the corridor to where it turned right at the first corner. Letta looked down it hopefully. There was nothing there.

'Hello?' she called, her voice echoing in her ears. She opened the first door she saw. A meeting room. Long table. Chairs.

'Hello?' she called again, and this time she thought she heard something. There was a door at the far side. She tore across the room and opened it. She found the source of the noise straight away. A sparrow was battering himself against the closed window. Its little wings were flapping helplessly. As Letta watched, it hit the glass one more time and then collapsed on to the sill. Letta turned to leave, just as someone spoke in the adjoining room.

'I don't want to hear excuses.' The voice was low and menacing. 'I want results!'

John Noa. Relief flooded through her. She opened her mouth to call him, but just then Noa spoke again.

'What about the wordsmith? Have you dealt with him?'

Letta froze. She closed her mouth. 'We dispose of him tomorrow night.'

'You think that is the solution to everything. I needed him here! Helping me! The people trust him and are used to taking instruction from him. Don't you think they might wonder where he has got to? Was he in league with the Desecrators? Did you at least find that out?'

The other man sighed. 'We tried, sir. We took out all of his fingernails. We starved him, beat him.'

No! a voice screamed inside Letta's head.

'He insisted that he had nothing to do with them, but that he could not, would not, go along with your plan.'

'Stop!' Noa said. 'Enough. I don't want to hear about your barbarity. Where is he now?'

'In the holding cell. If he hasn't died yet.'

Letta heard Noa sigh.

'Take him to the forest then and dispose of him.'

'Maybe it would be safer to kill him, master?'

'No!' Noa said. 'We do not kill. Nature will take care of those we need to eliminate. How long can an injured old man survive in the forest? We need not interfere.'

'We will do it tomorrow night, master.'

'Are you sure Fearfall won't talk and –'

Before Noa finished his sentence, Letta heard the door to the main room open.

'Sir!' A woman's voice. 'It's Amelia. She's had a bad turn. She can't breathe.'

Noa jumped to his feet. 'Where is she?' His voice was calm, crisp, but Letta could hear fear in it.

'This way, sir,' the woman said, and Letta heard feet rushing from the room.

For a moment, Letta felt as if she had forgotten how to breathe herself. Fragments of the conversation she had just heard raced about her head.

We took out all of his fingernails.

She tried to banish the images from her head. She had to get out of here. Then she could think about it. But her legs wouldn't move.

We took out all of his fingernails.

She had to get her breathing under control or she was going to throw up.

Three deep breaths, she told herself. *One, two, three.*

She felt a bit steadier. She put her ear to the door. There was no sound. Could the man be there still? Sitting quietly? Slowly she turned the handle. Through the tiny crack in the

138

door she could see the room was empty, the door open. She crept out, afraid to make any noise. She tiptoed across the room. At the far door, she stopped and looked tentatively out at the corridor.

Nothing.

She had to go back to where she had left Amelia. The woman would tell Noa she had been there. Her head started to pound. She ran along the corridor. She came to the corner and looked back towards the room door.

'Letta!' The word was like a gunshot. 'Letta?'

She turned around to face John Noa. He was frowning at her, a puzzled look in his eyes.

'What are you doing here?'

Think! Say something!

'I … I was looking for you. I was with Amelia and … and …'

John Noa put his hand on her shoulder, his eyes full of concern.

'You poor child,' he said. 'You have had a terrible shock. I can see that.'

Did he know what she had overheard?

'You were with Amelia?'

'She couldn't breathe.' Letta could barely get the words out.

'She has a breathing disease, my poor Amelia,' Noa said. 'She has these attacks regularly.'

Persuade him. Let him think you know nothing.

'I tried to find someone, to get help, but I got lost.'

'It's all right.' Noa's voice was soothing, talking to her in the way people spoke to frightened horses. 'We have sent for the healer. Amelia will be fine. Now, why did you want to see me?'

Letta shook her head. She couldn't do this. She couldn't pretend for another second. The man was a monster. He was so concerned about Amelia but he had allowed Benjamin to be tortured.

She had to get out.

'It was nothing,' she said. 'Nothing important. I have to go. I'll come back another time.'

Noa looked at her, his sharp eyes boring into her. 'You're sure?' he said.

'Yes,' Letta said. *Convince him!* 'I hope Amelia is better soon.'

'Thank you,' Noa said. 'You can find your way out?'

Letta nodded and walked away from him. With every step, she thought he would stop her or call the gavvers. At the door, she risked a glance over her shoulder. He was gone. She grabbed the door handle and pulled. The fresh air hit her in the face and she breathed it in greedily. She ran towards the gate, opened it and started down the steps. She had to fight to keep her attention from wandering. She needed to concentrate. It wouldn't do to fall now. She would think when she got home. For now, there were only the steps. She kept her eyes down, putting one foot after another.

She almost collided with the healer as she came to the last third of the journey. He stopped when he saw her, and stood back to let her pass.

'Is she still alive?' he said.

Letta nodded. 'I think so,' she said.

He pushed past her then, his heavy cloak brushing against the bare skin of her legs, leaving the smell of musty herbs in his wake. The wind gusted, and Letta felt rain on her face. Cold, stinging raindrops. She willed herself to walk on. She had to get home.

Benjamin! Benjamin was alive. His name flew above her like a firefly, circling, circling and then falling into oblivion.

CHAPTER 12

IMAGES of Benjamin flashed before her eyes, and in her mind, his suffering was her own. She could feel his poor hands, dry and cool, and in her head she could see the nails ripped from their cuticles. She remembered the first day she had visited Noa, when he told her Benjamin was dead. Had they been torturing him then? What did they want from him?

He could not, would not go along with your plan.

What plan? What was Noa planning that was so terrible that Benjamin would endure torture rather than agree to it?

She tried to remember everything that she had overheard at John Noa's house. The main thing was, they were going to dump Benjamin in the forest tomorrow – if he survived that long, if he hadn't already died from his injuries.

Noa did not actually kill people. Benjamin had explained that to her. Those who would not live in harmony were given up to nature. They were banished from Ark and had to take their chances in the forest. She hadn't realised then that they were beaten and tortured first. When their broken and bloodied bodies were thrown in the forest they were nothing but live bait for the wild animals. She couldn't let that happen to anyone else.

She had to contact Marlo again. She ran downstairs, already composing the note in her head.

I need you URGENTLY. Come at once. Letta

Outside, the day had dawned. Light snuck in through the high windows lighting the hard marble floor. People were moving towards Central Kitchen, going about their daily business. It all felt unreal to Letta. She wanted to open the door and scream at them to open their eyes and see Ark for what it was, a place built on treason and deceit. She swallowed the lump in her throat. She had to control her anger. Noa was a formidable enemy. She wouldn't beat him by being hysterical.

She would have to go and get food. If she didn't, Mrs Pepper would report her absence, and the gavvers would call to see where she was. She couldn't afford to have them walk in on her. She couldn't trust herself to behave normally. She would go now before it got too busy. After that, she would write the note and leave it with the Goddess. She walked to Central Kitchen with her head bowed, eyes cast down. She queued up, thankful that she didn't see anyone she knew. Mrs Pepper handed her two hard-boiled eggs and her bread ration along with a bowl of stewed apples. Letta took it silently and hurried out again, past the waiting people, the gavvers at the door, past the healer's, across the road, down the lane to her own back door.

Her hand flew to her mouth when she saw him, stifling the scream that sprang to her throat.

Marlo.

'But how –' she began. She hadn't even written the note yet!

142

'Sh!' he said. 'Inside.'

'What are you doing here?' she said.

'I had a dream last night. In it, you were calling me. So I came.'

She stared at him. He was like someone from another planet. There was something so unearthly about him, so otherworldly. Who believed so strongly in dreams that they obeyed them?

'A dream?' she said. 'Noa almost caught you yesterday. It isn't safe for you to be here. It isn't fair of me to ask you, but –'

He shrugged, the shadow of a smile playing about his lips. 'You saved my life, Letta, and risked your own for me.'

Marlo put his arm around her, holding her to his chest. She could hear his heart beat, and for a second, it reminded her of the sparrow caught in that room in Noa's house. She breathed in his sagey smell, feeling its comfort, its reassurance and something else as well. She felt so close to him and yet she hardly knew him. Marlo looked down at her.

'What's wrong?' he said.

She pulled away and looked into his eyes.

'Everything,' she said. 'Everything.'

It took her half an hour to tell him the whole story. Marlo listened without comment for the most part, and she had no idea what he thought, or how he was going to help her. She studied his face, trying to read his expression.

'When people are banished it can be very difficult to get information,' Marlo said. 'We know that the gavvers take them deep into the forest and abandon them. But there is no pattern, no routine to their actions. I need to talk to Finn. You stay here and carry on as though everything is normal.'

Marlo gripped her shoulders. She could feel his strong fingers through the thin material of her dress.

'You have to be careful now, Letta. If Noa senses you know

143

something… if he thinks you suspect him…' Marlo took her face in his hands. 'Trust me. Finn will know what to do, but for now you have to carry on. They will be watching. Give no sign that you are upset. Do you understand?'

He was right. In her heart she knew that, but it wasn't what she had hoped for.

'I'll be back by noon,' Marlo said.

She heard the door close as he left, the faint smell of sage the only sign that he had been there at all. She sat at her desk, her head in her hands.

She had to open the shop. Pretend everything was normal. Just for a few hours, she told herself. They would find Benjamin. They had to. She slipped the heavy bolts back and let the door swing open.

The rest of the morning passed in a blur. People came and went. She wrote out lists of words, prepared boxes for the builder's apprentices and tried to pretend that everything was normal. When the bell rang twelve times, she closed the shop and sat at her desk to wait. It was only minutes later when she heard the knock. She had been waiting for it, but she still jumped. Finn and Marlo hurried in.

They sat in Benjamin's study, Letta behind his old desk, and Marlo on the chair opposite. Finn stood beside the window, keeping one eye on the street.

'I am sorry to hear about your master,' Finn said.

'Can you help me to find him?' She couldn't keep the desperation out of her voice.

'We will try,' Finn said. 'We have heard nothing of your master. This is not something Noa wants people to know, so he will have taken precautions to ensure people don't find out.'

'He said it will happen tonight,' Letta said.

'Lately they have been using the West Gate and driving a few miles south, towards the river. There is no guarantee that they will use that route tonight, but it is probably our best chance.'

'They change the route all the time,' Marlo joined in. 'There are hundreds of miles of forest but they have been known to use some sites more than others.'

'Have you managed to rescue many people?'

There was silence for a second, then Finn spoke. 'No,' he said. 'Not many.'

'And if they don't use the West Gate?'

Finn shook his head, his eyes never leaving her face.

'Then we will lose him,' he said.

At that moment, she felt Marlo lean over and take her hand.

'Can't we follow them?' she said, remembering the morning she had seen Daniel taken.

'Not easily,' Finn said. 'They take the prisoners on a horse and cart with two gavvers positioned at the back, watching for any interference. We will post people near each gate from dusk on. That way at least we'll know which gate they used, but even that is dangerous. If they notice men hanging around after dark...'

Four gates. If only they knew which one! If they knew for certain all their resources could be placed there.

'Is there any way we could find out which gate they will use? I mean, for a fact. Who would know?'

'No-one,' Finn said. 'Only the gavvers and Noa. We had a source for a while in Noa's house, a man called Gorr, but he was discovered and banished about six months ago. Since then we have no-one on the inside.'

Letta's mind was racing as Finn talked. Could she get inside? If she were in the house could she find out anything?

'What about me?' she said looking from Marlo's face to Finn's. 'I could get in there this afternoon. What would I look for?'

Finn stood up abruptly.

'Are you mad? If Noa even suspected –'

'He would kill you,' Marlo finished the sentence for him.

'He will kill Benjamin if I don't,' she said. 'Please. Help me. If I got in on wordsmith business, how could I find out?'

Finn sighed.

'We don't know all that much about what goes on in that house, Letta, but we did get some information from Gorr. We do know that the Captain of the Guard, Cregg Whistlestop, writes the order.'

Letta nodded, trying to take everything in.

'We also know that all orders are signed by Noa himself,' Finn continued.

'So,' Letta said trying to figure it out, 'at some stage today the orders will cross Noa's desk?'

'That is almost certain,' Finn said.

Letta stood up and started to pace. 'So if I could get in there, into his office, I could see the order?'

'Letta, this is foolishness! I don't know if you could see the order or not. I don't know where he stores such things, if he stores them. I only know that he signs them.'

'But there is a chance…' Marlo's voice made Letta jump. She had nearly forgotten he was there.

'There is always a chance,' Finn growled. 'There's also a chance that she'll be caught and killed. Why don't you leave it to us? We will do everything we can.'

'But you said yourself, the odds are against you. It will be like hunting for sunbeams in a river. You might get lucky, but you might not. If we knew which gate, if we knew where they were

146

headed, then Benjamin would have a real chance.'

'You are right, but the cost may be…'

'My life,' Letta said. 'I know that, and I'm ready.'

Finn sighed again. 'Very well then,' he said. 'We'd better get to work.'

CHAPTER 13

Winter #487

Cold time of year

AS she climbed the steps to Noa's house, Letta realised she felt no fear. She had been in awe of John Noa before, looked up to him as the man who had saved the planet. She had grown up on stories of his great valour, his clever thinking, his vision. Now she knew that none of that was real. John Noa was a bully. That thought made her brave. He might be a very clever bully, but he was still a bully.

She had gone over the plan with Finn but even as Finn was talking, her mind was working independently. She wanted to trust her instincts, and her instincts told her that she could play a part. She would pretend that she was still the girl she had been yesterday.

She had almost reached the top of the steps. She rehearsed what she would say and how she would say it. She opened the gate. From the corner of her eye, she saw movement in the downstairs window, eyes always watching no doubt. She marched up to the door and knocked firmly. A gavver opened it. He frowned but said nothing.

'I come see John Noa,' Letta said. 'Tell him wordsmith here.'

The man looked her up and down, his eyes raking her from scalp to sole. Then he stood back and allowed her to pass.

'Wait,' he growled, before heading off down the long corridor.

She waited. A few minutes later, John Noa himself hurried up towards her. His face was creased in a frown and his eyes were full of concern.

'Letta?' he said. 'Is everything all right?'

She forced a smile. 'Yes, of course,' she said. 'I am so sorry to bother you again but you did say if I needed to talk to you – and I was worried about Amelia.'

'Amelia is much better today, thank you. Now come with me and we can talk in private.'

Letta tried to keep her mind blank as she followed him down the corridor to where it swung right and past two closed doors, one marked Laboratory, the other wordless. Finally, he came to his own study door. He opened it and Letta could see the huge desk and the chair behind it. Another two chairs stood on the far side. On the desk itself there was very little and Letta's heart sank when she saw how tidy the room was. She had imagined mounds of paper and files that would give her a hope of finding something useful.

'How can I help you, Letta?' said John Noa, sitting now behind his desk and looking at her, giving her his full attention.

She sat down opposite him.

'I came here yesterday to ask you if you might consider adding some words to the new List.'

She watched as the dark eyes clouded over. He sat back in his chair.

'New words?' he repeated. 'I'm not sure what you mean. Our aim is to curtail the use of language. As you know, throwing

149

words about to all and sundry is quite irresponsible, considering our history. What had you in mind?'

'Nothing too radical.' Letta smiled at him. 'I thought maybe we could introduce one new word. A word like "hope" perhaps?'

John Noa smiled. 'Hope?'

'Yes,' Letta said. 'I think it is a fairly harmless word, but it acknowledges that people do hope and –'

'Harmless?' His voice cut across her well-prepared speech. 'You think that "hope" is a harmless word? I'm afraid I would disagree with you there, child.'

'Would you?' Letta said, assuming a puzzled expression. 'May I ask why?'

Noa nodded. 'Hope looks to the future, does it not? We hope for things that we don't have now but wish to have some day. And that is what makes humans greedy, Letta. We are the only beings on this planet that refuse to live in the present. We are always looking for something else. A faster way to travel, a cheaper food to eat, a better song to sing. Do the deer that you live beside think like that Letta? Do the cows or the birds? No. Only man.'

'I never thought of it like that,' Letta said.

Noa stood up. 'Of course you didn't, Letta. You are too young and you have always lived in a time of peace. My experience, I'm afraid, is very different.'

He came out from behind the desk and put a hand on her shoulder.

'Hope is a lovely word,' he said. 'A relic from another time, but it's not practical, Letta, and it sends out the wrong message. Here in Ark, we don't hope. We do.'

Letta nodded. 'I see,' she said. 'I'm sorry. I didn't understand. I have wasted your time.' She bowed her head, hoping she looked suitably humble.

John Noa patted her shoulder. 'You did not waste my time, Letta. You are the wordsmith now. You have things to learn and I am happy to teach you. You are always welcome here.'

'Thank you,' Letta said.

'I will see you out,' Noa said. 'I have a meeting and –'

'No, please,' Letta protested. 'I know the way and I have taken enough of your time.'

John Noa nodded. 'Very well, then,' he said. 'If you are sure?'

'Perfectly,' Letta replied and turned quickly, heading for the door.

She walked down the corridor, not looking back. There was no-one about, though she could hear voices coming from somewhere above her. The second door she passed was open. Letta stopped and looked inside. She looked over her shoulder and then into the room again. A laboratory, she thought, slipping inside and closing the door behind her. The walls were dyed white and the room had only one window, a narrow opening with a wide sill on the inside. One wall of the room was lined with capacious tin vats. Letta approached the nearest one cautiously. The vat was full of water, and in the water she could see pulped paper, thick and stodgy, congealing in clumps. Curious now, she fished some of it out. She held the sodden paper for a moment and she could see that it had once been written on and still had streaks of red ink running through it. And then she saw it. A piece of paper still intact clinging to the side of the vat. Carefully she peeled it off. The letters were already blurred but Letta knew what it said.

Future: A time yet to

'*Come,*' Letta said softly. '*A time yet to come.*'

With a rush she understood what was happening here in

151

this sterile room. Noa was destroying words, recycling the small cards, pulping them to make new paper. The words that Benjamin had collected. The words that Letta had transcribed. Tears pricked her eyes. Why? Why had he charged them with the task of finding every remaining word if he had always intended to destroy them?

Nothing wasted, nothing lost. That was what Noa preached. And she had believed him.

She felt as though all the air had been sucked from the room. They had not been saving words for a time when man could be trusted with them. They had been destroying what was left of language.

She got up and went back to the door, opening it slightly. She felt less trapped with the door open. The walls were closing in on her. She had to forget what she had just seen and concentrate instead on her mission.

Someone was coming. She pressed her body against the wall. She could make out John Noa's voice and one other, also male. She held her breath as they passed within inches of her.

'That is your responsibility then,' Noa said.

'Yes, sir,' the other man replied, and they were gone.

Letta waited until the sound of their footsteps had totally disappeared. She counted to ten in her head and then another ten. She peeped through the crack in the door. All seemed quiet. She opened the door and surveyed the corridor. There was no sign of Noa or anyone else.

As quickly as she could, she scampered out the door and back to Noa's office, all the time waiting for the voice that would halt her in her tracks. The door to the office was closed. She grasped the cool metal handle and turned it. The door opened. The office was empty. *Now!* The voice in her head screamed.

She crossed the floor quickly and stood behind the desk. There was only one pile of papers. She flitted through them, trying to ignore the shake in her hand. Orders for the harvesting of wheat. Results from the laboratory. A list of names. She scanned it quickly. No sign of Benjamin's name. She had reached the end of the pile when she heard the approaching voices. Two of them. Both men. Noa almost certainly. Letta looked around the room, trying to subdue the wave of panic rising in her chest. Under the desk. It was her only hope. The desk was old-fashioned, closed on three sides, made of heavy, dark wood. She threw herself to the ground, pushing her body into the farthest recess of the desk, arms wrapped around her knees. Then she heard the door open.

'Well done, Len. That was a job well done.'

Noa.

She heard the footsteps crossing the floor, the chair being pulled out, and then his feet were inches from her body. She tried to make herself smaller, straining away from him. Her heart was beating so loudly she couldn't understand why he couldn't hear it.

Noa sighed. 'I am glad you have decided to come with us, Len. The scientists are convinced it will work – and it is both quick and painless. Nonetheless, we will need good men, like yourself, to make sure it all runs smoothly.

'Yes, sir,' the other man said. Letta didn't recognise the voice. There was silence for a moment.

'I wish it could have been otherwise.' Noa's voice again. 'But man is a parasite now, nothing more. We have to deal with the situation we find ourselves in. And I have found a solution. Many favour extinction, but I do not think that is the answer, my friend. Nature abhors a vacuum.'

153

The other man coughed, a small apologetic cough as though he only spoke with great reluctance.

'About the wordsmith, sir –'

Letta felt the blood of her body go cold. Noa was talking. She forced herself to concentrate.

'Benjamin and I go back a long way. I never thought he would betray me.'

The other man muttered something Letta didn't catch.

Noa stretched his legs under the desk. Letta cowered away from them. *Please. Don't touch me.* His shoes almost brushed her leg. She could feel the heat from his body, smell his sweat. She heard the other man's chair scrape on the floor as he stood up.

'I'll leave the orders for you to sign, sir.'

'Yes,' Noa said. 'Thank you.'

Letta heard the second man walk across the floor. The door opened and closed. Noa pulled his feet back in. Letta breathed a little easier. She didn't know how long he sat there, but to her it seemed like hours. Her right foot had fallen asleep and she couldn't feel it at all. She wanted to massage it but was afraid to move. It reminded her of the cave she used to play in as a child. A small cramped space that smelt of moss and wild flowers. She closed her eyes and tried to stay in that place, to distract herself from the terror she was feeling. If Noa found her, she knew there would be no hope of mercy. As the minutes ticked by, she tried to hold the image of the cave in her head. She remembered the sound of the small stream that flowed past it on its way to the sea. These were the days when she had learnt the names of the wild flowers. Maybe if she concentrated she could still remember them. Noa coughed.

Bluebell, crocus, primrose, cowslip…

She pulled her knees closer to her chest.

Dandelion, mouse-ear, angelica, nettle…

Noa stood up. She heard him cross the floor. The door opened and closed. Letta was too afraid to move. What if it was a trick? She chided herself for being ridiculous. If he knew she was there he would have confronted her. She rubbed her foot and felt shoots of pain as the blood started to flow again.

Then she crawled out. She put her feet under her, but she had to cling to the desk in order to stand. She was alone. She almost cried with relief. Then she remembered.

I'll leave the orders for you to sign.

She saw at once that there was a new stack of papers on the desk. The first page had to do with food supplies. The next was a register from Mrs Truckle, listing all of her new pupils. And then she saw it. Benjamin Lazlo. She held her breath, scanning it as quickly as she could.

This evening, midnight, South Gate.

Her heart soared. She knew where they would leave from. Underneath that was details of the men who would guard him.

Timilty, Rudder.

Finally, she saw the word *Banish*.

She replaced the page carefully.

She had to get out of here. She had two choices. The window or the door. She hurried to the window. Outside was a sheer drop. Not an option. It had to be the door. She pressed her ear against it and listened. She couldn't hear anything.

Maybe she could go back to the laboratory. Anywhere would

be safer than here. She opened the door carefully. A woman's voice sounded somewhere down the corridor.

'Bring down here! Come now.'

Letta closed the door, her heart thumping. She could hear the women drawing nearer. Then the voices disappeared. They had obviously gone into a room. Letta bit her lip. She had to get out of this office. She opened the door again.

She stepped out onto the corridor and started to walk. It felt like she was walking on a tightrope, waiting for the moment when she would lose her balance and fall. She hurried on. She could see the front door. Just a few more strides. She turned the heavy knob and pulled. The door fell open. She hurried out, pulling it closed behind her, and headed for the gate. She looked over her shoulder. Still nothing. Quickly she found the steps and started her descent. It wasn't as easy as the last time she had climbed down. Darkness had fallen and the wind had risen again, howling about her, blowing her hair into her eyes.

The South Gate.

Midnight.

That gave them a real chance. Once more, hope swelled in her heart. She would see Benjamin tonight. No matter how badly injured he was, she would nurse him back to health. Despite the cold she felt a faint glow of happiness. When she finally got off the stone steps she walked as quickly as she could towards home, conscious of time slipping by.

She had to talk to Finn. They had to get ready for the night ahead.

He couldn't settle. His limbs felt like they had a life of their own. He had told Amelia that he needed air but it was silence he craved.

He stood on the beach looking out at the sea. Benjamin haunted him at every turn. They had been such good friends. Neither one of them was a scientist, but they had been passionate about the environment. They had both been laughed at, ridiculed for their doom-laden prophecies, but they had stood together, shoulder to shoulder.

Benjamin had written stirring articles, using his mastery of words to try to wake people from their fug of complacency. It was Benjamin who had led the final campaign against the oil companies, when they rushed to grab the oil and precious minerals from the Polar caps after the ice had melted and left them vulnerable to an attack from man.

And yet.

Even Benjamin would not see things through. He would not cross the final hurdle with him. He did not see that man had no further use as he was presently constructed. Language was what made him different. Language was also what made him arrogant. Man, after all, was only a newcomer here on Earth. He would soon be forgotten, though it would take thousands of years to repair the damage he had caused. What was thousands of years to the universe? Nothing. It would pass like seconds. Nature would shake herself and get ready for the next species to gain dominance. Like the dinosaur, man would be as nothing. Unlike the dinosaur, he would still exist, wordless, tame and in harmony with his fellow creatures. Without words, he would never again be dominant. Nothing wasted, nothing lost.

If only Benjamin could have understood that. The cold crept into his bones. He was lonely. So many of his friends were gone. He still had Amelia, though. She was his soul mate, the one he turned to when he couldn't bear his life a second longer.

A wave washed in near his feet, wetting his shoe, then slouched away again. He had met her on a beach, her and her sisters, on *a bright summer day before he had understood how bad things would get. She had been so young, so innocent, and he had fallen in love. He had been in love ever since.*

He sighed and turned away from the sea and headed home. He would talk it through with her again, the entire plan, though he was sure he was doing the right thing. Amelia was logical, she would point out any flaws. He couldn't afford for anything to go wrong. Amelia would help him. She was the only one who truly understood him. She was the only one who would stand by him until the end. Of that he was certain.

Melting #284

(1) Heat making liquid
(2) Time after ice melted

LETTA heard the eleven bells ring as she looked on to the darkening street.

'The South Gate at midnight,' Finn said, frowning thoughtfully. 'On foot, with only three of us, we couldn't hope to keep track of it. And there isn't time to put our people in place. We have to think of some other way to track it.'

There was silence for a second as they all listened to the wind outside, moaning in its mad flight through the town.

'I had a dream last night,' Marlo said, his voice tight and stretched. 'I saw a trail of blood on the forest floor.'

Letta shivered. *A trail of blood.* Then her eyes fell on the row of red inkbottles. Ink? Ink would stain the grass, like blood. Her heart started to beat faster. If they could attach a bottle…

'What is it?' Marlo asked.

Letta ignored him and hurried out to the corridor behind the shop, where Benjamin stored bottles. She pulled out the boxes that held the smaller, glass vessels. They rattled as she pushed those boxes out of her way. In behind, against the wall, she found what she was looking for. A large plastic bottle, a relic from one

159

of Benjamin's trips. It was the length of her arm and as round again. She picked it up and carried it back to Marlo and Finn.

'What's this?' Finn said.

She placed the bottle carefully on the floor. 'This is how we will know where the cart went. Help me fill it.'

'With what?' Marlo asked, his head on one side, eyebrows raised.

Finn slapped his knee and laughed. 'Ink!' he said, before Letta got a chance to answer. 'Ink! That's genius, Letta! Come on, hurry. We don't have much time.'

One by one, they emptied the small bottles of ink into the large container. Letta watched the red dye climb up the side of the bottle and in her mind she saw again the pulped paper in that room at Noa's house. What fools he had made of them! Everything he had told them, everything they had believed and built their lives on – all of it false. The thought scalded her.

Marlo touched her arm. 'We'll need to puncture it,' he said. 'One hole should be enough. Not so small that it gets clogged straight away. Not so big that the ink runs out too quickly.'

Letta nodded, keeping her eye on the ink as it poured from the bottle in her hand.

'Then we need to attach it to the cart.'

'Thin string would be best,' Finn said. 'Do you have any?'

Letta knew she had seen some, but where? Then she remembered: 'Benjamin's office. He uses it to tie up word boxes.'

Letta felt she was drowning in questions. 'We'll need to stop the cart and attach the bottle without them seeing us,' Letta said, while Marlo was fetching the string from the office. 'How can we do that?'

'Distraction,' Finn said with a smile. 'We cause a distraction. We could have Marlo lie on the street in front of the cart.

You could pretend to be his sister. You stop them, say your brother is ill. While all that's happening I will be attaching the bottle and –'

'No!' Letta felt the word burst from her. 'This is my plan. My risk. You and Marlo create the distraction. I attach the bottle. Besides, I'm smaller than you. I can get under the cart without them noticing.'

Finn shook his head. 'You have no experience in these matters, Letta. Leave it to me.'

Letta grabbed his arm. 'No, Finn. I have to do it. If they catch you, they will kill you. I am the wordsmith and for some reason Noa likes me. He will at least give me a hearing.'

'Will this do?' Marlo came in holding a few strides of twine wrapped about a piece of wood.

Finn took it from him. 'Yes,' he said, pulling the string, testing it between his hands. 'I think it will.'

Marlo looked from Finn to Letta.

'Do we have a plan?

'I think so,' Letta said. 'What do you say, Finn?'

'All right,' Finn said. 'We'll give it a try and may the Goddess help us this night. We'll wait at the dry-stone bridge on this side of the South Gate. When the cart comes, Marlo will lie on the road. I will stop them and say that my son has fallen ill with fever. That'll be your chance, Letta. Get under the cart and attach the bottle. You will have about thirty seconds. If I put up too much of a fight they might arrest me. Once the bottle is in place, we can do no more. We'll wait till first light and follow the ink.'

Letta nodded. She could see it all in her head.

'I think it will work,' she said.

'Time we were leaving,' Finn said. 'Have you a spike and a hammer, Letta, to puncture the bottle?'

Letta went to Benjamin's tool kit and took out the sharp stone spike he had there and the hammer with the smooth wooden handle. She could almost feel his hand on hers as she stroked the cool wood. *Please let him be still alive. Please.*

The plastic punctured easily enough. Finn had made a very small hole. He held the bottle up and nothing happened.

'Too small,' he muttered and Letta held her breath. He inserted the spike and hit it one more time, gently, with the hammer. A drop of red fell on his great paw. He smiled and put his finger against the hole.

'Now all we need is a stopper.'

'A piece of cork?' Letta suggested.

'Try it,' Finn said.

Letta took one of the little stoppers they used for the ink bottles and with a small sharp knife started to whittle it away until there was nothing left but a sliver.

'That should do,' she said.

'Give it here,' Marlo said.

Finn removed his finger and Marlo jammed the cork in place. Finn held the bottle up. The cork held.

'Next the string,' Finn said.

Marlo took it and wound it around the neck of the bottle.

'Now,' said Finn. 'All we need do is tie the end of the string to the shaft of the cart. What do you think?'

'Let's go,' Letta said.

Finn put the bottle under his great coat and Letta pulled on her own coat before carefully opening the back door.

The wind hit her in the face as soon as they were outside. The sky was black, full of waiting rain. There was no moon. Letta could feel the darkness pushing in on her, thick and suffocating. She struggled against the wind, the cold piercing her bones. The buildings on either side of her were only shapes, great hulking beasts sheltering from the weather. In her head she tried to keep track. The potter, the weaver. Then the rancid smell of sheep hide alerted her to Mel the shearer's where the wool from the sheep was turned to yarn to make clothes. Maggoty Mel they had called him when they were schoolchildren running around on these streets in the early summer, when the hides were piled high outside Mel's door. Maggoty Mel. It seemed like all of that had happened in a different place, a different world.

Finally they saw the bridge looming out of the darkness and beyond it the South Gate. They stood against the cool stone wall and waited. Beside her, Marlo put his head down against the wind, but Letta felt braver with it lashing her in the face, the rain cascading down her cheeks. She almost missed what Finn said, so loud was the wind.

'It's coming,' he said, and Letta strained to hear what he had heard. A few seconds later she heard the rolling sound of wheels on the rough cobbles. The cart. Finn thrust the bottle into her arms.

'Go!' he hissed at Marlo, and Marlo instantly sprang from the shadows and threw himself on the ground. The cart came closer. Finn stepped away from the wall. Letta clutched the bottle to her chest, her hands wet and slippery on its smooth surface.

'Hey!' Finn shouted. 'Stop! Help!'

At first, Letta thought that they hadn't heard him, but then the horse shied and she heard one of the gavvers swear.

'Whoa!' he shouted, and the horse's hooves skidded on the wet ground. Finn grabbed the harness and held fast. *Now!* Letta thought and dashed from the wall.

'Get away!' She heard the gavver call out as she slipped between the wheels of the cart.

'Boy sick. Fall down. Need help!' Finn shouted against the wind.

'Move him!' the gavver called.

Letta pressed the bottle against the rough shaft of the cart, lashing the twine around it and tying a hard knot. Her fingers slipped as she tried to fasten it and she had to start again.

'Get him up or we run over him!'

'Please, sir.' Finn's voice was pleading. Then she heard a thump as one of the gavvers jumped from the cart. She couldn't hear the conversation they were having but she could imagine it. She checked the bottle one last time and pulled out the cork.

And then she heard it. A moan. Benjamin. She had been so intent on attaching the bottle that she had almost forgotten that he would be there, on the cart. She heard the gavver jump back on. Heard the driver crack the whip. She grabbed the back of the cart and pulled herself up just as the horse lurched forward and the cart moved. *Benjamin!* She didn't know if she had said it out loud or only in her head. All she could hear was the wind. He was alive! She reached out to touch him, feeling rough sackcloth and the shape of his feet. She pulled hard with her arms just as the cart lurched again swaying violently on the rough cobbles and throwing her back onto the road. Her shoulders hit the cobbles first, knocking the air out of her. For a second, she lay there with her arm outstretched towards the cart in a hopeless gesture as the rain lashed her and the roar of the wind drowned out the noise of the cart. When she stood up, there was no sign the cart had ever been there. She sat back on her heels and felt as though something inside her had just collapsed, like falling through a trapdoor. She hardly noticed Finn until he was lifting her up off the ground and pulling her back to the bridge. His big hand wiped the rain off her face and he tucked her under his arm as though she were a child of five.

The bell rang eight times before the first fingers of dawn appeared. The wind had settled. It was still there but only a tame version of itself. Letta knew how it felt. The storm inside her had also quietened. She was worn out from the emotion of the night, the lack of sleep, the incessant reviewing of what had happened. She couldn't explain why she had jumped on the cart. It hadn't been part of the plan, nor had she realised that Benjamin would be there, right beside her, breathing, feeling. It was as if she had blocked it out in the planning stage. As if to think of Benjamin would have been such a distraction that she wouldn't have been able to cope. And he was alive! She just wanted to hold his hand and comfort him, to stay with him in the dark forest until morning. Finn had been shocked. He'd spoken to her about it when they got back to the shop.

'What were you thinking? Did you not realise that they would have felt your weight on the cart? What were you going to do when they reached the dumping site?'

She had no answers for him. Besides, she also had the practical things to worry her. Had she attached the bottle properly? Had she removed the cork? She couldn't remember. All she could recall was the sound of Benjamin moaning. The feel of his feet under the sacking. What was he doing now? He had spent all these hours lying in the open, his wounds bleeding, wild animals on every side. A trail of blood on the forest floor.

Marlo and Finn had taken her back to her house and stayed with her, and she was glad of their company. They were worried. She could see it in their eyes. Finn had a large bruise under his

165

right eye, where the gavver had struck him. Marlo was quiet, no doubt reliving all that had happened. She had to remind herself that they went on missions like this all the time. This was not new to them the way it was to her. She was filled with admiration for them. Was it only a few weeks ago that she had despised the Desecrators and all that they stood for?

'Can we leave soon?' Letta asked as she saw the sun send out gentle rays in the morning sky.

Finn shook his head. 'I don't think you should come with us, Letta,' he said. 'If the shop is closed it will arouse suspicion.'

Letta jumped to her feet. 'You can't be serious,' she said. 'You can't expect me to sit here while Benjamin is thrown somewhere in the forest.'

'But won't they come looking for you if the shop is closed?' Marlo asked.

Letta knew they were right. They would come looking for her. She needed a reason to be gone. Could she say she was going on a word-hunting mission as Benjamin often did? She didn't know if he informed Noa or the gavvers before he left. She could put a note on the window.

She ran to her desk and started to write.

Closed. Two days. Use drop box. Wordsmith

She showed it to Finn. He frowned.

'Very well then,' the older man said. 'Get ready. Bring whatever water you have. We'll go first. You don't want to be seen with us. Follow in a few minutes. Meet us at the bridge.'

Within minutes they were gone. Letta hurried around the house, collecting her water ration, wishing she had time to go and get more. She took Benjamin's bag, his tool kit, his maps, a woollen sweater for him and all the herbs she could find.

When she was ready she put up the sign in the window and opened the front door. Light flooded in. The storm had blown over and the sky was clear and baby blue. Mrs Truckle stood looking at her.

'No harm,' Letta greeted her, though inwardly she was cursing the day Benjamin had asked the old woman to keep an eye on things. Mrs Truckle nodded towards the sign. 'Where you go?'

Letta felt the colour mount in her cheeks. She didn't like lying. 'Word finding,' she said.

'Word finding? Where?' The little woman had her head on one side, her small button eyes squinting back at Letta.

'The forest,' she said. 'Have Benjamin's maps.'

Mrs Truckle frowned. 'You tell gavvers?' she said. 'Benjamin always tell gavvers.'

Letta hesitated. If she told the truth, Mrs Truckle would probably drag her to the Round House to get permission and she might be too late to go with Finn.

'Yes,' she said, fastening the leather satchel. 'Have to go now. Weather good.'

Mrs Truckle caught her arm. 'Food? Come now. I talk to Mrs Pepper.'

'Have food,' Letta lied. 'Need to go.'

'On your own? You too young. Bring Werber.'

Letta pulled her arm away. 'No,' she said. 'Go now. Alone.'

She hurried away before her old teacher could say any more, but she could almost feel the old woman's unease and she knew that Mrs Truckle was the kind of person who liked to get to the bottom of things.

She couldn't worry about it now. She had to get to the bridge and meet the Desecrators. If they were still there.

CHAPTER 15

End #168

Last part

LETTA could see Finn and Marlo waiting for her as she approached the bridge. She breathed a sigh of relief.

'Come,' Finn said, making for the gate.

'What should I say to the gavvers?' Letta asked with one eye on the two hulks guarding the gate.

'They won't give you any trouble,' he said and marched on ahead of her.

Letta had no choice but to follow him. Finn and Marlo hurried through, eyes down. Letta followed them. The gavvers looked away.

'Some of them are easier to pay off than others,' Marlo said, with a smile, and Letta found herself nodding as if such things happened every day.

She looked around. In front of her the forest opened its gaping mouth. Silence reigned. There was no bird song. No sound at all, except for the slight ruffle of the wind as it passed through the trees. To Letta, it sounded as though the forest was breathing, quietly, steadily.

'We go through here,' Finn said. 'Keep your eyes open for

the ink.'

Finn disappeared into the gloomy passageway that lay open ahead of him.

Within seconds, the trees closed in about her and made it feel like it was dusk again. Her eyes raked the ground looking for the tell-tale red splashes.

'There!' Finn's voice sounded unnaturally loud. He was hunkered down and Letta could feel his excitement. She went closer and saw it for herself. The deep red of the beetroot ink lay on a flat leaf of butterbur. She tore the leaf off and pressed it to her face. There was no mistake. Beetroot. Marlo clutched her hand.

'We're going to find him,' he said.

'We have to hurry,' Finn said, but he patted Letta gently on the shoulder before turning and heading off through the trees. An hour later, they were still walking, chasing every drop of beetroot ink. Letta could feel the musty dampness of the forest soaking into her bones. Her legs ached; the ground was heavy with fallen leaves and treacherous with tree stumps and sudden holes. Thorn bushes arched out of the undergrowth, their long necks clawing at her skin. Every fifty strides or so, the forest threw up other paths branching right and left. Each time they had to stop and wait while Finn searched for the red ink that would show them the way. Letta ploughed on, slightly comforted by the sound of Marlo trudging behind her. Every few minutes she looked up to catch glimpses of the sky through the dense canopy, an intricate cloth of blue and grey furrowed with twisted bands of cloud. Then, she had to go back to looking at her feet trying not to fall over, trying not to twist or break an ankle.

There was a strange atmosphere in the woods. A hushed kind of waiting clung to everything. Nobody willingly ventured in here.

When the last earthquake had taken place, wild animals hitherto held in captivity broke free and established new territories for themselves under cover of the dense forests. Tigers, lions and snakes had all been spotted here. During one particularly cold winter, some of the animals had ventured out and encroached on the town looking for food. Letta had listened to the terrifying stories people had told over the years. Never, in her most vivid nightmares, could she have imagined herself in here. She concentrated on her feet again. More than once, she looked up only to find herself walking through a spider's web, the sticky silk clinging to her face and hair. Images plagued her as she walked. Benjamin lying on the open ground all night in the driving rain. His hands bleeding. Animals stalking him.

She tried to push them away and imagine seeing him again, taking him home. With a sickening lurch she realised she could never take him home. Where would they live? Maybe the Desecrators would give them shelter? She felt something shift inside her, a dropping feeling as though she had jumped from a cliff and down below her was nothing but darkness, uncertainty and fear. What future did they have? She had no idea.

They had stopped again. Finn went off to investigate the new pathways while somewhere in the distance an animal roared. A wolf? A bear? She looked about her, wondering again what was out there, what lurked in the dense mess of trees and rocks.

'This way.' Finn nodded to his right and they were walking again. Hours passed. The sky was streaked with mauve, the sun had disappeared. Would they find him before nightfall? A few minutes later, Finn called a halt and they sat on a fallen tree to eat their meagre rations. From his bag, Marlo took bread and a hard, grey-looking cheese along with an apple for each of them. Letta handed round water and they sat in silence, glad of the respite. As soon as the food was eaten, Finn was on his feet again.

'What time is it, do you think?' Letta asked.

'Evening,' Finn said and started to walk again.

Half an hour later, he stopped.

'What is it?' Letta said.

'Don't you smell it?' Finn sniffed the air loudly.

'Smoke,' Letta said. 'Could it be smoke?'

Marlo shook his head. 'Out here?'

'This way,' Finn said hurrying in the direction of the sharp, acrid smell.

A few minutes later he held up his hand and gestured to them to be quiet. Letta sniffed the air, turning her head to where the wind carried the smell at its strongest. Wood smoke.

Finn hurried them on, moving stealthily. Letta followed him, trying not to make any extra noise. She could hear it now. The crackling of a fire. Finn waved them in behind an enormous oak. Letta leant against the great tree and looked to where Finn was pointing. Letta stretched her eyes, unable to believe what she was seeing. A ring of fire. Someone had built a circle of fire in the middle of the forest.

'There's someone in there,' Marlo said, raising his voice to be heard over the crackling of the flames.

Finn moved forward as far as the next tree. Letta and Marlo followed him. There was someone there, moving about. A small figure dressed in black.

Finn beckoned and they moved again. This time they could see her clearly. A small woman in dark clothes. Long hair streamed down her back, giving her the appearance of a girl, until the light from the fire caught her face and then Letta could see the deep lines on her tanned skin and the splashes of grey in her hair.

The woman was pouring water from a rusty can along the line of the fire. In the middle of the circle was a bundle of rags.

Finn signalled to Letta and Marlo to stay while he stepped forward. Letta watched him as he approached the circle of flame.

'No harm!' she heard him shout.

The woman didn't answer.

'No harm!' Finn said again. 'Can you help us?'

'Who you?'

The woman's voice was rusty, the words struggling out of her throat as though they were causing her pain.

'Outcasts,' Finn said. 'Looking for a friend who was banished.'

'And how is it I am knowing that what you say is the truth?'

The woman bent down and picked up a stout wooden branch, the top of which was swathed in cloth. She thrust the branch into the flames and it lit at once. She said nothing but Letta could see that this was now a weapon.

'It is the truth,' Finn said. 'We are not gavvers. We are here to find our friend.'

'How many you be?' The woman lifted the torch lighting Finn's face but her eyes scanned the environment.

'There are three of us,' Finn said.

Marlo took Letta's hand and they stepped out into the light. Letta could feel the heat coming from the flames and stroking her face.

The woman looked at her. 'Who you looking for?' she said.

'My master,' Letta answered. 'Benjamin Lazlo. We know they dumped him near here.'

There was a long silence. The woman never took her eyes from them. No-one moved.

Then the woman picked up her watering can and doused the flames in front of them.

'Enter!' she said.

Letta followed Finn into the circle.

'Over there,' the woman said, pointing at the bundle of rags.

For a second, Letta didn't understand. She turned her head slowly to the bundle at the heart of the circle. The bundle moved.

'Benjamin?' Letta crossed the distance between them in three strides and threw herself to the ground beside him.

His face was drawn and grey, half covered in a scraggy beard. His hair clung to his head, damp and matted. His eyes were closed. She gripped his hand. He moaned, a deep guttural sound that pierced her heart. Instantly, the old woman was beside him. Letta watched as she lifted his head and pressed a small flask to his lips.

'Hush now, hush my friend,' she crooned. 'All is well.'

Benjamin's face relaxed. The old woman put his head down on the hard ground.

'What do they call him?' she said, without looking at Letta.

'Benjamin,' Letta said, stroking the skin of his hand, trying not to look at the bloody mess that was his fingers.

'And you?'

'Letta,' she answered.

'I be Edgeware,' the old woman said. 'Now, we need move him. The fire keeps away wolf and his friends but not for long. They came last night for look. The fire jittered them so they not stay around too long, but they be back. Their hunger will be stronger than their jittering.'

'We will carry him.' Finn had suddenly appeared beside them. 'Where do you live?'

The old woman hesitated.

'You don't know whether to trust us or not,' Marlo said.

'I want no dealings with Noa's kind,' Edgeware said. 'I rather live here with the beasts. At least they be what they seem to be.'

Marlo nodded.

'I have heard of you. They call you The Black Woman of the Woods. I just didn't believe you existed.' He smiled. 'We have met people you rescued.'

'They save selves,' Edgeware said. 'I just give them helping hand. Like this one.' She nodded towards Benjamin.

'I couldn't move him so I keep vigil with him. I thinking he would die here. Now, maybe no. I be taking you to my dwellin'. Follow me.'

Without a word, Marlo and Finn leant down and picked the old man up. Letta kept a firm grip on his hand. He muttered something and then went quiet.

Stepping out of the fire circle, Letta felt the cold again. It had grown dark and the air was now frigid. She couldn't imagine anyone living in this place. How did Edgeware survive? Where did she get food and water? She glanced at Benjamin. She had thought she would never see that face again.

He had been in her life for as long as she could remember. A steady, gentle presence. Always there, never faltering. It had taken this to make her realise that she loved him. He had been mother and father to her, friend and mentor. In the first days, after her parents left, he had distracted her, taking her on long walks, talking to her about his craft. Later, when they didn't come back, he had started to train her as his apprentice, directing her, giving her a purpose. She'd always thought of him as a stopgap, someone who would take care of her till the people she loved came back. Now she realised he was the person she loved, and he was the person who loved her, and she didn't want to lose him. She bit her lip. She wouldn't lose him. Somehow, they would come through this.

The forest thinned out as they walked until they came to a clearing. They followed the strange woman across an open field. In the half-light, Letta could see that the ground was rutted and covered in a carpet of dense white flowers, making it look as if a heavy mist had fallen on the starved scutch grass.

Before them lay the remains of a village, clusters of deserted houses crouched behind waist-high weeds, brambles and tattered shrubs, with their eyes blinded and their little doors kicked in. Letta had never seen a place as lonely.

Edgeware led them on till they came to a cottage set away from the others. It was a sturdy little house, with a reinforced wooden door and small windows. Around the perimeter was a dry-stone wall and Letta could see torches set in the stone at regular intervals. They followed her through a gate in the wall and up the winding path to the door. There they stopped.

Edgeware lifted the heavy beams that guarded the door, kicked it open and went through. Then she beckoned them in. The men had to bend their heads to go through. Letta followed, glad to be in out of the cold. Inside was a small room, neat and organised. There was a makeshift bed in the corner and there Edgeware told the men to leave Benjamin.

As soon as he was settled, Letta knelt on the floor beside him.

'We need bandage for fingers,' Edgeware said.

Letta could only nod. Her throat felt tight and constricted and she felt tears prick her eyes.

Edgeware slipped away.

Letta stroked Benjamin's hand. 'You're going to be all right, master,' she whispered into his ear. 'You have survived worse things than this.'

Edgeware came back with a basin and old rags. She took a piece of cloth and soaked it in the water. Then, very gently, she started to remove the black clots that clung to the nail bed. Benjamin groaned.

'Can you take over here, bairn?' Edgeware said. 'I need to get him potion for the pain.'

Letta nodded. She took the cloth and very tentatively started to clean away the dried blood. In her heart a fire of pure rage was burning bright, but she ignored it, focusing on the work in hand. A few minutes later, Edgeware was back with a herbal drink. She pressed the cup to Benjamin's lips. He opened his eyes for a second.

'Just drink,' Edgeware said.

As soon as he had swallowed the liquid, he relapsed into his previous comatose state.

'He be right weak.' Edgeware said. 'Right weak.'

'Can you make him better?' Letta said, stopping in her work to look straight into the other woman's eyes.

Edgeware shook her head. 'I can nay make people better or worse,' she said. 'They do that their own selves. He be an old man. He be badly treated by ignorant people that can nay see themselves for the fools they be.'

'Why would they do this?' Letta asked. 'Why?'

The old woman shook her head. 'Who knows?' she said. 'Maybe he tell us when he be able to.'

Time passed slowly after that. They cleaned his hands and Edgeware put a salve on the raw flesh.

'What's in that?' Letta asked looking at the thick cream clinging to the open wounds.

'Oak bark, lobelia, comfrey, marshmallow root, mullein leaf, skullcap, black walnut, aloe and calendula in a base of beeswax.' The old woman recited the list of herbs like a mantra.

Letta had never heard of most of them.

'Oak bark be natural antiseptic. Mullein leaves ease pain. I still have small store of beeswax since before the wild bees became extinct.'

'You are a healer,' Letta said.

Edgeware smiled. 'If you like,' she said. 'Now let him sleep. Sleep be the greatest healer of all.'

Edgeware moved away, but Letta stayed there holding the old man's hand. In the background, she could hear the gentle hum of conversation between Finn and Edgeware and she could smell garlic cooking but she didn't move. She remembered a night long ago, when she was about nine or ten. She had woken from her sleep with a fever. She had called out for Benjamin and he had sat there all night with her because she was afraid to go to sleep.

She looked at his worn old face and her heart filled with love for him. He had been through so much. Was it all to end here in this cabin deep in the forest? As if in answer to her question, the old man opened his eyes.

'Letta!' he said. 'Letta!'

CHAPTER 16

#357
Remember

Keep in mind, no forget

'HOW are you, master?' she said gently.

He looked up at her, the old grey eyes unusually bright.

'I have so much to tell you, so many things you should know. I promised your mother you would have nothing to do with politics. It had cost her so much already.'

His eyes had grown dull and his breathing more laboured. Letta shook her head.

'It's all right, master. Be calm now.'

The old man turned his head towards her and even that little movement seemed to cost him great effort. She had to put her ear to his mouth to hear him.

'John Noa is not what we thought. He wants to make us all wordless, Letta. Permanently. We would never be able to communicate again. Never.'

A fit of coughing shook the old man's body and he lay back on his pillow, defeated.

'What will happen to us?' Letta asked. 'Will we become extinct?'

'"Extinction" is the saddest word,' Benjamin said. 'Noa told me that when I first met him.'

'Why did Noa hurt you, master? Why did he arrest you?'

'He wanted to help me, save me.'

'Save you from what?'

'You don't understand. In the old days, before the Melting, no-one would listen. No-one. The politicians just talked and talked. They used words to keep the people in ignorance.'

'It's all right, master,' Letta said, laying her hand on his arm. 'Don't upset yourself.'

'What Noa wants to do is insane,' he whispered. 'I couldn't agree to it. I don't want to be one of the elite. I don't. What have I done, Letta? I trusted him.'

'Don't worry, master. It will all work out.' She tried to make her voice soothing but he was so weak she couldn't be sure he was hearing anything she said.

He grabbed her arm, his fingers digging into her flesh. 'Don't drink the water. Remember that, child. Don't drink the water. Don't let anyone drink it.'

His hand fell away and he closed his eyes. Soon he was asleep, his laboured breathing replacing the silence. Letta watched him, noticing the deep lines in his face, the grey in his hair. It seemed he had become old overnight. She stroked his cheek, talking softly to him, reassuring him, comforting him.

Later, she walked out of the house feeling shocked and numb. *He's ill*, she thought. *Why else would he talk the way he is talking? John Noa plans to make us wordless? Don't drink the water. It doesn't make any sense.*

'Letta!'

Marlo's voice cut across her reverie. Letta watched him stride across the yard towards her. The air was heavy. She looked up and saw that the sky too seemed loaded, as if it would soon snow. Somewhere overhead a bird screeched and Letta realised how quiet it was. A silence had fallen on the forest, broken only by the moaning of the wind.

'There you are!' Marlo said, putting his arm around her. She shivered despite herself. 'How is he?'

'Weak,' Letta said more to herself than anyone else. 'He thinks Noa plans to make us wordless. He keeps telling me not to drink the water.'

She looked up at Marlo, trying to judge his reaction.

Marlo shrugged. 'Let him rest. Talk to him again after he's slept.'

Letta nodded.

The day passed slowly, with Benjamin lapsing in and out of consciousness. In the background, Letta was aware of Marlo and Finn coming and going, talking in hushed tones. Edgeware continued to dose him with her various concoctions, leaving little bottles beside the bed, mixing potions that filled the house with strange smells, but nothing seemed to help.

'He be an old man,' Edgeware said to Letta. 'You can nay expect too much. Old people get tired, you know. After a while they nay care so much.'

'But he will get better.' Letta pushed her.

'Perhaps,' Edgeware said, but Letta didn't like what she saw in her eyes.

As night fell like a thick blanket, Letta again went to sit with Benjamin. Edgeware bandaged his hands again and left a noxious brew for him to drink when he woke.

'I sleep now,' she said to Letta. 'I come to you in a few hours. Call me if you be jittered. The wolves might come close to the house. You'll hear them, but Finn lit the torches outside earlier. That will keep them at bay.'

'Thank you for everything,' Letta said. 'I still don't understand why you've done all this for us.

The old woman sighed. 'I can nay do much for your kind,' she said. 'But I try to show them that there are people who can behave like humans were meant to behave. I remember the old days. The human race made a lot of mistakes, but we did good things too. We had minds of our own. We made decisions. It wasn't all bad.'

Before Letta could say anything, the old woman turned and left the room. Letta went over and sat beside Benjamin. His breath was coming in soft little gasps like the rabbits Letta had seen in the wheat fields as a child.

Soft little puffs of air.

Outside she thought she could hear moaning. *It could be wolves gathering,* she thought. *Or maybe the wind.*

The old man woke just before the dawn. Edgeware had insisted that Letta sleep for a few hours while she kept watch and, to her own surprise, Letta had slept. When she returned she found Edgeware nodding by the bed, her chin bouncing gently on her chest. Letta had sent Edgeware to her bed and resumed her vigil about an hour before the dawn. The old man had been restless but had not regained consciousness.

When he turned his head, Letta could see that he was barely able to open his eyes.

'Master,' she said, 'you awake!'

He squeezed her hand.

'There are things I need to ... tell you, Letta. I wish I could pass this burden to someone else ... someone older ... but you are the wordsmith now.'

'What, master? What should I know?'

'John Noa called me to his house to make me an offer. He offered me immunity ... from ... what he planned to do.'

A fit of coughing suddenly racked his body. Letta lifted his head and waited anxiously until it subsided.

'It's all right, master,' she said. 'You can tell me later. Rest now.'

He lay back on the pillow and Letta could see a blue glow about his mouth.

'No time,' he said. 'Let me finish.'

She stroked his hand. 'Go on, then,' she said.

'John Noa plans ... to make the people ... wordless.'

'Wordless?' What could he have in mind? A shorter List? *No* List?

'He's determined. He thinks man is still a ... liability.'

'Master?' Letta felt her heart pounding.

He opened his eyes again. 'Letta,' he said, 'you are the wordsmith now. For centuries ... centuries ... writers have stood between the rulers and ... the people. You have to ... stop him.'

Letta put her hand on his cheek. 'I will, master,' she said, tears rolling down her face. 'I will.'

'They loved you very much, you know, your parents. They would never be ... away ... if they could help it.'

'I know that, master,' she said.

He tightened his grip on her hand.

'In my study, in the bottom drawer, is a package, for you, Letta. Do not open it until all of this is over. Then, if there is a future ... if you manage to stop him ... open it then.'

'But what is it, master? Why do –'

'No questions, child. Just remember ... the birds still fly south, remember that, child.'

Letta had no idea what he meant. Was he delirious again?

His breathing got more laboured. He gripped her hand.

'You have been ... like a daughter to me, Letta,' he said. 'You can't let Noa do this ... to us.'

182

Letta tried to speak, but her throat was too tight, tears rolling into her mouth and down her neck. Around the room, the fireflies were gathering. Words she couldn't say dancing about her head.

Love. Heart. Warmth.

'Master,' she managed to say, but he hushed her and with the last of his strength pulled her to him.

She put her head on his chest. She could just hear the faint beat of his heart and feel his hand on her hair.

'No need,' he said. 'No need for words.'

She closed her eyes, listening to him breathe, and a calmness descended.

Outside she heard a lone bird greet the day, its song bright and full of hope. The sun shone weakly through the window and warmed her neck. Benjamin exhaled, one long breath, a breath full of resignation. Letta waited for him to inhale, but there was only the sound of her own heart in her ears.

And then, she knew, he was gone.

She had stayed with him for as long as she could. She didn't wake the others, wanting these last few hours alone with him. Her mind was racing with all he had told her but her heart was numb. She tried to remember the happy times they had spent together, things he had told her, but she couldn't concentrate. He was depending on her and she would not let him down.

She paced the floor, trying to assemble the facts as she knew them. Noa planned to make people wordless. He had offered to save Benjamin but Benjamin had refused his offer. Noa had murdered him. That was all she knew.

The immensity of her promise hit her. How could she stop Noa? She had no idea what it was he planned to do. Images of the Wordless haunted her.

Edgeware came to her as the first flurries of snow filled the window. She looked at the old man, then took Letta in her arms. Letta was glad to feel the warmth of the older woman, but she still couldn't feel anything emotionally.

Within minutes, Finn and Marlo joined them. They sat together around the bed while Edgeware chanted old verses that she said would shelter his fleeing spirit. Letta had never heard anything like it.

Hallowed, hallowed be thy name
You shall nay want
For thou be great
As you be in your beginning
Be now
And ever shall be
Hallowed, hallowed, hallowed.

Then, with the help of Marlo and Finn she wrapped Benjamin's body in a white linen sheet. At midday, they buried him behind the cottage as snow fell on Letta's hair and rested on her upturned face. The others left her alone then, to say her last goodbyes. Anger consumed her. Hot, fierce anger roaring inside her so that her ears rang and her stomach churned.

She looked back into the dark forest but there was nothing to see apart from the snow, a white screen between her and the rest of the world.

Benjamin. She would never see him again, never hear his voice, never hold his warm hand. His soft, reassuring presence in her life was gone for ever, like a clock that had stopped ticking.

Marlo's voice woke her from her reverie,

'There you are,' he said. 'I was worried.'

Of course he was worried. She was in the forest, alone. How quickly she had grown used to her new surroundings, lulled into a mindless security in a matter of days.

'I'm sorry,' she said. 'I needed time to think.'

He offered her his hand, and she took it with some reluctance.

'I talked to Finn,' Marlo said. 'You can live with us. If you want to. Would you like that?'

She could see the concern in his beautiful eyes, the blue-grey shining in the white light. She hesitated.

'Thank you,' she said. 'I would love to go and live with you, but –'

He frowned.

'But?'

'I have to go back, Marlo. There are things I have to do.'

As soon as the words were spoken, she realised she had made her decision. She had to try to do what Benjamin had asked of her.

'You should know something.' Marlo spoke slowly. 'We are planning a revolution. Finn has already recruited people from Ark, from Tintown. It is only a matter of time before we overthrow Noa. You could be part of that.'

'There isn't time,' Letta said. 'We know he plans to make us wordless. We need to know how he's going to do it.'

'I don't understand,' Marlo said.

'I hope I can be the wordsmith. I think that is important to Noa.'

Marlo's face fell.

'You will go back and work for him, even now, after all that has happened?'

Letta smiled. 'I will go back and work *against* him, Marlo. That's different.'

Finn, however, was not as easy to persuade. They sat around Edgeware's table and talked late into that night. Edgeware said little, but Letta could see that she listened to every word. Finn continued to push for Letta to come and stay with them.

'You are too young to take Noa on all alone, Letta,' he said finally, and Letta could see that he was coming to the end of his patience. 'In time we can overcome him. We already have the makings of an army.'

'We don't have time,' Letta said. 'I am the wordsmith: I can get Noa to trust me, like he trusted Benjamin. I can find out what he plans to do and then we can stop him.'

'If he hasn't killed you by then,' Finn said.

There was silence for a second as those words hit home.

Then Edgeware spoke. 'I think Letta be right,' she said.

Everyone stared at her. The old woman took up her cup and sipped from it. 'You will nay stop him from the outside. He be too clever and too well protected. If Letta gain his confidence, happen it be easier to defeat him.'

'And what if he realises what she's up to?' Finn's eyes were hard as he glared at the old woman.

Edgeware didn't flinch. 'Then he be killing her, and we all be wordless. If she nay does do it, she live on, but mankind, as we know it, be destroyed.'

She put her cup down. No-one spoke. The stark reality of Edgeware's words brooked no argument. There was no going back now. Letta only hoped she could do what was required of her.

'You will have us behind you at all times,' Finn said, as though reading her mind. 'Whatever we can do, will be done. We need you to keep in touch, to let us know what is happening.'

Letta nodded. 'Of course,' she said.

'What about you, Edgeware?' Finn said. 'Can we persuade you to come and live with us?'

The old woman shook her head.

'Whatever days be left to me, I will see out here in the forest,' she said. 'I am having no need of the company of men.'

'Have you no family?' Letta asked quietly.

The old woman shook her head.

'I be having a son once,' she said, playing with the handle of her cup.

'What happened?' Letta said, realising that she was straying into territory that older people didn't like. Edgeware looked up at her, her eyes clear and bright.

'Noa made him wordless,' she said.

Letta felt as though the breath had been knocked out of her.

'Wordless?' she said, thinking of the people she had seen in Tintown.

'Why do you say Noa made him wordless?' Finn asked.

'Because he did,' she answered him, without looking up from her cup.

'How?' Letta asked, trying to make sense of the shifting sands.

Edgeware laughed, a mirthless sound. 'He cut out his tongue.'

She had spoken so softly that Letta thought at first she had misheard. But one look at Marlo's face and she knew there was no mistake.

He cut out his tongue.

'Why?' Letta had to force the word out.

187

Edgeware shrugged. 'Who be knowing that?' she said. 'It be a time before List. An experiment, done in secret. He kidnapped the children. It be his first attempt to control words, but it be too complex. Many of the chosen ones bled to death. My Thomas didn't. He survived. His body did. But his spirit be dead from that day. He hanged his own self one morning. He be seventeen.'

Her words hung in the stale air of the little room for a moment. Letta felt she could almost touch them.

'How did you find out? About Noa, I mean?' she said.

Edgeware was silent for a minute, but then she started to speak again. 'A couple months after they be taken, the children who didn't die arrived back. They walked out of the forest. None of them could communicate, or they be too afraid to. My Thomas could write. Noa didn't know that. I took him home and got the story from him. They telling them their families be killed if they tell anyone, but Thomas and I be close in heart always. He telled me everything.'

'Was that when you went to live in the forest?' Finn asked the question quietly, but Letta could hear the steel in his voice.

The old woman nodded. 'I couldn't stay there. I took Thomas and everything we owned and walked back into the forest. I thought I nay would survive, survived, but somehow I did.'

'But Thomas didn't,' Marlo said.

Edgeware shook her head. 'No,' she said. 'He died here and he be buried here.'

The words were simply spoken, but Letta knew it explained why Edgeware stayed. She didn't want to abandon him.

Letta was reluctant to leave the old woman and Benjamin. It was strange to her that she took comfort in him lying under the forest floor. It seemed like a better place than back in Ark, a safer place. The old woman hugged her before she left.

'Go safely,' she said.

'Thank you for everything you did for me and for Benjamin,' Letta replied. 'I hope some day that I will be able to repay you.'

''If you be able to stop Noa you will more than repay me,' Edgeware said before letting her go.

Almost before she knew it, Letta was once more following Finn through the dense forest, listening to Marlo's steady steps following her. The snow had stopped falling but had left a deep carpet under foot. The wetness soaked Letta's feet leaving her feeling cold all the time. She barely noticed, though. Her mind was too preoccupied by the future and what she might do and where it would lead her.

By the time she saw the South Gate of Ark loom out of the mist, she had the bones of a plan.

The water tower was deserted. He stood on the narrow walkway between the tanks. He rehearsed what he would do. The Green Warriors had taught him all they knew about the chemical. He was almost ready. He walked through it in his mind until he was certain he hadn't forgotten anything. Then he climbed down the stairs, one foot after the other, gripping the rusty banister, his hand slippery with sweat.

How many to keep?

The Green Warriors, Len, the chief gavver, Amelia and a handful of craftsmen. That should be enough.

The wordsmith? Letta was a sweet girl and it made his heart heavy to think of losing her, but no, they would have no need of a wordsmith. He was confident that Benjamin had removed most of the words that were out there. Though perhaps Amelia would want to keep her. That was something he would discuss with her.

He made a mental note to destroy his own library. There would be time enough to destroy what remained in the wordsmith's shop when it was all over. By then, words would be of no use, and of no interest.

Before the Melting, the Wordless had been aggressive at first but soon became docile and lost the will to live. He would leave that to nature. There was only so much he could control.

CHAPTER 17

#395

Son

Male young

'WHY do you think Fearfall the scavenger lied to me about finding Benjamin dead?' Letta asked Finn before they parted company.

'I don't know,' he said. 'We can bring him in and question him.'

'Wouldn't that be dangerous? Wouldn't he report you the first chance he got?'

Finn shook his head. 'He wouldn't know where he was or who had questioned him.'

Letta frowned, trying to process what Finn had just said.

'When?' Letta said. 'When can you question him?'

'We need a few days,' Finn said. 'We need to watch him for a while, learn his movements. Then we'll take him.'

Shadowy images raced across Letta's mind. People being taken in the dead of night. Bodies washed up on the beach. People talking in hushed whispers.

'You'll let me know?' she asked.

Finn nodded.

She was sorry to see them go.

Marlo had hung back for a moment to talk to her privately. 'Remember,' he said, 'you're not alone. You can always contact us.'

'Or call you in my dreams,' Letta said with a smile.

'That might not be quite so reliable,' he said and took her hand, his thumb stroking her palm. She felt the blood run to her face. His skin burning hers. Could he feel her excitement?

'Do think about coming to live with us, Letta. It's not a bad life, you know.'

'I know,' she said, trying to keep her voice steady. 'I just need time, Marlo. I need to carry out my promise to Benjamin. Maybe I won't be able to but I can at least try.'

'You will,' Marlo said, his mouth on her ear, his breath warm against her. 'You can do anything if you want it badly enough.'

Later, walking through the familiar streets, she thought again about what he had said. She'd missed his touch as soon as he'd left her. She wanted so badly to go and live with him. To see him every day, to feel his arms around her. But she had to focus on other things. She was the wordsmith. That was her destiny. She wouldn't walk away from it. She just hoped he would wait for her.

As she walked up Cedar Street, she saw a crowd gathered outside the cobbler's shop. *Of course*, she thought. The last day of November. The Changing of the Shoes, when people got fitted for new footwear. Shoes were swapped from older children to younger ones, the shoes of the dead were passed to the living, men and women found themselves entitled to a new pair or were disappointed when Rua the cobbler said their shoes could be repaired yet again.

Letta had been best friends with Rua's daughter, Eva, when they were at school. She had died from a fever when she was twelve. Rua was a hearty man with a big laugh and was well liked in Ark, though people felt he was mean with his materials and certainly new shoes were not given easily. He made the shoes mostly from cotton or hemp, but field workers were entitled to leather made from dead animal skins. She shivered, remembering the skins hanging in the sun behind the cobbler's house. Letta's own shoes were well patched but she knew there was no question of replacing them yet. She stood for a minute, watching the crowd hanging about outside the shop. It was always a happy day, this Changing of the Shoes, with a festival atmosphere and today was no different. There was lots of laughter as Letta walked on by, and she was struck by how her attitude had changed. Once, she would have seen this as proof of her community pulling together, one big happy family living lightly on the planet. Now she knew differently. This was how Noa exerted his control, pulling their strings, a menacing puppet master, hiding in the shadows. If the people knew what he was really like!

They would know. She would see to it that they did. Approaching her own shop, her stomach rumbled ominously. Edgeware had given them bread and frozen berries to take with them. Finn had tapped into the main water pipe to give them water, but now she was hungry. It was past breakfast time and not yet dinner time. Tuesday. Nettle soup. Baked potatoes and goat's cheese. Her mouth watered.

She caught a glimpse of her reflection in the tin cladding of the shop. She looked thin and bedraggled, she thought. Her red hair was long and knotted, her face white and pinched. She ran her fingers through her hair. She was the only redhead in Ark.

She scurried round to the back door and let herself in. The warmth hit her like a wave, the warmth and the smell of paper and beetroot. She breathed it in, glad to be home.

Over the next hour, Letta set to putting her house to rights again. She checked the drop box and laid out the orders ready to start on them later in the day. Everywhere, images of Benjamin haunted her. She found it hard to concentrate. She heard three bells ring just as the knock came on the outside door. She took a deep breath and went to open it.

Carver, the gavver, stood there, leaning nonchalantly against the wall. 'You back,' he said, pushing past her and walking across the floor to the counter.

'Yes,' she said.

List sounded strange to her now. She had grown used to speaking the old tongue. She would have to be careful.

'Where you go?' the gavver asked, flicking through a box of cards that sat on the counter.

'Word search,' she said. 'Near Tintown.'

'You no tell Round House.'

'I must tell?' She tried to make herself look innocent. She needed him to think she didn't know any better.

He frowned. 'Yes,' he said. 'Must tell.'

They both jumped as the door opened again

It was Rose, the healer's wife.

Letta was startled by the change in her. Gone was the small, tidy woman with her hair pulled back into a neat bun. This woman's hair flowed down her shoulders. Her clothes were dirty and unkempt and she was barefoot. Letta was about to go to her when the woman advanced, her eyes wild, her hands clenched in two tight fists.

'Where he?' she said, glaring at Letta.

Letta glanced at the gavver, but he was standing watching the scene playing out in front of him.

'Please,' Letta began, but the other woman gave her no

194

chance to speak.

'You said you find him. You said friends help. What friends? Who? Where my boy?'

She was screaming now, flecks of white foam gathering at the corner of her mouth. 'Answer!' the woman screamed.

Letta said nothing. Her mind was racing. If Rose told the whole story with Carver standing there!

The woman came closer, her face pushed up against Letta's face so that she could feel the other woman's breath on her cheek, smell her sweat. Her fingers dug into Letta's shoulders.

'Who friends? Desecrators? Desecrators take my son? My Daniel?'

Letta reached out a hand to try to calm her but the woman slapped it away.

'I call gavvers. I tell. Desecrators take Daniel. You help. You Desecrator. Desecrator!'

Rose lunged at Letta, but Letta was younger and faster. She grabbed the flailing arms and held them tight, but she couldn't stop the torrent of words.

'Desecrator! Where Daniel? Tell! Tell me!'

'Gavvers took Daniel, Rose. You know that. You saw them. You saw him on the cart.'

'No!' the woman hissed at her. 'You! You Desecrator!'

Letta felt rather than saw the arrival of the healer. In seconds, he had taken his wife away from Letta and held her firmly in his arms.

'She no well,' he said to Letta, his eyes darting to the gavver standing by the counter.

Rose was still struggling, but she had stopped screaming and instead made little high-pitched noises like a bird caught in a trap.

'Please, take her home,' Letta said.

The man nodded and half-pulled his wife across the street. The woman kept looking back at Letta but all resistance had gone from her.

Letta watched until they disappeared inside their own front door. She turned to the gavver. He hadn't moved but a small smile played about his mouth.

'Woman mad,' he said.

'Yes,' Letta said, trying to hold his gaze.

'Sometimes mad people speak truth. Ha?'

Letta didn't answer but she felt her face flush red and hot. The gavver walked out without a backward glance.

Back at her desk, Letta sat with her head in her hands. What would become of poor Rose? Was she already insane? She couldn't imagine Ark supporting her if she couldn't contribute. Why had Letta ever said she would help her? Did Carver already suspect something or was he just trying to unsettle her? She tried to read the expression on his face. He had seemed amused if anything. If she was going to win Noa's trust there mustn't be even a whisper that would bring disrepute on her head.

She got up and walked to the window. The street outside was quiet – the workers were still in the fields, the children in school. Over at the healer's the blinds had been closed and the door shut. She was just about to turn away when she saw Carver bend his head as he came through the healer's front door. He glanced across and saw her. For a moment they locked eyes, then he turned and walked up the hill. The healer stood framed in the door behind him. He turned away when he saw Letta at the window. Then all was quiet again.

Letta sat at her desk, trying to compose herself. No-one would heed poor Rose. Like the gavver, they would think she had gone mad with grief. But Carver wasn't stupid. What had he learnt when he followed Rose home? She bit her lip. No point worrying about it now. Time would tell.

In her head, she played and replayed her last conversation with Benjamin. Noa intended to make them wordless. But how? He couldn't cut out all of their tongues. Could he? Would he offer her immunity? Probably not. She wasn't valuable enough. Maybe she would find out more when they spoke to the scavenger. She went back to her work, slowly transcribing her words onto their cards, comforted by the ritual and the earthy smell of beetroot.

It was two days before she heard from Marlo.

She had just gone to the tailor to be measured for a dress. The rules were clear. A dress would be issued when the edge of the cloth came half a stride over the knee. Tala Green had measured her, the nail of her thumb scratching her bare skin. Yes, she'd said, and handed her someone else's old dress, then waited while Letta removed the one she was wearing.

She left the tailor's as the last glimmer of the day faded. It was evening time, a dark, wet November evening. She looked up and there he was. He had a hood pulled over his head and his coat was heavy with rain.

'Marlo!' she said.

He pushed back the hood. His eyes danced in his head.

'Were you expecting me?' He smiled.

'Yes,' she said, her heart turning over. 'No. I don't know. I hoped you would come but I wasn't sure.'

This was it. They must have Fearfall. That was why Marlo had come. She turned to face him. 'You have him?'

Marlo nodded. 'As good as. He'll be at the pump house tonight. Finn sent me to get you.'

'We should go then,' she said, not looking at him.

He took her arm. 'What's the matter?' he said.

'Nothing,' Letta answered. 'Nothing.'

'You seem – angry. Are you?'

She shook her head. 'No,' she said. 'It's just…'

'Yes?' he said, and she could see the gentleness in his eyes.

'I'm not sure it is right to kidnap someone like this. I've heard about it before, Desecrators taking people, but –'

'But you never thought you would need our services?'

'I suppose,' Letta muttered.

Marlo walked away from her. 'This is hard for you,' he said. 'Your whole world has disappeared. I understand that. Don't worry about the scavenger. No-one will hurt him.'

Letta said nothing but she noticed the coolness in his voice.

'Maybe you would rather stay here?' he said. 'I can come back and –'

'No,' Letta said. 'This is my doing. I should at least be there.'

'Let's go then,' he said.

They hurried through the town, down to the West Gate.

'We have paid the gavver,' Marlo said to her. 'But it is better if he doesn't see you. I will distract him. You go through and wait for me in the trees on the far side.'

Marlo went to talk to the gavver, and as soon as they were deep in conversation Letta slipped through the gate and made for the trees beyond the scrubland. She didn't have long to wait. Marlo joined her and, with a slight nod, set off through the trees. Letta followed him, trying to imagine where he lived. He had said it was an old pump house but she couldn't imagine it here in the depth of the forest. She hurried to stay with him as they went deeper and deeper into the gloom. She could see nothing but trees. Row after row of trees swallowed by shadows.

As they walked, a branch lashed her face and she cried out. She put her hand to the welt and felt the warm dampness of her own blood.

'Let me look,' Marlo said, his voice soft and husky. He took her chin in his hand and with his finger smoothed the blood away. Letta tried not to wince. Marlo stroked her cheek softly, his thumb gliding along her skin, brushing her mouth. His hands were warm and callused. Letta's heart accelerated; a shiver went through her body. Reluctantly, she pulled away, the cut already forgotten.

Marlo took her hand in his, and they walked on. She had just begun to doubt the existence of the pump house when it loomed up out of the darkness.

The building was of grey, lichen-spattered stone, the roof above it had partially caved in but its tall chimney still stood, blackened with time, no longer belching out filthy black smoke into the heavens. Marlo took her arm and brought her towards the door. The deserted building, windows boarded up like a blind man, stared sightlessly down at her.

Marlo turned the key in the lock and the door fell open. With one last glance over her shoulder, she stepped inside. Behind her, she heard the door close.

The air smelt of damp and rot.

All around her was inky black. She moved one foot forward shakily. She felt giddy, terrified she was going to walk into an enormous pit. She put her hands out to balance herself. She felt Marlo's warm hand on her elbow and she turned to follow him.

They were in a cavernous hall, a high, gloom-filled room, its shadows pierced by shafts of light from a row of small windows far above them. Letta stumbled after Marlo as he led her across the bare concrete floor.

Frigid air assailed her face. Only the reassuring warmth of Marlo's hand on her arm made her keep on, even though her ankle throbbed and she could only see shadows in the bleak light. Then they stopped. Marlo knelt down. Letta frowned, trying to see what he was doing. His finger seemed to gauge the dark beams of the floor and then with a sharp tug he flipped up a metal ring. Marlo caught it and tugged, grunting with effort. Under his pale hand a trapdoor swung open. Cat-like, he swung deftly onto a ladder and disappeared into the hole.

'Ready?'

Letta grasped the top of the ladder and started to climb down. In seconds, she was standing on the floor beside Marlo.

He turned abruptly and opened a door in the wall behind them and Letta was plunged into a different world. Before her it was all warmth and colour and people. A vast room, its ceiling high and lofty and flanked with small lamps and candles. Under her feet, a floor of dark, weathered timber, honeyed with age and glowing gently in the half-light. The candles cast a mellow glow around the room, throwing shadows softly onto the walls.

A team of men and women were painting an enormous cloth which had been hung from the ceiling. The cloth was pulled tight and across it Letta could see an effusion of colour: cornflower blue, violet, coral. It was like nothing she had ever seen before; like nothing she could have imagined. She moved towards it, mesmerised. As she approached, the artists looked up from their work.

'This is Letta, the wordsmith,' Marlo said.

They nodded at her, and one woman smiled. 'No harm,' she said.

'No harm,' Letta whispered back.

'Finn?' Marlo looked at one of the men.

'They're not back yet,' the man said. 'Might take a while.'

Marlo nodded and turned to Letta.

'I'm on dinner duty tonight,' he said. 'Do you want to help?'

'Of course,' she said.

'I'll get started,' he said. 'But first you should have a look around.'

He was gone before she could protest.

She looked around. She had never seen or imagined a place like this. The high walls were painted in blocks of vivid colours stretching far above her: wild raspberry, ochre and emerald green. The colours flowed into one another, so that she couldn't be sure where one ended and another began. Punctuating the banks of colour were beautiful, intricate tapestries, heavy brocades interlaced with shimmering threads, but it was not the walls alone that held Letta's attention. A narrow shelf ran along the whole length of the room and on it people had placed their treasures, little things that they had obviously carried with them to this place. Letta had seen such souvenirs before but there was power in the fact that these were not the treasures of one person or of one family but of many. There was a quaint china cup decorated with lime green leaves and powder pink roses, a bottle fashioned like a heron with a long narrow neck. There was a carved sandalwood box, a scattering of shells with opaque pink underbellies and an old copper coin which had been lovingly placed on a tiny wooden plinth.

She examined the floor beneath her feet. What should have been a cold and dusty stretch of concrete had been covered in old lengths of wood, then divided into squares with some kind of black dye. Each square had a picture in it and each picture told a story. Letta crouched down to get a better view. The area all around her feet was dedicated to wild flowers: bluebells, cherry and cowslip, dandelion, gorse and yarrow. She walked through them to the next set of images. Letta could tell at once that a different hand had drawn them. One square showed people being swallowed by a giant wave. Letta bent lower to see the detail: a mother clutching her baby to her breast, a pair of young lovers holding hands, an old grey man leaning on a stick, a sea-bird captured mid-flight, and towering above them, the crushing mountain of black-blue water. The next square showed a cityscape with a fissure running through it. On either side of it, buildings were tumbling into the abyss. The picture was so vivid, the horror so real, that Letta could feel fear emanating from it.

Intrigued, she crossed the great room to where she could see Marlo in an alcove, working away.

'The pantry,' he said with a grin, when he saw her. The alcove consisted of a big table and row after row of shelves packed with produce. Letta gasped. She had never seen so much food outside of Central Kitchen.

'Where … how …?'

Marlo smiled.

'We forage in the wild for most of our food,' he explained. 'Then, it gets preserved.'

He picked up a jar full of something dark purple in colour.

'Jam,' he said. 'Made from wild berries. We'll need that. And cheese.'

'Cheese?' Letta said.

'Nettle cheese. It's good. You should try some. Leyla makes it.' He picked up a large pot and lifted the lid.

'And soup. Always soup.'

Letta looked around perplexed.

'What do you do for bread?'

Marlo shrugged, walking past her with the pot of soup.

'We do without,' he said.

'And water?'

Marlo shrugged again.

'We do whatever is necessary. We cannot live without it.'

Letta remembered how she had seen Finn tap into the main water pipe in the forest. She noticed another cupboard, its door slightly ajar. Curious, she opened it. It took her a second to realise what she was looking at. Row upon row of small, sharp utensils. Rough knives hewn from stone or wood or metal. Small enough to be concealed in a closed fist. Below them great wooden clubs. They were weapons. They were homemade but no less deadly. Marlo followed her gaze.

'We have to be able to protect ourselves, Letta,' he said, quietly closing the door. Weapons. As Letta processed that thought music flooded the building. She looked up, entranced. The notes swirled around, deep and booming. She recognised Leyla, the saxophone player. In front of her were dancers swaying slowly at first, puppets pulled on invisible strings. Then the music took hold of them, rising and falling to some ancient beat that only they could feel. Letta's head was filled with images of leaves. Crisp autumn leaves swirling in the wind.

The music was unbearably beautiful, the dancers at one with it, the air vibrating with it. And then it changed. The dancers were still and the saxophone started to speak, in sad, quiet notes; notes that ripped Letta's heart from her chest; notes full of tears and regret. She felt the hot sting of tears in her eyes and a deep pain somewhere inside her.

Then Leyla began to sing:

Down in the valley
The stream flows on
In the heather morning
Quiet as a swan.

The soft smell of lavender enveloped Letta. Her mother's face swam in front of her. She wanted to run from the music. Run from the images it dragged from her so casually, filling her heart with a new and unfamiliar pain and a terrible yearning.

And then the music ended.

CHAPTER 18

FOR a second, Letta didn't move, ignoring Marlo, who had stopped working and was looking at her with one eyebrow raised. She went straight to Leyla. The older woman looked up as Letta approached.

'Why did you play that sad tune? Why? How can you bear it?'

Letta could hear the anger in her own voice but she couldn't hold the words back.

Leyla looked at her and smiled. 'Music comes in all colours, Letta, just as we do. Before I knew the word for Creators, I called us colour-catchers, the musicians, the painters, the dancers. That's what we try to do, catch the colours in our own hearts and share that with other people. Colour-catchers. I think I still prefer that word,' she said. 'One of my colours is sadness, my friend.'

Letta looked back at her, uncomprehending. Leyla sighed.

'That last piece I played is full of regret for loved ones I have lost, things I have seen.'

'But,' Letta managed to say, 'you should try to forget those things. They are not things you want to remember.'

Leyla shook her head. 'I need to remember them, child. I need to remember how much I have lost. We all do, despite what Noa says.'

Leyla reached out and touched Letta's hand.

'Have you seen him recently?'

'Noa?'

Leyla's voice was so low, Letta could barely hear her.

'Yes, I have,' she said.

'And Amelia?'

Letta nodded. 'She lives with Noa. Why do you ask?'

The woman hesitated for a moment.

'You are Freya's girl, aren't you?'

Letta felt something shift inside her.

'You knew my mother?'

Leyla nodded. 'A long time ago. The song I sang earlier was her favourite.'

Without another word, Leyla stood up and went to talk to the dancers. Letta wrapped her arms around herself, suddenly cold. She had seen something in the older woman's eyes. Something so deep it frightened her.

Her thoughts were interrupted by Marlo's voice. 'You seem upset?'

'No. I mean yes. No, I'm not exactly upset, not really. It was just Leyla's music. That's all. It was sad.'

Marlo nodded. 'You are not used to music, Letta, and it affects you deeply. Before the Melting, people heard music all the time and they became used to it. It had no effect. It lost its power. That's what Finn says.'

'I'm not sure it's a good thing,' Letta said, the words out before she could censor them.

'You don't think music is a good thing?' Marlo narrowed

his eyes and she could see he was trying to understand her. 'Why?'

'Well,' Letta said, 'it is unsettling. It makes you think of things, feel things. Its fine when it's happy, but when it reminds you ...'

She couldn't continue. Her throat felt tight and she was afraid she would cry.

Marlo took her hand. 'John Noa banned the arts because he didn't want us to be unsettled. He didn't want us to think for ourselves. He didn't want us to be any different from the sheep in the fields. But we *are* different, Letta.'

Letta looked into his eyes.

He continued: 'Music calls to that bit of us that is different. There are lots of words for it. Soul. Spirit. Heart. Music makes us feel that we are not alone. That is its power.'

She nodded but didn't offer any of her own ideas.

'Come,' Marlo said, taking her arm. She followed him across the floor, her mind in chaos. She wanted to ask Leyla about her mother, to find out more, but Marlo was walking purposefully and she knew she couldn't go back. On the far side of the vast room, there was a door and, as they approached it, it opened and a woman came through.

'They are ready,' she said to Marlo.

Letta's stomach tightened. She had almost forgotten why she was there.

'We should go in,' Marlo said.

Letta took a deep breath and followed him.

She was in a corridor. Beyond her, somewhere in the distance, she could hear raised voices.

'Wait here.'

Marlo went ahead to a door towards the end of the corridor. Letta waited. She tried to imagine what was happening behind that door. Had he told them anything? Were they torturing him? She reminded herself that this was all for the greater good, but the uneasy feeling wouldn't go away.

She jumped when Marlo suddenly reappeared beside her.

'Put this on,' he said, handing her a black hood. As she watched, he pulled one over his own head. A black hood with two holes cut into it for his eyes. He was like something from a nightmare, a stranger. Even the blue–grey eyes looked cold and vengeful.

'Put it on,' he said again. 'You don't want him to recognise you.'

She pulled the hood over her face. All at once, she was plunged into darkness, the smell of the cloth suffocating. She pulled it round till she could see through the eyeholes. The world was telescoped into a narrow band.

Marlo led her into the room, the hood warm and cloying, a pulse beating in her throat. Smith Fearfall was sitting on a chair. Around him stood Finn and two other big men, all hooded. The room was small and entirely empty except for that chair. Fearfall's head snapped around when Marlo and Letta entered, eyes wide like a startled hare.

'What you want from me? Where my boy?' His voice was high and taut, fear bubbling from his lips and making his pupils dilate.

'No harm will come to the boy.'

Letta recognised Finn's voice, though it had a hard edge to it that she hadn't heard before.

'I've told you we don't speak List here. So speak as you wish.' Another voice, one of Finn's colleagues.

'What do you want?' Fearfall spat the words at them. Letta recoiled, despite herself.

'Information,' Finn said. 'Answer our questions and you can go home. You and your boy.'

The boy? Was the boy here? Letta tried to catch Marlo's eye but he was staring at the scavenger.

'I know nothing,' Fearfall said. 'You have the wrong man.' But his eyes darted around the room as though following invisible shadows.

'I don't think so,' Finn said. 'You found the body of the wordsmith. Isn't that so?'

'Yes,' Fearfall said, focusing on Finn.

'Where?'

'In the forest, near the river.'

'And he was dead?'

'Yes.'

There was silence for a moment.

Then Finn sighed. 'Now, Smith, I need the truth.'

'That is the –'

'No!' Finn banged the wall with his fist. Fearfall jumped in the chair.

'No,' Finn said again, more calmly this time. 'That is not the truth. We know it is a lie, and so do you. So we will start again. You didn't find the wordsmith, did you?'

'I did. I did find him. By the river.'

Letta felt her own anger stir. Lies. All lies.

Finn dropped his voice a tone. 'Do I have to remind you that we have your son?'

The scavenger's face drained of colour. Letta felt cold all over. They were holding the child.

'You wouldn't –' he began, but seemed unable to finish the thought.

Finn walked over to him and bent down till their eyes were level. 'We will do whatever we have to do. Tell me the truth and no harm will come to your son.'

209

'Desecrator!' The word was barely there and yet it pulsed with anger and hatred.

Finn ignored him. 'Why did you lie?'

There was silence in the room. Letta watched Smith Fearfall clench and unclench his hand. No-one dared breathe. Finn didn't move.

Finally Fearfall spoke. 'John Noa,' he said.

'Noa told you to lie?'

'Yes.'

'Tell me!'

Finn walked away from him.

Fearfall dropped his head to his chest. 'He told me to say that I found him in the forest. He said to say he was dead. That's all.'

Letta felt as though a fist had hit her. She remembered how she had felt when she heard that news, *savaged by wild animals.* He'd said *that* about Benjamin.

'Did you see the wordsmith at all?'

'No,' Fearfall answered.

'How did Noa know you?'

'I am a scavenger. I bring him things.'

'Things?' Finn stopped pacing and looked at the man.

'Things that are of interest to him.'

'What was the last thing you brought to him?'

Fearfall looked away.

Finn waited a second. 'Smith?' he said, and this time his tone was laced with menace. Fearfall jumped as though he had been struck.

'I don't know. A canister. I thought the Green Warriors would want it.'

'And did they?'

The question was asked casually but Letta could feel the tension in the room.

'Yes,' the scavenger said.

Finn paused. He looked at Letta. In the distance, she thought she heard a child cry.

The interrogation continued.

'Now, Smith,' Finn said, 'you are doing very well. A few more questions and you will be on your way home.'

'May the Goddess curse you,' Fearfall said glaring around the room.

'The canister. What did it look like?'

'I'm not telling any more,' Fearfall said sulkily. 'I've said enough.'

Letta wanted to scream in frustration. Why wouldn't the man just tell the truth? As though reading her mind, Marlo put a restraining hand on her arm.

'What a pity!' Finn said. 'I had hoped to avoid unpleasantness. Dean!' Finn turned to the man beside him. 'The boy is outside. Get him. You know what to do.'

Letta felt as though her heart had stopped beating.

'Yes, sir,' the other man said, and turned to leave.

'No!'

The word came out more like a groan from Fearfall. Letta saw tears in his eyes.

'Leave him,' he said. 'What do you want to know?'

'Tell me about the canister,' Finn said.

Fearfall shrugged. 'It was silver. About a stride long.'

'Did it have markings?'

Fearfall shrugged again. 'Letters,' he said. 'It had a string of letters written on the side of it. Now give me back my child!'

'What were the letters?' Finn pressed him.

The scavenger shrugged. 'I don't remember,' he said.

'Try!' Finn's voice was cold.

Fearfall's eyes darted around the room like those of a trapped animal.

'I don't remember,' he said again. 'N, I think.'

'N?' Finn said. 'What else?'

Fearfall shook his head.

'We will find out one way or another, you know that,' Finn said. 'You might as well tell us.'

Again Fearfall shook his head.

'Do you want to see your boy again? Do you?'

'N-I-C-E-N-E.' Fearfall coughed the letters out as though they were barbed hooks.

Finn hesitated. 'Nicene?' he said.

Fearfall nodded.

'Very well. You shall have the boy back and you will leave here unharmed. However, next time you lie for Noa, it will not go easy for you. Or the boy. Remember that, Fearfall. One word to Noa and it's all over. Now, let's go over your story one more time.'

In the distance Letta heard a child scream. The scavenger froze.

'No harm will come to him,' Finn said evenly.

The child screamed again.

No! Letta thought, her heart pounding. *I can't do this.* She turned and left the room, not looking back.

Once she was outside the door she could hear the child clearly, sobbing now. She followed the sound and it led her to a narrow room further along the corridor. She flung the door open, not knowing exactly what she expected to find. In the room, Fearfall's son, the small boy she had seen in Tintown, was crouched on the floor, looking up at a young woman wearing a hood.

'We won't hurt you,' the girl was saying. 'Please stop crying.'

But Letta could see the terror in the child's eyes.

'Bad people! Bad people!' he screamed, the words like pellets flying around the room, his voice taut and full of fear.

Letta pulled off her hood. 'It's all right,' she said, kneeling down beside him. 'It's all right now.'

'Keep your hood on,' the girl said urgently, but Letta ignored her.

Instead, she put her arms around the child and held him close.

'Don't be afraid,' she said to him. 'Don't be afraid. Your father come soon.'

The child looked up at her, big brown eyes stained red from crying.

'Bad people,' he said again, but Letta could see that he was calming down.

'Hush!' she said. 'All well now. All good.'

Just then, the door opened and a hooded man stood there.

'Put on your hood!' he said to Letta. 'Give me the boy.'

She recognised his voice. It was the one Finn had called Dean.

Letta stood up. 'Let me take him,' she said.

'Hood!' Dean said sharply.

Reluctantly, she pulled on the hood. The little boy didn't seem to mind. He clung to her hand and followed her.

On the corridor, Fearfall was being held by two more hooded figures. The boy pulled away and rushed towards him. Fearfall picked him up, holding him tight, kissing his head, murmuring words of comfort.

'Go!' Finn said, appearing behind them, Marlo at his side.

The small group moved on. As they passed Letta, the scavenger stopped, and Letta felt he was looking right at her despite the hood.

'I'm sorry,' she said. 'But –'

'Desecrators!' He spat the word at her. 'Vermin!'

With that, Dean pushed him on, and they all disappeared through the door. Letta pulled off her hood. She took a deep breath of fresh air. She barely noticed Finn and Marlo coming to her side.

'Nicene,' Finn said. 'Any idea what that is?'

Letta shook her head, finding it hard to look at him.

'Something from the old days?'

'Certainly,' Finn said. 'Gas or a chemical most likely. And it may be nothing, but –'

Letta said, 'I might know someone who would know,' thinking about the old man she had met in Tintown. He'd been a scientist in the old days, she remembered.

'Will you stay here tonight?' Marlo asked her.

'It might be safer,' Finn added.

Letta didn't want to stay. She felt very uncomfortable about all that had happened. She wanted space to work it out. Her own space.

'That is kind of you,' she said. 'But I think I should go home. I might be missed.'

'Very well,' Finn said. 'Marlo will take you.'

He seemed exhausted, now that the questioning was over. He walked past her slowly, touching her arm as he did so.

'Go safely,' he said.

CHAPTER 19

#192

Scavenger

Person collects old things, rubbish

THERE was no light in Tintown. Letta walked hesitantly, terrified she would miss her step and fall. She tried to remember her route that last day she had been here. This time, there were no children running about, but she could sense people in the shadows, watching her. She hurried on. Was there someone following her? She strained to hear but her own heart was beating so loudly she couldn't be certain. She stopped. A stone skidded somewhere behind her, tapping her ankle as it passed. Someone blocked her path. A man. She couldn't make out his features but she could hear him breathing.

'Who you? What you want?' she said, trying to make herself sound confident.

'You here again?'

The voice was low, menacing. She tried to remember where she had heard it before. 'Who you?' she said again.

'Go home,' the man said. 'Don't come back. You hear?'

He took a step towards her. Now she could feel his breath on her face. She had to get away. From behind her, a hand grabbed her shoulder.

215

'Trouble?'

She turned. A man stood behind her, tall and broad.

'Well, Smith?' His voice was low but firm.

Smith! That is how she had known the voice. Smith Fearfall. The scavenger.

'Girl no business here,' Fearfall said. 'No business.'

'That true?' The man squeezed her shoulder.

Letta looked up. She could see him now.

'Kirch,' she said.

It was the son of the old man she'd met the last time, the scientist. She could scarcely believe her good fortune.

'Yes,' he said. 'Kirch. Have you business here?'

'I come see your father,' Letta said.

'Does that answer question, Smith?'

Kirch Tellon's question to Smith Fearfall was a challenge. Letta was sure of that.

'Girl is trouble,' Fearfall said but he turned and walked away.

'Come.' Kirch Tellon took her hand. 'Follow me.'

Letta followed him, in and out, past huts piled one on top of the other, through the rank smells, the misery and the sense of hopelessness. Kirch stopped at a hut on the end of a row.

'Smith Fearfall not bad man,' he said, turning to her. 'Desecrators took him and his son. Boy frightened bad.'

She could hear his screams still. *Bad people! Bad people!* The terror in his eyes.

'Why you talk to father?'

Tellon's voice woke her from her stupor.

'I want ask him …,' she stammered, 'about something before Melting.'

Kirch frowned.

Letta pressed on. 'And I bring healing herbs.'

Kirch ducked under the low door into the hut. Letta followed. The house was not in complete darkness. A small candle glowed in one corner, enough to let Letta see the old man, slumped in a chair by the far wall.

'My father no like dark,' Kirch said by way of explanation. 'I try keep light here before he sleep.'

There was a strange smell in the room like putrid meat. A dead animal? As Letta came closer, she realised that the smell was coming from the man's leg, the gaping wound was now covered in yellow puss and a black clot of bluebottles hovered above it. Letta's stomach heaved.

'What name?' she whispered.

'Solam,' he said. 'His name Solam.'

'Get water,' she said to Kirch, and started to unpack her bag.

'Only rainwater,' Kirch said.

'Better than nothing,' Letta retorted.

Rainwater was so polluted that people would no more drink it than sea-water. But, for this, Letta thought it could do no harm.

'And fetch rag,' Letta ordered before kneeling down in front of the old man.

'Solam,' she said gently. 'I brought herbs, make you feel better.'

She pulled the small bottle of water from her bag and held it to his lips. He drank slowly, barely wetting his tongue before pushing the bottle away.

Kirch came in and handed her a small bowl of cloudy water and a piece of grey cloth. From her bag, Letta took a tincture of calendula that the healer had given Benjamin when he had cut his leg on rusty metal. She knew it had the power to kill infection, but first she had to clean the wound. She dipped the cloth in the water and started to dab at the edges of the incision. She had to stop constantly to bat away the flies, but

217

she persisted until the edges of the cut were clean. Then, as gently as she could, she applied the tincture to the gaping cut. Despite her attempts at gentleness the old man stifled a groan as the tincture hit the wound, but Letta soothed him, talking to him, while she continued with her work.

'Nearly done now,' she said, patting his hand. 'Nearly done.'

She tied the rag around the infected leg, which would at least keep the flies away.

'Thank you,' the old man said when she had finished.

'Girl need to ask you something,' Kirch said as Letta packed her bag again.

'No,' Letta said. 'You need to rest. I come another day.'

'No,' Solam said. 'Ask now.'

Letta sat back on her heels and looked up at him.

'Nicene,' she said. 'It was … is a chemical. I think. Stored in a silver canister.'

'Nicene,' the old man repeated softly. 'Long time ago.'

He was quiet for a moment, and Letta held her breath.

'It was to be used on criminals. It destroyed the part of the brain responsible for language.'

'List, father,' Kirch said. 'Talk List.'

Letta could hear the fear in Kirch's voice. She turned to him. 'Please,' she said. 'There is no need.'

Kirch shrugged.

The old man continued. 'The left temporal lobe. That is the part of the brain that understands and produces language.'

'My father scientist before Melting,' Kirch said, his voice cracking.

'May the Goddess forgive me,' the old man whispered.

Letta leant closer.

'It was we scientists who discovered Nicene. Hans Nicene

218

was one of the foremost scholars of his day. He discovered the chemical while he was looking for a cure for dementia. Nicene is soluble in water, tasteless, odourless, colourless. It is also very efficient.'

'Efficient for what?' Letta prompted.

'Once ingested, Nicene destroys the left temporal lobe. After that, you can't speak, can't read or write, can't understand language. You are totally isolated from all other living things. And you can't invent a new language either.'

There was silence for a moment and Letta tried to imagine the loneliness of that.

'It was to be used on criminals,' the old man went on. 'Only on the most heinous of criminals, those who could never be allowed back into society. The human rights groups kicked up a bit of a fuss at first, but they got no support. Not when people saw the type of people Nicene was to be used on. Sadistic serial killers, people who harmed children…'

Letta nodded, hardly daring to breathe.

'But of course it didn't stop at that,' the old man continued.

'How do you mean?'

'The mentally ill were the first to be drawn in. The government started to use Nicene secretly on people with mental illness. It kept them quiet, easier to deal with.'

He stopped and Letta handed him the bottle of water again. This time, he drank deeply.

'Then it was terrorists or anyone who disagreed with the government. They too were silenced. Nicene was one hundred per cent successful and there was an added, unforeseen bonus.'

Letta waited.

'They died soon after the treatment.'

'It killed them?'

The old man shook his head. 'No,' he said. 'Not exactly. Medically, it shouldn't have shortened their lives. No. Nicene himself saw it for what it was. They died of despair.'

His chin dropped to his chest and he studied his hands. Letta had a fleeting image of Edgeware's son, hanging from a tree. The old man looked up at her.

'Why are you interested in Nicene?' he asked. 'Like all science, it was lost after the Melting, thank the Goddess. I had never thought to speak of it again.'

'No reason, really,' Letta lied. 'I am the wordsmith and someone mentioned it. It's my job to record all the words we can find.'

The old man laughed. A small bitter sound.

'So that you can destroy them?'

'So that we can remove them from circulation,' Letta said, packing her bag, 'until man can once more be trusted with them.'

She didn't dare confide in these people. She knew nothing about them. It was dangerous enough not to have spoken List. She touched the old man's hand.

'Thank you,' she said. 'I hope your leg is better soon.'

'Wait,' he said. 'How is John Noa? You see him?'

'Yes,' Letta said. 'I see him.'

'And the Deer sisters? They still there?'

'Amelia Deer is there.'

'There used to be three of them, three sisters, good-looking girls. I can't remember their names. Noa was besotted with them. Only humans he ever truly loved. There was a falling out. Amelia stayed with Noa.' The old man's words were more for himself than anyone else, Letta thought.

She stood up.

Kirch moved back and let her pass in front of him. 'I'll walk with you,' he said.

Letta didn't argue with him, though her head was teeming with all she had heard, and she desperately needed to be alone and figure it out.

'I hope you know what you are doing,' Kirch said when they reached the gate.

Letta looked at him. What did he know? Or suspect? He put his hand on her shoulder and looked into her eyes.

'If you ever need help, you know where to find me.'

'Thank you,' Letta said. 'I have to go now. Go back to your father. Take care of him. Here.' She rooted in her bag until she found the tincture. 'Use this. It will help.'

He took the little bottle from her.

'Thank you,' he said softly. 'But I think he is beyond our help now.'

Letta watched him go back towards Tintown and her heart ached for him. How could she have lived all this time on the edge of that hell-hole and not known what went on there?

She turned and faced the gate looming out of the darkness.

Letta spent much of the night awake, going over all she had learnt.

Don't drink the water!

That was what Benjamin had said to her and she had thought that he was delirious. She knew now what those words meant. Had Noa already put the chemical in the water? If he had, then he wouldn't drink the water, and nor would any of the chosen ones. But maybe he hadn't put the chemical into the water yet?

She would have to work on that principle, she decided. Anything else was hopeless.

When morning came she felt weary but she couldn't rest. Her head was still teeming with ideas, half-formed plans and desperation. *I have to get out of here*, she thought. *Water! I'll go and get water.* She grabbed her coat and headed out. The day was still young and cold. The snow had disappeared but the air was icy and the wind blew from the north. Her feet found their own way down the little incline into the square where Werber was busy handing out water. What would he say if he knew what John Noa intended for them? An old man was taking his full bottle and walking away as she approached.

'No harm, wordsmith,' he greeted her.

'No harm,' Letta responded. She was surprised that he knew her, though already it seemed people were accepting that she was the wordsmith. Still, each time they greeted her, she had an urge to look around to see where Benjamin was.

Benjamin. She felt the familiar ache as she thought his name but she pushed it aside and walked over to Werber. He smiled when he saw her.

'No harm, Letta!'

'No harm,' she answered.

'Come for water?'

'Yes.' She smiled. 'Thirsty.'

He pulled a cup from under his table and filled it from a bottle on the ground.

'Drink!' he said to her.

She sipped from the cup gratefully.

'Good water,' she said. 'Cool.'

He nodded.

'All water comes from the tower?' she asked, nodding towards the water tower that stood on the hill behind him.

'Yes,' Werber said, and she could hear the pride in his voice. 'Water pumped into tower to be cleaned.'

Pumped. A specialist word for those involved in water.

'How cleaned?' she said frowning.

'Chemicals,' Werber said without hesitation.

Chemical. Another specialist word.

Letta gave him what she hoped was an admiring look. 'You work there, Werber?' she asked.

A flush coloured his skin. He looked around to check that no-one was listening. 'Sometimes,' he said. 'Sometimes.'

He started to fill her bottle with water from the tap.

'You work there this week?' Letta pushed him.

'This morning,' he said proudly.

'You clean the water?'

He nodded. 'Not allowed talk about it.'

'I understand,' Letta said and took the bottle from him, her mind racing.

He wasn't allowed to talk about it because water in Ark equalled survival. The water tower was heavily guarded and, because Noa feared that the Desecrators could take the water plant and gain control of Ark, everything to do with water was heavily secured. She remembered the basics from school. The dirty water was brought in barrels to the tower, where it was cleaned. The clean water then went into big tanks, where it was stored until it could be piped out to the water stations. That was all she knew, and she was certain it wasn't enough. She needed to know everything about the water plant. Everything.

CHAPTER 20

BACK at home, Letta went to search for a word list that dealt with water treatment. When she found it, she was surprised at how long it was.

Filtration, evaporation, tank.

She was still lost in her own reverie, when she heard a gentle tap on the back door. She hurried to open it. As she did, two bodies pushed past her, followed by a sharp burst of frigid wind. She closed the door quickly.

'You have to come with us,' Marlo said, as soon as he entered the shop.

'The gavvers have had a complaint,' Finn said, checking that the front door was securely bolted.

'About me?' Letta said, trying to think what she might have done that they could know about.

Finn nodded. 'The healer claims you are in league with the Desecrators.'

'Oh,' Letta said, remembering the hatred in Rose's eyes.

'It's serious,' Marlo said, his brow furrowed.

224

'Yes,' said Letta. 'It is serious.'

'He says you told his wife that you had friends who could help her get her son back.'

Letta could see the Goddess in her mind, hear herself promising to help Rose.

'Rose is traumatised. Why do they believe her?'

Finn shrugged. 'Carver doesn't trust you. Ever since Marlo was here he's had his suspicions. He's building a case.'

'How do you know all this?' Letta couldn't stop herself pacing the floor.

'We have people everywhere,' Finn answered. 'Even amongst the gavvers.'

'Take what you need and come with us,' Marlo said, his voice full of urgency. 'You'll be safe in the forest.'

Letta shook her head. 'No, Marlo,' she said. 'I would never be safe again. If I run now, they'll know it's true. As it is, they only have Carver's suspicions and the accusation of a mad woman.'

'Do you think Noa might not believe them?'

'Maybe not,' Letta said. 'I don't know. I think he trusts me.'

Marlo frowned. 'And if he doesn't?'

'He and Benjamin were best friends when they set up Ark. He would find it hard to believe that I, of all people, would betray him.'

'Maybe,' Finn said. 'Let's leave it another day and see what happens. Our informer will let us know if Carver plans to make a move.'

'Can you do some research on the water tower?' Letta asked them.

'What kind of research?' Marlo asked.

'I need to know about the gavvers. What are the shifts? How many of them? All of that.'

Finn nodded. 'We have a friend who works as a water gatherer. We can ask him.'

'Why do you need to know?' Marlo asked.

Letta told them about her visit to Tintown and her conversation with Solam. When she finished, the two men were quiet for a moment.

Then Finn stood up. 'We will do anything we can to help you, Letta. You only have to ask.'

Marlo gripped her hand. 'We'd better go,' he said. 'You don't need the gavvers to find us here.'

Letta closed the door behind them, re-running everything she knew about the water tower until her head ached.

An hour later, she went to lie on her bed, exhausted. She was just about to fall asleep when she heard a noise downstairs. She sat up.

I didn't go to Central Kitchen, she thought. *Didn't show up for dinner. It could be Mrs Truckle looking for me.*

She jumped up and ran down the stairs. She didn't want the old woman to have to come looking for her. Mrs Truckle was getting old and the stairs would tire her out. She opened the door before she realised her mistake. It wasn't Mrs Truckle. It was Carver. Between his teeth he had a piece of grass and he chewed on it as he watched her.

Letta eyed him coldly. 'Yes?' she said.

'You think me fool?'

Letta said nothing.

He spat the grass onto the floor. 'I know what you are.'

The words hit her like darts. She opened her mouth to say something but no sound came out.

'Rex!' Carver clicked his fingers and another gavver appeared beside him. 'Take her!'

226

In a heartbeat, the second gavver had snapped a chain lock on her wrists, and was bundling her out the door.

She tried to yank her arms away from him but he held her firmly, laughing at her paltry efforts.

'Come!' he said and shoved her onto the street.

She was in a cell. Seven strides by three. There was no light. The sky was just visible through two bars high up on the outside wall. The door was big and solid and black. There was nowhere to sit, so she leant against the wall, feeling the cold air through the bars. All about her was the smell of damp and decay.

She didn't know how long she'd been there, but it had still been light when they'd thrown her into this cell. She hadn't seen them since. It was eerily quiet.

She remembered the day she had spoken to Hugo. Was it through the same window? Her jaw tightened when she thought of how they had treated him.

Just then a scream rent the air. A man's scream, she thought, somewhere to her right. Instinctively she rushed to the door. There it was again. Another scream from the same direction. A cold shiver ran down her spine.

She dropped to the floor and sat there, feeling the cold seep in through her thin dress. She wouldn't betray Marlo and Finn, no matter what they did to her. She wouldn't talk. Not one word. If this is how it is to end, let it be, she thought. I will not betray them. She almost wished the interrogation would begin so that she could get it over with. She hated this waiting, twitching at every noise.

Another scream cut through the air. She jumped despite herself. *Torture.* She tried to push the word away. Then she

227

remembered Benjamin's hands, and panic threatened to overcome her. She couldn't think about it. Wouldn't think about it.

Did Noa know she was here? Had he ordered her arrest? How much did they know? That was the thought that worried her. What did they know?

She was stopped in her thoughts by the sound of boots. A key turned and three bolts slammed back. With a loud creak the door opened. Her heart was beating rapidly. Carver. And another gavver she hadn't seen before.

'Get up!'

She didn't see the kick coming. Carver's boot crashed into her hip. Pain shot through her. Her stomach lurched. She could taste acid in her mouth. She stifled a cry. She wouldn't let him see how vulnerable she was. She struggled to her feet, her eyes locked on the black boots. He took another step towards her.

The second gavver looked away. She braced herself for a blow, but none came.

Carver smiled. 'Not so smart now, are we?' he said.

In her head, all Letta could register was that he was speaking in the old tongue.

He leant in closer. 'Where are they? Your friends, the Desecrators. I know they're planning something. I want names. I want to know where they live. I want to know it all.'

His voice was strangely hushed. She had to strain to hear him.

'And you –' His finger prodded her arm. 'You are going to tell me.'

She opened her mouth to speak but he was faster. He caught her hair in his fist. She felt her scalp constrict. Pain. Ripping, burning pain. He pulled harder. She felt tufts of hair come away from the root. Despite herself she cried out.

Carver laughed. 'Feel more like talking now?'

She could feel his spit on her face.

He put his lips to her ear. 'We are only starting, only starting.'

He turned to the other gavver. 'Close the door, Wallum.'

Letta swallowed hard. Carver released her, throwing her against the wall. She stumbled but managed not to fall. Carver took off his jacket.

Suddenly a new voice broke the silence. 'What is this?'

At first she didn't recognise the speaker, and she found it impossible to drag her attention away from Carver. It was Carver's own reaction she noticed. The way his mouth turned down, how the light went out of his eyes. She glanced across.

Noa.

'What is going on here?'

The words fell like icicles from his mouth. Carver seemed to shrink before her.

'Desecrator, sir,' Carver mumbled. 'Reason to believe.'

'Get out!' Noa snapped the words at the men, never taking his eyes from Letta.

A noise like rats scuttling across the floor and the gavvers were gone. Letta felt herself breathe again. She looked up at Noa but something in his eyes had changed. Gone was the grandfather figure he had presented before. In his place, Letta saw only a shell full of venom, and all of that venom was directed at her.

'So, Letta,' he said, 'I understand you are in trouble?'

'Yes,' she said. 'I am but I don't understand why.'

He ignored her.

'You have been associating with Desecrators, they tell me.'

What did he know?

'What do you mean?' she said.

He sighed. 'That's the trouble with words, isn't it? So inexact.

229

So much room to wriggle and squirm and play with the truth. Don't you think, Letta?'

'Yes,' she said.

He knows something, Letta thought, her mind working furiously.

'So, they made contact with you? What did they tell you? What did they promise you?'

She had to tell him something that had a grain of truth in it, something he might believe.

'I didn't know,' she said. 'You have to believe me. Someone called to the shop, the day Daniel was taken.'

'The boy?'

'No,' Letta said. 'Not a boy. An old man. Hugo was his name.' *He's already dead*, she thought. *You can't do any more to him.*

'Go on,' Noa said, but Letta could see the hesitation in his eyes.

'I was upset about Daniel. He was so young, you see. I was upset, and Hugo said he had friends who could help. I told Rose that and – I promise you I had no idea he was a Desecrator. I hate the Desecrators. I hate everything they stand for. I wanted to talk to you, to tell you.'

'Enough!' he said, raising his right hand.

He doesn't believe me, Letta thought desperately. *He knows I'm lying.*

Noa leant in closer. Seconds ticked by. She could almost see his mind working. Then he took a step back.

'I believe you, Letta,' he said finally. 'But you took a terrible chance. I know you are young, but you have to grow up fast now. Save your sympathy for the planet. Do not waste it on delinquents like Daniel.'

'Yes, master,' she said, bowing her head in what she hoped looked like humility.

Noa smiled, a slow, lazy smile. 'The gavvers have a job to do. The healer's wife made a complaint. A serious complaint. That had to be investigated.'

He stared at her for a second, and she could see that his eyes were no longer focused.

'Come! This is no place for us to talk. Follow me!'

She watched him stalk out in front of her and then quickly followed him, hearing the heavy door of the cell slam behind her.

'Come!' Noa said again, putting his arm around her. 'Come see what we captured.'

Why was he doing this? Why had he come to her rescue at all? Was this a test?

She followed Noa, almost running to keep up. For an old man, he was incredibly fit. Before she knew what was happening, they were descending a flight of old stone steps.

'This leads directly to one of our holding cells,' Noa explained. 'When I was building Ark, I thought we would keep grain here in this underground bunker, but we soon found a more urgent need.'

At the bottom of the steps, a narrow corridor led them past a number of doors and finally to the first cell, a small room with a barred door. Letta looked in but it was empty. At the next door, a woman was standing looking in. Her raspy breathing left no doubt as to her identity.

Noa stopped. Through the bars, Letta could see someone manacled to the wall. Her hair hung down limply about her face and her feet were bare. She was looking at the floor. As they approached she looked up. Letta drew in a sharp breath. She could feel the colour draining from her face. It was Leyla, the saxophone player. John Noa turned to Amelia, who was standing staring into the cell.

231

'My dear,' he said, 'what are you doing down here?'

Amelia looked up at him. 'I came to beg you –' The air rasped through her lungs as if the life force was being sucked from her.

Noa stroked her cheek with his finger. 'Stefano has cut some roses for you,' he said, speaking gently, as though to a child. 'Roses in winter – think of that! There is nothing the Warriors cannot achieve. Why don't you go up and put them in water?'

'Please, John.' Amelia grabbed his hands, clinging to him. 'Please forgive her.'

'I don't think you understand,' Noa said. 'We can talk about this later.'

'But John,' Amelia persisted, 'she was once my sister. The only one I have left. You have to help her. I will take full responsibility.'

Her sister! How could Leyla be Amelia's sister? Did Marlo know this?

'Please, John.' Amelia grabbed his arm.

Listen to her, Letta pleaded silently. People said that Amelia was the person closest to Noa. If Leyla was her sister, he wouldn't let any harm come to her. He loved Amelia and that would make a difference. A weight shifted from Letta's heart.

'Go now,' Noa was saying to Amelia. 'Go. I will take care of everything.'

Amelia backed away from him as though afraid to lose eye contact, lest he change his mind. Letta stood listening to the gravelly noise of her breathing as she left them. Noa watched her till she disappeared around the corner, his eyes soft, his lips pursed.

'Carver!'

The word snapped across the hall and suddenly the gavver was standing beside them.

'Sir?' he said, ignoring Letta.

Noa nodded in Leyla's direction.

'Did we get any useful information from her?'

'Not much,' Carver said. 'Like all of them, she has nothing to say.'

Noa nodded and looked at Leyla again, a frown creasing his face. He leant closer to the bars.

'Who are they, Leyla?' he whispered.

Leyla looked away from him.

'One name. One name for your life.'

No reaction.

'The life of your child.'

Letta watched as Leyla lifted her head and stared back at him. For a second, her gaze shifted to Letta, and Letta could see the pain in her eyes. *She's pregnant*, Letta thought. *Will she not save her child before all of us?*

'One name, Leyla.'

Noa's mouth was against the bars.

Leyla looked up at Letta.

'Be strong, girl!' she said. 'Like your mother. Like all the women in your family.'

She turned to Noa, then opened her mouth and started to sing, her eyes sparking with defiance.

Down in the valley
The stream flows on
In the heather morning
Quiet as a swan.

Letta saw Noa's face suffuse with colour.

'Damn you!' He spat the words at the woman in the cell. 'Terminate her.'

'Yes, sir,' Carver said, moving towards the cell. 'We'll take her to the forest and –'

'No! Do it here,' Noa said, grabbing his arm. 'We can't take any chances. They might be watching for her. And, Carver?'

The gavver looked at him, waiting.

'Do it now.'

No! A voice inside Letta screamed. *Not Leyla.*

But Carver was already opening the cell door.

'Come!' Noa said, putting an arm around Letta's shoulder. 'Enough of this.'

Letta heard the deadening sound of a blow, and Leyla cried out in pain.

Letta longed to turn around and fight for Leyla, or at least to hold her in her arms and say goodbye. But she knew it was impossible. Carver would kill her too. Instead, she followed Noa back up the stairs and out onto the street.

The walk up the hill to Noa's house was a silent one. Letta walked behind Noa, her dress clinging to her back, cold sweat drenching the fabric, her hip still aching from Carver's boot. Images of Leyla's face taunted her.

You have to keep it together, she told herself. *Think! You need to reassure him, convince him you are on his side. That's the only chance Leyla has.*

He opened the door and strode ahead, not looking back to see if she was following. As she walked down the corridor towards his office, she felt herself calming. She could do this. She had to.

She sat opposite him, the great desk between them. As soon as he sat down, he picked up a document and started to read. Letta waited. Was she supposed to talk?

Finally, he looked up. 'You had something you wanted to discuss?'

His eyes were like a hawk's, she thought. Alert and wary.

'I had a thought, master,' she said, hardly daring to look at him.

'Yes?'

'I think the List should be even shorter.'

'You do?' he said, with a half-smile. 'So you have changed your mind. And why is that?'

I have to make him believe me, Letta thought. *This is it. I won't get another chance.*

'I've been thinking about what you said the last time we talked,' she said, 'and I don't think Ark will survive if the ordinary people have that many words.'

'Go on,' Noa said, and Letta could see he was watching her, judging her.

'I see it with people every day,' she said. 'Even though their words are limited, they still come up with ridiculous ideas, they still spend their time giving out about Ark, complaining about animals running wild on the streets. They are never happy. And then I thought, maybe we could have a much shorter List and a law against idle chatter. People should use words for function not for nonsense!'

For a moment, Noa said nothing, then he threw back his head and laughed.

'What did I say?' Letta asked, trying to look as though he had hurt her feelings.

'You sound like me when I was a young man,' he said. 'So strange to hear the old arguments again.'

'Again?' said Letta, and now she wasn't acting. What did he mean 'again'?

Noa stood up and walked to the window.

'Before the Melting,' he said, 'the government found a way to remove language from the criminal elements in society.'

Nicene, Letta thought, trying to hide her excitement.

Noa turned to her, his blue eyes sombre.

'Not everyone agreed with it, of course, as a device, but it was effective.'

'How?' Letta asked. 'How did they do it?'

'Not by way of List,' Noa said. 'They found a way that was less kind and more deadly.' He hesitated.

'Did it work?' Letta asked eagerly.

The old man sighed. 'Yes. It worked. It worked very well.'

'Can we use it then?' Letta said. 'Can we do what they did?'

'I never wanted to go that way with Ark,' Noa replied. 'I thought, you see, that we could create a sort of Eden here, where the lamb could lie down with the lion. I thought we could use language in a limited way, to communicate, but man is always so arrogant, so arrogant.'

Letta could see the despair in his eyes.

'But we could use it?' she pushed him. 'Against the Desecrators?'

'Yes,' said Noa. 'Against Desecrators. The gavvers tell me they are gathering support. They are planning to move against me.'

'No!' Letta said, jumping up. 'They can't be.'

'They use words to corrupt the people, to fool them into believing, just like they did before the Melting.'

'We have to stop them,' Letta said. 'Surely there is a way to stop them spreading their – filth?'

She found it easy to act the part of the outraged wordsmith. She only had to remember how she used to feel about the Desecrators.

'Don't worry, little one,' Noa said. 'I have a plan. We may not need List any more.'

'Like that method you mentioned, before the Melting?'

'Yes,' he said. 'Just like that.'

236

He was staring at her again and then he seemed to make a decision.

'You should go now Letta,' he said. 'I am glad you told me about Hugo. I will speak to the gavvers and explain. Go now, child.'

Letta nodded. 'Thank you, master,' she said, and turned to go..

'One last thing,' he said. 'In a day or so, I will send you some bottled water. I want you not to drink any other water but that until I tell you otherwise. It is important. Can you do that?'

He is going to do it, Letta thought wildly. *He is going to put the Nicene in the water tank, but he has decided to spare me.* She tried to show no sign that she knew what was going on.

'Of course,' she said. 'But why?'

He waved his finger at her. 'Sometimes, Letta, we have to follow orders and not ask questions. Can I rely on you?'

'Of course,' she said again, standing up. Her legs were shaking. Her head felt light.

Noa had turned back to his work. Rage stirred inside her. She stood for a second looking at his bowed head and imagined killing him. She had never felt an impulse as strong in her life. This man did not deserve to live.

He looked up. 'Was there something else?' Cold blue reptilian eyes.

'No,' Letta said. 'Nothing.'

Her thoughts were in turmoil as she made her way back to the front door. She had to tell the others that she knew the water was about to be poisoned, and she also had to warn Finn that they were going to kill Leyla.

Amelia appeared from one of the closed doors just as Letta approached it. Her face was white and drawn, her eyes too bright, like someone with a fever.

'Leyla is your sister?' Letta said softly.

'Yes,' Amelia answered, 'my sister.'

'There were three of you?' Letta said, remembering what Solam had told her in Tintown.

Amelia looked at her, eyes boring through her. For a moment there was silence. Then Amelia spoke again.

'Yes. Three. My other sister was lost,' she said. 'But Leyla and I survived.' Amelia looked down the corridor as though searching for something or someone. 'Leyla once worked with us, here, building Ark, but she and John –'

'They didn't get on?'

'She was a musician. When John banned all music, Leyla couldn't, wouldn't accept it. She was always stubborn. My father spoilt her. His little colour-catcher. That was what he called her.'

'What will happen to her now?' Letta asked.

Amelia shrugged. 'John will protect her. She doesn't deserve it, but he will do it for me.'

I have to let her know, Letta thought. *She can still save her. Even if it means Noa's anger is directed at me, I have to say something.*

Letta shook her head. 'I don't think so,' she said. 'He has already ordered them to kill her.'

Amelia's eyes flashed for a second, then her hand shot up and slapped Letta across the face.

'How dare you! John would not do that,' she said, air hissing through her mouth. 'Get out of my house.'

Letta turned, opened the door and left. She could only hope that Amelia's anger would extend to Noa, and that she could stop him destroying Leyla once and for all. It would be worth any pain if that happened, but in her heart she knew it was already too late.

Overhead, a gull screamed and Letta quickened her step. She had to talk to Finn.

Back at home, she threw herself into Benjamin's chair and let the tears that had lodged in her throat fall freely. She hugged her knees to her chest and tried to stay calm. She replayed the scene at Leyla's cell. Had Leyla known all along that Noa would kill her? Had she hoped for mercy? What had she meant about the women in Letta's family. What women?

Marlo came in so quietly that she didn't hear him till he appeared in the door.

'I'm sorry,' she said. 'I'm so sorry.'

He was beside her in a heartbeat, kneeling beside her chair.

'Sh!' he said. 'It's all right.'

'You know about Leyla?'

'Yes. We thought we had lost both of you.'

His hand caressed her arm. She looked into his eyes.

'Leyla –' she began.

'Finn has gone to see what he can find out.'

'How did they catch her?'

Marlo got up and walked to the window. 'They had done the show at the bridge, when the gavvers arrived. They ran. They had a head start. It shouldn't have been a problem, but –'

'But?'

She could hardly bear to hear the answer.

'Leyla tripped. Fell. She'd been getting cramps in her legs.'

'Cramps?'

'She's pregnant.'

'She and Finn?'

'Yes,' Marlo said. 'The gavvers frog-marched her through

the town. People in the street stopped to throw stones at her. There was almost a riot. In the confusion, Finn managed to give her a blade.'

Letta's heart leapt. 'To attack them with?'

He shook his head. 'He gave her the blade, Letta, so that she can cut her wrists, take her own life – if she needs to.'

Letta looked at him and all her words deserted her. *Take her own life.*

'She won't tell them anything,' Marlo continued. 'But, well, we don't know how much she can endure. She's vulnerable.'

'You don't have to worry,' Letta said softly. And then she told him all she had heard outside the cell door. 'They are going to kill her, Marlo. She didn't tell them anything.'

When she had finished, Marlo was silent for a moment, taking it all in. then he looked up at her and she thought her heart would break at the pain she saw in his eyes.

'I'll get Finn,' he said and then he was gone.

CHAPTER 21

FINN looked twenty years older, Letta thought, as she put a cup of burdock tea in front of him.

'Did she see you?' he asked, hugging the hot cup to his chest.

'Yes,' Letta said. 'She did. I think they wanted her to betray me. It was a test. I'm sure of it.' She waited for a second. 'Finn!' she said. 'Did you know that she was Amelia Deer's sister?'

Finn's head snapped up. 'Amelia's sister?'

Letta told him what she had learnt.

Finn shook his head. 'I never knew,' he said. 'She never mentioned –'

Marlo put a hand on Finn's shoulder. 'She must have had her reasons,' he said.

Finn stood up. 'I'm going to talk to some people,' he said. 'See what I can find out. If they have killed her, I need to know what they did with her body.' He stopped for a minute. Nobody spoke. Finally, Finn turned towards the door. 'We'll meet back here this evening,' he said as he walked away.

'I can't believe this is happening,' Marlo said as the door closed behind Finn. 'If Noa has killed her and her baby…'

'He is capable of anything,' Letta said. 'His plan to put the Nicene in the water is getting closer too. There can be no doubt about that now. But we still have no idea exactly when he will do it.'

'Any chance Werber would tell us what's happening?'

'We can't trust him,' Letta said, putting down her cup. 'When I receive the bottles of water, I suppose that will mean the Nicene is about to be added.'

'We'll have to warn people not to drink the water,' Marlo said.

'Yes,' Letta answered, but in her heart she knew that was impossible. Who would listen to them?

'I'd better go back home,' Marlo said. 'People are anxious about Leyla.'

Letta nodded. She didn't want him to leave, but at the same time she needed space to think. He touched her arm before he left, and once more she got the faint, bitter scent of sage. Then he was gone.

Next morning, Letta got up early and headed for the beach. The fresh air might clear her head, she thought, and give her some clue as to how to proceed.

When she reached the beach, the tide was coming in, the sand soft and wet under her feet. She stood looking out at the water, not really seeing anything, until a flock of small birds rose up noisily in front of her. They circled over her head twice, three times, and then set off out across the ocean.

Benjamin's voice in her head was so clear it was as if he was standing right beside her. *The birds still fly south.*

Of course! How could she have been so slow? If the birds still fly south, then they must be going somewhere. There must be another place, far from here. Were her parents there? Her heart quickened. They could be. That was what Benjamin had been trying to say: *Don't lose hope*. She had to survive this, she needed to be here if they came back. She had to. And she wasn't going to be wordless.

As she turned to leave, something caught her eye: a lone figure walking slowly towards her. A woman with her head down. As Letta watched, she walked past the men loading barrels of sea-water, past the small stone jetty. Letta waited until she came nearer. With a start, she realised that it was Amelia. Letta had never seen her outside Noa's house before. Curiosity kept her standing there, waiting for the older woman. Amelia's progress was slow but Letta didn't move. Amelia stopped a few strides away from her.

'You were right,' she said, her voice flat, the words curdled and sour. 'He has killed her.'

There was an emptiness in Amelia's eyes that Letta found frightening.

'You didn't know her,' Amelia said, as though talking to herself. 'She was unique. Talented as well as beautiful. We washed up here after the Melting. Three sisters. John took care of us. He had a good heart. He only wanted to save the planet. Was that so wrong?' She looked at Letta, her eyes searching the girl's face.

Letta said nothing.

'Leyla turned against him. Became a Desecrator. It broke my heart.'

'And now she's dead,' Letta said quietly. 'I'm sorry.'

'There are worse things than dying,' Amelia said.

'I agree,' Letta said, her eyes searching the other woman's face for any clue that they were both referring to the same thing.

'Soon all of Ark will know that,' Amelia said.

She was talking about the Nicene. Letta was sure of it.

'And you? Will you stay with Noa? Will you be part of it?'

Amelia shrugged. 'What choice do I have?' she said. 'A broken old woman who can't even breathe efficiently. How long would I last without Noa?'

'We all have choice,' Letta said.

'Who knows what the future will bring?' Amelia said. 'We can only wait and see.'

'Or we can influence it,' Letta said, not wanting to let her off the hook. 'You have great power, Amelia.'

The other woman laughed, which brought on a bout of coughing, a wet, desperate cough that left her gasping for air.

'Are you all right?' Letta put an arm around Amelia's shoulder and lowered her on to a rock.

'I have no power,' Amelia said. 'I couldn't even save my own sister.'

'I know what it is to lose someone,' Letta said.

'Your parents,' Amelia said softly, not meeting Letta's eyes.

'Yes,' Letta answered. 'And Benjamin.'

Amelia nodded. 'Benjamin was a good man. Sometimes I did try to influence the future, you know, without much success. But I tried. I tried to let you know.'

In a flash, Letta knew what she was talking about.

'BENJAMIN NOT DEAD. That was *you*, wasn't it? You left that note for me.'

Amelia shrugged. 'What does it matter now?'

'It mattered to me then,' Letta said. 'It mattered an awful lot. It gave me hope and it meant I got to say goodbye to him.'

Amelia lifted her hand and touched Letta's cheek, tears in her eyes. 'You are so like your mother,' she said.

'My mother? You knew her? Leyla told me she remembered her too.'

'How could we forget her?' Amelia spoke so softly that Letta had to strain to hear what she said. 'Freya. Poor little Freya. She was the youngest and the most adventurous of us. The bravest too, braver even than Leyla.'

Suddenly, Letta could hear Leyla's last words to her.

Be strong like your mother. Like all the women in your family.

'She was your *sister*.' Even as Letta spoke the words, she knew they were true. 'That was her song, the one Leyla sang. I *knew* there was something familiar about it.'

Amelia turned away from her, looking out to sea.

'She sang it to you all the time. You were the focus of her whole life, of all of our lives. We came to Ark with nothing, three sisters orphaned and alone. John took us in and cared for us. You were born in his house and lived there for the first four years of your life. John adored you.'

'*What?*' Letta struggled to process what she was hearing. 'Why did I not know this? Why did no-one tell me?'

'Your mother betrayed us, Letta. She set off, she and your father, against John's orders. She abandoned Ark, abandoned me, abandoned you, Letta. I couldn't accept it. I told John that I never wanted to hear her name again. I couldn't bear to look at you. John sent you to live with Benjamin and warned the people that you were not to be told about your family background.'

'How could you do that?' Letta could hear the bitterness in her own words. 'She was still your sister.'

Amelia sighed.

'They were both my sisters. They both betrayed John, but more than that, they betrayed Ark. That I couldn't forgive.'

'Please, Amelia,' Letta said, 'help us.'

Amelia shook her head, sighing deeply.

'I will tell you this,' she said. 'Carver doesn't trust you. You may have convinced John, but Carver won't give up. Be warned.'

Without another word, Amelia got up and walked away, not looking back. Letta stood watching her, hearing her hoarse breathing get fainter as the distance grew.

Somewhere in the ether she could hear Leyla's sweet voice:

Down in the valley
The stream flows on

Later, back at the shop, Letta couldn't rest. She felt as though she were trapped in Ark as much as Amelia was. She stood looking out at the street and let her mind wander over all that had happened. Her whole world had imploded, but in a strange way, she felt more real, more alive because of it. She had always seen herself as special in Ark. She was the wordsmith's apprentice, part of John Noa's team. The ordinary people were somehow separate from her. They didn't have as much language or the right to speak it. They didn't have information or power.

She realised now that it was that sort of thinking that had made Noa into the monster he had become.

She thought about the Desecrators and their way of life. Among them, she had got a glimpse of what life could be and, having got a glimpse, she was hungry for more.

And she thought about her mother, tried to imagine those three young women so full of hope and enthusiasm for the new world. Leyla was dead, Amelia transformed into a pitiful old woman and Freya …

Finally, she pulled out a box of words that Benjamin had brought back from a field trip and that had not yet been sorted. She was laying them out on the counter when a noise startled her.

A few minutes later she looked up to find Werber at the door.

'No harm!' he greeted her, his round face wreathed in smiles. 'Bring you water.'

Letta felt as though her heart had stopped. In his hand, he carried a box with six large bottles of water in it.

'I bring to Green Warriors in morning. What wrong, Letta?'

'Nothing,' she managed to say. 'Nothing wrong. Thank you.'

He wagged his finger at her.

'Thank you no List word!'

Of course it wasn't. List didn't accommodate please and thank you. Not any more.

She nodded. 'Leave water there,' she said pointing to the counter.

Werber hefted the box onto the counter.

'Good water,' he said to her with a smile.

Once he was gone, Letta allowed herself to panic. The water was being distributed. That meant that Noa was about to use the Nicene. She had to stop him. She sat at her desk with her head in her hands and tried to think. She didn't hear Marlo come in. She looked up and found him, dressed as the cat collector, looking down on her. She jumped to her feet.

'I am so glad to see you,' she said. 'Where's Finn?'

'At the pump house,' Marlo said. 'In a bad way.'

'Leyla?'

Marlo nodded. 'We don't know where they've buried her.'

'Listn, Marlo,' Letta said. 'Noa's going to put the Nicene in the water. Any minute. I have got my bottles of uncontaminated water, and Werber is delivering some to the Green Warriors tomorrow. It's time.'

They sat in silence for a moment.

She shivered at the thought of the water bottles in her house. It was as if the evil emanating from the house on the hill was a physical thing. She could almost touch it.

A sound from the direction of the back door startled Letta. 'Did you hear something?' she hissed at Marlo.

Without a word, he slipped out the door, and made for the stairs to the Monk's Room. Letta got up and walked through the shop and out to the door at the back. She opened it cautiously. There was no-one there. She looked down the lane just in time to see a figure dressed in a long black coat disappear around the corner. A woman? Whoever it was, they had left in a hurry. As she turned to come back in, the drop box caught her eye. She opened it and saw a single sheet of paper. She picked it up. Three words:

TOMORROW AT DAWN

She recognised the handwriting. It was the same person who had written BENJAMIN NOT DEAD a lifetime ago.

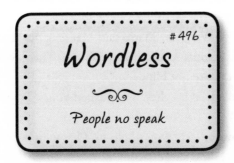

CHAPTER 22

Wordless #496

People no speak

FOR the remainder of the day, Letta and Marlo struggled to think of a way to get into the tower. She didn't tell him about her mother. It was all too raw, the story too new to share it with anyone else, even Marlo. Instead she concentrated on her mission. She had to find a way to be there at dawn.

'It's impossible!' Marlo said, when he got back from observing it. 'We can't get past the gavvers. Werber was right about the extra security.'

'One more time,' Letta said pacing the room. 'Who can get in there? Who is allowed in officially?'

'Not much happens there, to be honest,' Marlo said. 'Salt water comes in. It's desalinated in one big tank. The fresh water goes into a second tank to which they add chlorine, to purify it. Then the clean water is piped out.'

Silence stretched between them. Letta stared at her hands, straining to come up with another route into the tower. When she looked up she found Marlo's eyes looking back at her. He held out his hand to her and she put her own hand in his. He caressed it with his thumb. He smiled at her then and her heart raced.

I need to focus, she thought. *Focus.*

'The water-cleaning process may be very simple and auto-mated, but there must be people who are officially allowed into the tower.'

'The Green Warriors,' Marlo said, standing up. 'And no, Letta, you cannot disguise yourself as a Warrior. The gavvers may be stupid but they're not blind.'

Letta smiled. 'Who else?' she pushed him.

'Werber?'

Letta frowned. 'He won't help us. I know he won't.'

'Amelia?' Marlo suggested.

In her mind's eye, Letta saw Amelia walking along the beach. 'That's it!' she said, nearly knocking Marlo over in her excitement.

Marlo's eyes widened. 'You think Amelia would help?'

'No!' Letta said. 'Not that. Listen!' She grabbed Marlo's arm. 'I met Amelia today on the beach. While we were there, men were filling barrels with sea-water.'

'Water gatherers,' Marlo said. 'What about them?'

'The *barrels*!' Letta had to stop herself from shouting at him. 'The barrels go into the tower.'

Marlo frowned. 'I have no idea what –'

'I could *hide* in a barrel.'

The words hovered in the air between them.

'Not you,' Marlo said. 'I'll do it.'

'You won't fit,' Letta said. 'You won't, Marlo, but I will.'

Marlo shook his head. 'It's too dangerous.'

'It's the only way,' Letta said and, as she said it, she knew it was true.

'It means that I can get into the tower. When he puts the Nicene in the water I'll be there. I can talk to him. And if that

250

doesn't work I will be close enough to overwhelm him. He's an old man.'

He adored you. If what Amelia said was true, maybe that would help too.

'You have to help me,' Letta said gently.

'What do you need me to do?' he asked.

Over the next hour they refined and polished the plan. Marlo would identify a barrel and remove some of the water. They couldn't empty it altogether: the water needed to slosh when the barrel was moved, or it would be noticed. He would also put a small hole on the side so that Letta wouldn't be short of air. Finally, he would distract the workers.

'That won't he hard,' he said. 'It's a low-security job, and I know one of them, Colm.'

Letta nodded.

'While you are in the tower,' Marlo continued, 'we will marshal as many people as we can find.'

'To do what?'

'We might not be able to get into the tower, Letta, but we can cause confusion outside it, keep the gavvers occupied so they can't interfere with what you're trying to do.'

Letta frowned.

'We will be armed. Finn managed to get some Black Angel guns last week,' Marlo hurried on. 'And they won't be expecting us. We can easily take down the gavvers guarding the tower.'

Letta remembered the cupboard she had seen at the pump house and the crude knives lined up, waiting to be called on.

'We have all night to raise an army,' Marlo went on. 'We already have supporters, waiting for the call. Finn has been working for months to recruit people. More than thirty men have signed up from Tintown in the past few days. They are

251

being led by a man called Kirch Tellon. He said he knew you.'

'He does,' Letta said, remembering the quiet man and his father.

'You should let us do this altogether Letta,' Marlo pressed. 'It's too dangerous for you alone. We could storm the tower and –'

'And then what? Noa could put the Nicene in the water in a second, long before you had a chance to overpower him.'

Marlo didn't answer but Letta knew that he had accepted what she said.

'How is Finn?' she asked, after a moment.

Marlo shook his head. 'I've never seen him like this. His heart is changed somehow. He loved her very much. There are no arranged partnerships amongst the Creators, you know. People get together because they love one another.'

With his last words, something struck Letta. A thought that seemed to have come from nowhere. *John Noa loves Amelia.* She didn't know why that might be important, but she knew it was.

'I'd better go,' Marlo said. 'I'll see you at the beach. Five bells?'

'I'll be ready.'

After Marlo left, Letta went on pacing the floor, going over the plan. The barrel would get her into the tower. When Noa came she would plead with him. Persuade him. If that didn't work, she would overpower him physically, knock the Nicene out of his hand so it didn't go in the water supply. She was certain she could do it, once she got close enough to him.

She was distracted by a noise outside the window. She went to the door and looked out.

On the street, a small group of men stood in the fog. Their arms and legs were bare and they wore their hair long. They

252

were the Wordless. She opened the door and walked onto the street. The men were trying to communicate with the people who passed by. Letta could see them grabbing on to people, grunting, gesticulating.

They're trying to tell them something, Letta thought sadly. The Wordless persevered, stopping anyone who came near. Bruno, the tinsmith, pushed them away roughly and walked on. A woman crossed the street to avoid them. Letta could see the aggression growing on their faces. As she watched, a small boy tried to cross in front of the group. Without warning one of the men lashed out, his hand catching the back of the child's head. The boy fell face first right in front of Letta. In a heartbeat, the Wordless dispersed, even as the child's cries cut through the air. Letta knelt down beside him. He looked up at her with enormous frightened eyes.

'Allove!'

The scavenger's boy. She remembered him from the pump house.

He gazed back at her, stunned from the fall. Then she could see recognition dawn slowly.

'Bad people! Bad people!'

Letta jumped. The child was terrified of her, she could see that.

'You!'

She looked up. Smith Fearfall was staring down at her. He looked from the child back to Letta as if in slow motion.

'You were there that night. You are one of them.'

Fearfall reached down and grabbed her arm. She could feel his nails dig into the soft flesh.

'Desecrator! Desecrator! Call gavvers!'

Letta didn't wait to hear any more. Yanking her arm away

from him she pushed him as hard as she could, felt him stumble, and then she ran.

Adrenalin coursed through her body. Her feet pummelled the rough ground, her arms pushing people out of her way. Behind her, she could hear shouts and jeers but she didn't look back. She was sure there were people in pursuit but she didn't care. All she could think about was getting away. Up ahead, she saw the cobbler's shop and behind it the lane where she had played as a child. She had to get there before they caught her. She tried to go faster but her breath was catching in her chest now, her side was hurting her and she could feel a stitch developing.

Thump! Something hit her on the back. She pitched forward but managed to stay standing. She glanced back. A small crowd was fifty strides behind her, howling like wolves. She turned the corner, sprinting past the front door of the cobbler's and made it into the lane.

She knew this area like she knew her own face. This was where she had played with Eva, the cobbler's daughter. In front of her she could see the high stone wall that marked the end of the lane. A dead end. She fell to her knees in front of it. Her hands moved urgently along the ground until she felt it. A cold metal ring. She pulled. At first it didn't move. She pulled again. This time she managed to lift it. The old manhole cover was big but it moved easily enough. Holding on to the edge of the stones, she lowered herself down. Her feet hit the ground. She found the groove cut into the cover stone, and pulled it across, as she had done so many times when she had played hide-and-seek with the cobbler's children. It didn't fully close and she could hear the crowd now. They were at the top of the lane. Another tug, and the stone sealed the crawl hole. She waited, her breath coming in gasps.

She could feel their feet above her. Hear their muffled curses. What if one of them knew about this hiding hole? She closed her eyes and hoped that they did not.

Minutes passed. They were still there. Still muttering, still searching. Then she heard a high-pitched whistle. Gavvers. More running. Then finally silence.

She stayed where she was, not daring to move. She had to be sure they were gone. Every so often, a siren rent the air. They were still looking. Carver wouldn't rest now. He had proof. An eyewitness.

But she had to get to the beach. She had no idea what time it was.

She raised her arms and gently slid the cover across. Grabbing the stones on either side she lifted herself up. She climbed out carefully. The lane was empty. She crouched there for a moment, ready to run. The wall, to her right, loomed out of the darkness. There was a door there that led to the cobbler's small back yard. She turned the wooden knob carefully. The door opened. On a line, strung across the yard, hung the hides the cobbler used to make his leather. She touched one, gingerly. The smell was overpowering, just as she remembered it from when she had played there as a child.

She crossed the small yard and exited through a gap in the fence. It had started to rain, dark clouds gathering overhead. Within seconds she was back on the street, head down heading for the potato fields. She trudged up the hill feeling the bustle of the town falling away behind her. As she crested the hill, she stopped to catch her breath. She never heard the man behind her till his hand clamped on her arm. She screamed. The hand covered her mouth.

'Quiet!' a voice said.

She looked around.

'Finn!'

In his hand Finn held a wooden club.

'I have to meet Marlo. At the beach.'

She could hardly get the words out.

'Come quickly,' Finn said. 'We don't have much time.'

The latest intelligence said that the Desecrators were about to strike. An outright rebellion this time, drawing on the disaffected, not only in Ark but also in Tintown. They had spent months raising an army. Time had run out. He knew that he had to make his move now, but he couldn't concentrate.

Why did it have to be Leyla? He paced the floor feeling like a caged lion. Of all the Desecrators, they have to drag her in. He could feel Amelia's pain but could do nothing to help her. Everyone in Ark knew Leyla had been arrested. If he had not dealt with her, they would have sensed his weakness and attacked. He had seen it with the wolves many times and knew man would be no different.

No. Leyla had had to die. Amelia would understand, eventually. She was clever. He could have concocted a story to ease her grief. Maybe he should have said that she had died of natural causes.

A heart attack.

Amelia would have believed him, she had always believed him. He buried his head in his hands.

No! He couldn't have done that, couldn't have used words to deceive her. He was not a hypocrite. Amelia would understand. She had been fond of Benjamin, but she hadn't opposed his decision when it came time to get rid of him. She would support him now too. When she recovered from the first wave of grief, she would know that what he had done was right.

She had been quiet when he told her, her face white, her eyes wide. He remembered her grief when she lost her younger sister. The long nights by the window, waiting. He had tried to hold her, but she had been like a block of ice in his arms. It was understandable, he told himself, they were sisters no matter what Leyla had become. He would save Letta for her. That would mean something. Letta was her own flesh and blood. Amelia would forgive him.

Why then did he feel such crushing anxiety? It was like the walls were closing in on him. There was tightness in his throat like a noose. He pulled at the shirt buttons at his neck. He needed air. He turned quickly, stumbled, almost fell. He reached for the wall to support him.

He had to calm down. It would be time soon. He would take Werber with him. The boy was loyal and stupid. Werber could guard the door while he ...

He couldn't trust any of them now. Not the gavvers, not even Carver. No! He would go into the tower with only Werber; Werber and the grey wolf.

The gavvers had told him Leyla had gone to her death still singing.

CHAPTER 23

Tower

#449

Tall, narrow building

THE air was thick and suffocating as they headed for the beach. Finn strode on ahead with Letta struggling to keep up. The walk seemed endless. Up the hill, past the potato fields, then down the winding path. On the beach, Finn pulled Letta down behind a rock. She looked up at him in alarm, but he put his finger to his lips.

'Better the water gatherers don't see you. Stay there. I'll find Marlo.'

She sat on the sand, leaning against the rock, and waited. Excitement coursed through her. The next few hours would be the most crucial of her life.

'No harm!'

Marlo appeared beside her.

'Well?' she said.

He nodded. 'All good. I managed to find a barrel they had filled and I emptied out half the water.'

'Good,' Letta said.

'You know the platform over there where they load the barrels?'

Letta nodded. 'I know it,' she said. 'I've seen them pull the horse and carts alongside.'

'Yes,' Marlo said. 'They roll the barrel on to the cart and take it through the town and up Noa's Hill to the water tower.'

'What happens after that?'

'At the tower,' Marlo said, 'they attach a pulley to it. The horse pulls the rope and the barrel goes up to the top of the tower. There are two more men up there. They roll it in, open it, and tip the salt water into the tank to be cleaned.'

'But –' Letta objected.

'I know,' Marlo said. 'Just listen. They take the last load at six bells and leave the barrels outside the tower till morning, when they lift the last load in and start again.'

'But I need to be in the tower tonight. I can't wait till morning.'

'I've thought of that,' Marlo said. 'When they drop the load, one of the workers will make sure that your barrel goes up to the top of the tower. It will be left there overnight.'

Finn slipped in beside them. 'Then you climb out –' he said.

'And wait for Noa,' Letta finished for him.

Finn nodded grimly. 'It's not too late to change your mind.'

'Did you speak to Colm?' Marlo asked Finn. 'He's the water gatherer I told you about, Letta. He's a good friend.'

Finn nodded. 'He knows what to do. The last load leaves shortly, though. Colm will distract his colleagues while we put Letta in the barrel. I'm to give him the signal when we are ready.'

'I am ready,' Letta said, though she felt light-headed and was breathing too fast.

'We will be outside the tower at dawn,' Marlo said. 'You'll get your chance to talk to Noa.'

'You'll have ten or fifteen minutes,' Finn said. 'Then we're coming in.'

'I'll just check the beach. See if they are ready,' Finn said, and disappeared again. Letta sensed he wasn't altogether happy with the plan but at least he was giving her a chance.

Marlo moved in closer to her. She could smell his warm sagey smell and feel his breath, soft on her cheek.

'I wish I could take your place,' he said.

'I know.'

'Take this,' he said, placing a knife in her hand. It had leather bindings around the handle and the sharp steel looked cold as ice. She pushed it away.

'No!' she said. 'I can't. What would I do with it?'

Marlo placed the handle in her hand again.

'Put it in your boot. Please, Letta. For me.'

She looked into his eyes and closed her fingers around the handle.

'I won't use it,' she said to him, shoving it into her boot.

'I will never meet anyone like you again, Letta. Go safely. Please.'

He put his hands either side of her face and pulled her closer to him. Her fingers touched the skin of his bare arms and she felt as though a current ran through her, and then her lips found his and they were kissing. Kissing like they would never stop. She felt his hands in her hair and she buried her face in his neck, breathing in his smell, never wanting to leave his arms.

'When this is all over –' Marlo began.

She pulled away reluctantly, her breath unsteady.

'Yes,' she said. 'When this is over.'

Seconds later she was running down the beach, Finn to her right, Marlo to her left. At one point she stumbled, and Marlo grabbed her arm. She sneaked a glance at him. His jaw was set. Worry lines creased the soft skin around his eyes. He caught her looking at him and he smiled and she wished that the world could stop for a minute and let her savour that smile.

The water gatherers were nowhere to be seen. The two men lifted her onto the platform where six barrels stood.

Marlo took the lid off one of the barrels.

'Quickly,' Finn said, and swung her up in his arms. And then her feet were in water, her legs, right up to her hips. The cold was like an electric shock. She couldn't stand upright. She bent her knees, feeling the water soak into her skirt, making it feel heavy, pulling her down. She put her hands on the side of the barrel for balance.

'All right?' Marlo's voice was tight with anxiety.

'All right,' she said. And then she heard the lid bang into place, and darkness descended.

She couldn't stop shivering. It was so cold. She bit her bottom lip to try to stop the spasms but it didn't help. She could hear the sea and the odd sea bird outside and feel the salt wind. She touched rough wood and the cold metal head of nails and then something slimy that made her pull her hand back quickly, until she realised that it was just a clump of seaweed. *I mustn't panic*, she thought. *Just relax. Think about something else.*

And then the barrel moved. Gently. A mere tap. Her shoulder hit the side. She pushed her hands against the wood and braced herself. The barrel tilted violently. She almost screamed. Her head hit the side of the barrel. She sat down, not caring that the water was now above her waist. The barrel tilted again. Salt water splashed her face. Her body was jerked and slammed from side to side. She stifled another scream. Tears flowed down her face. Her body hurt at every point, bruises on top of bruises, and then all was quiet again.

'Hup!' a man shouted outside.

She realised she was on the cart. The cold was now seeping into her bones. She hugged her knees to her chest and waited. More loud bangs as the other barrels were loaded. Shouts from the men.

'Hup! Forward!'

And then the cart moved.

She braced her feet against the side of the barrel. Better she thought. Definitely better. Soon she could almost predict the rhythm of the horse. Over and back. Over and back. The sounds of the beach faded and she knew they were heading in the direction of the town. In her mind's eye she could see the fields on either side, almost see the high hedges. It seemed to take for ever but suddenly there was the sound of people all about her. Disembodied voices shouting greetings, giving instructions, and then they were moving away. She knew that they were headed for the winding path that led up the cliff to the tower. Had they reached it yet? Suddenly the barrel slipped, smashing into the one behind it. Letta's head bounced off the surface. Blinding pain caused her to see flashing lights. They had reached the path. She was sure of it now. She could hear the men encouraging the horse.

'On, boy! On!'

The path was as twisted as she had imagined. She could almost see the horse, picking his way carefully through the stones, loose clinker scattering behind his clumsy feet. With every twist her stomach lurched until finally she felt acid in her mouth, followed by a flood of saliva, and then her stomach heaved and she vomited all over her skirt. She sat back exhausted, wiping the vomit from her mouth with the back of her hand.

It can't be much further, she told herself. It can't be. She was afraid the cold would kill her before she ever got to the tower.

Or that she would hit her head so hard that it would knock her out and she'd slip beneath the water and drown. No! She wouldn't let that happen. She was going to get to that tower and stop Noa. The cart lurched again as the horse stumbled. She wrapped her arms around her head to protect it, felt the skin tear as her hand made contact with the rough wood. She winced as the blood dripped down her arm and onto her face.

On and on they went, falling from side to side, the smell of vomit overpowering, the taste of blood on her lips. Ache piled upon ache with the relentless movement of the barrel. At one point, her head hit the lid so strenuously, that she almost bit right through her lower lip. She cried out, despite herself, and was terrified they would hear her. Nothing happened. Letta curled her body into a ball, her arms wrapped around herself, her eyes closed. And still they climbed, the horse doggedly pulling the cart, the men shouting instructions. Then, when Letta honestly felt she could endure no more, they stopped.

'Hold, boy! Back now!' she heard the man call.

She could hear the men clearly.

'That's it,' one said.

'I'll untie the horse.'

'No. Me. I do it. You go home.'

'My turn.'

'Go, man! Go home to your new mate!'

They both laughed then. Letta scooped up water to wash the blood off her face. She heard the man retreat.

'See you tomorrow.'

'Tomorrow!'

Then nothing. She waited. Had they both left? A few minutes more. Then the barrel jerked.

'Hup, boy!'

She felt the barrel being lifted. It swung right and left, then tapped off the wall of the tower, sending her flying. Her shoulder submerged in the water and then the barrel was swinging again. Right, left. She tried to move with it to lessen the impact. How much farther? She couldn't bear to think how high the tower was. She had been afraid of heights all her life. She thrust the image away. Concentrate on the motion: Right. Left. Bang! The barrel hit the wall again. Her head bounced off the side. And then it stopped. She shifted position and the barrel swayed. She knew then that she was hanging from the rope, at the top of the tower. Still outside the tower. She tried to remember what Marlo had said.

The horse pulls the rope and the barrel goes up to the top of the tower. There are two more men at the top. They roll it in, open it and tip the salt water into the tank to be cleaned.

Were the two men still there, waiting for her barrel? Her heart raced at the prospect. If they were, they would open the barrel and tip her into the tank.

She waited. Maybe she would be left here, forgotten. She had a vision of her dirty wet face staring up from the bottom of the barrel, swinging like a metronome, while life went on outside.

Then another thought assailed her. Had Colm managed to get the barrel up here and then been forced to leave? Would she be here all night waiting to be discovered in the morning? The minutes stretched. The cold was unbearable now. Her teeth were banging together, her jaw ached. And all the time she was straining to hear something, anything.

She didn't know how long she'd been there. She tried hard not to move. Moving caused the barrel to swing and made her stomach lurch. And then suddenly she felt a massive pull as the barrel was hauled to her right. She could hear the man grunting with the effort. She prayed it was Colm. Then a loud bang. Her body shuddered from the vibration.

'There!' she heard the man mutter to himself.

Was it the same voice? She couldn't tell. Did he know she was in here? Maybe not.

Footsteps.

Footsteps receding.

Then silence.

She didn't dare move. She had to be sure. Somewhere in the distance she thought she heard a door slam. Had she imagined that? *Wait. Patience.*

She counted slowly to one hundred. Then another hundred. Gingerly, she tested the lid. She pushed. It stayed firm. She pushed again, harder this time. Panic threatened to drown her in its wake. She knelt up in the barrel and with all her strength pushed against the lid. *Crash*! The noise was deafening as the lid flew off and landed on the steel platform.

Letta cowered, covering her ears with her hands, all the stress of the past hours catching up with her. She waited for the whistles, the sound of running feet. But there was only silence. Gradually, her heart slowed. She placed her hands on the sides of the barrel and levered herself into a standing position. After three attempts, she managed to throw her leg over the edge, and let herself fall to the floor.

Only then did she take in where she was. The barrel stood on a narrow platform. The tower had a roof to protect the water from contamination, but there was a large gap in the wall behind her through which the barrel had come. It had stopped raining but a bitter wind gusted through the opening, making her feel as if the entire tower was open to the elements.

In front of her were two large tanks, one raised slightly higher than the other, both tanks filled to the brim with water. Pipes made from woven canvas connected the tanks. Letta had heard about the filters invented by the Green Warriors that allowed water to travel from one tank to the other, but did not allow salt to pass through at all. The lower tank was the desalinated water to which the warriors added chlorine. This was obviously where Noa would put the Nicene.

A narrow walkway stretched between the tanks. To Letta, the walkway appeared to float there, with nothing either side but a steep void.

To her right she could see a staircase leading down to the hall below. *I have to get to the stairs*, she told herself. Looking down made her dizzy, so she tried to look straight ahead. Carefully, with her back still pressed against the wall, she took off her boots, now sodden and heavy, cursing the vertigo that made everything so difficult.

The knife was still there tucked inside her sock. She took it out carefully and laid it on the floor beside her. Then she took off her wet socks. Feeling her bare feet on the ground helped her to feel more balanced. She picked up all her belongings, and slowly, never leaving the safety of the wall behind her, she headed for the stairs.

When she got there, she sat on the top step and tried to catch her breath. She was sure she was going to be sick again. She knew it was illogical, but the feeling of standing up there, with nothing below her but that gaping blackness, terrified her. Yet she had done it, she told herself, wiping the cold sweat from her face. She had done it.

The staircase was a dilapidated structure with gnarled wooden treads and a rough banister. It stretched down to a cavernous space below, an entrance hall of sorts, whose floor was tiled with blocks of stone. There were two large windows on one wall chequered with small lozenge panes sunk in black lead. The walls were covered in flaking limestone plaster that had once been painted in a grey–green colour. The only decoration was a circular slab of pure white marble, engraved with the image of a grey wolf's head. Letta stared at it, transfixed.

She would go down there, she thought, and find somewhere to hide and wait. Werber had been certain that there would be no-one inside the tower at this hour. Besides, there was nowhere to hide upstairs with the tanks, and she knew she would be overcome with vertigo if she stayed. She walked down slowly, clinging to the old wrought-iron banister, flaked with rust, as the stairs curved in on itself, making her feel disoriented and slightly dizzy. Beside her, a narrow window extended almost to the roof but it was already too dark to see anything. Finally she reached the bottom.

A fluttering noise made her look up just in time to see a family of bats fly across the vaulted ceiling and disappear. On the wall opposite the large windows she saw another door, almost invisible, flush to the wall, with only the shadow in the plaster betraying it. Carefully, she pushed against it and felt it give. A corridor stretched in front of her about twenty strides long. Her bare feet glided noiselessly over the stone floor. A few strides later, she noticed the flooring had changed. Now she was walking on cold marble. The paint on the walls was new, not flaking as it was everywhere else. The smells had changed too. Before she had only smelt damp and decay. Now what assailed her nose was sharp and clean and medicinal. In front of her was a laboratory of some sort. Two long benches neatly arrayed with glass bottles of different shapes and sizes. The room itself had one long window on the far wall, with a wide ledge beneath it, but it was too high for her to see through. But best of all there was a line of hooks on which hung three white suits. Boiler suits, she thought they were called.

'Yes!' she muttered to herself.

Within seconds she had divested herself of all her wet clothes. She used one suit to roughly dry her body and then put on the second suit. It was too wide and too big but she turned up the legs and arms and pulled it around her as tightly as she could. She was still cold but she felt cleaner. She thought about putting the second suit on over the first one for heat, but she was afraid it would make her too clumsy. When the time came, she would have to be able to move quickly. She picked up the knife and sat on the ledge under the window to wait for Noa.

It was time. The Green Warrior handed him the canister. He held it up to the light. It looked so innocent. But he knew its power. He had banked two full weeks' worth of water. Man could only survive for one hundred hours without water. At first, the people of Ark would drink, going to the water stations as they always did. Then, he would open the pipe in Tintown, where they would be grateful for the extra water. Finally, the Desecrators and the rebels in the forest would find the main pipe unguarded, and from it they would steal what they needed. No force required from the government.

The water would flush them out, driven on by their own thirst.

He tried to imagine the days that would follow.

The silence that would descend.

Eternal silence.

CHAPTER 24

THE night passed slowly. It was cold in the old tower. Letta put her boots back on and shoved the knife in beside her bare foot. Then she crossed the hall again and perched half-way up the stairs. For the first hour or two she sat waiting to hear a noise at the front door or see it move, but eventually she relaxed. She had no idea if or when he would appear.

Her body ached, her head was beaten and bruised from her trip in the barrel, but she blocked it out trying to focus on what she had to do.

She let herself remember the feel of Marlo's lips on hers, the warmth of his arms holding her close.

She saw the dawn break. A soft shaft of light fell from the high windows. She stood up and, balancing on the tips of her toes, managed to see the outside world through the narrow window. The sight below made her draw her breath in sharply. Out at the far boundary wall stood row upon row of people, a raggle-taggle army, strewn out in no particular order.

The wall was high and the very top of it was lined with shards of broken glass. But the rebels had scaled it. Even as she

269

watched, a man appeared at the top of the bulwark. An ally on the ground took a step back, then slung a metal hook with a rope attached, in his direction. The hook found purchase, and instantly the man shimmied down, and jumped to the ground, joining his colleagues.

There were no gavvers to be seen. In the dark of the night, the rebels must have taken care of the ones who had been on duty at the tower. But more would come. She was sure of it. Noa would not come here to do this final act without backup.

A shiver ran through her. She tried to shut out the images of carnage that tormented her. The Creators were no match for the gavvers. She looked at the lines of people again. Creators, people from Tintown, all standing together, facing death and, above them, barely visible in the distance, Noa's house. Had he already seen them?

She tried to find Marlo in the crowd but the light wasn't strong enough. She knew he was out there though, waiting.

A slight movement caught her eye. She strained to see what it was. A grey wave coming across the fields. Gavvers. Had Marlo and the others seen them?

The harsh sound of stone scraping on stone interrupted her thoughts. She was alert instantly. She stood up, bracing herself. Her hand went to her boot and she pulled out the knife. She climbed the stairs, her feet clumsy on the pocked treads, never taking her eyes from the hall below.

There it was again. No doubt this time. Stone moving. Stone growling somewhere beneath her. She looked down, just in time to see the grey wolf turn, to the right, then to the left. As she watched, the marble circle was pushed up from beneath, and the stone slid to one side. The wolf had moved and, in the void beneath, Letta could clearly see the top of a man's head.

She looked up. The staircase seemed higher than she remembered it. She didn't want to go back up there to the top of the tower but she had no choice. Noa was about to make his entrance. Sweat broke on her forehead. She put her hand on the banister and started to climb the remaining steps.

She had almost reached the top of the stairs before she glanced down again. In a pool of early morning light, she saw Noa's hunched figure emerge from the hole in the floor. He straightened up, trembling slightly as though harried by some inner gust of air. And then a second head emerged. A head, and then a body. Werber. He stood beside Noa like a startled ghost.

'Stay!' she heard Noa say. 'Let no-one in.'

'Yes, master,' Werber's familiar voice floated up to her.

If they looked up now they would see her. She tried not to breathe. She put her foot on the next tread. Would it creak? She couldn't remember. The tread took her weight with a slight groan. She stopped. Had they heard her?

'No-one comes up the stairs.' That was Noa's voice. 'Do you understand?'

She climbed the last two steps quickly. Silently, she slipped through to the tanks.

She thrust the knife into her pocket and made her way along by the wall. The empty barrel stood there, as if waiting for her. She crouched down behind it. Timber creaked beneath her. He was climbing the stairs. Was he coming up alone? She listened hard. One set of footsteps. That meant Werber had stayed below, as ordered.

Her heart quickened. There it was again, another step and then another. He had reached the top of the stairs. Could he see her? She thought she heard him sigh.

Then more footsteps, nearer now. Her body tensed. He stopped. There was an eerie silence. Moving stealthily she peered around the side of the barrel. He was standing with his back to her, out on the walkway between the water tanks, looking down to where the clean water was held. His head was bowed as though he were praying and he was holding something in his hand.

Noa turned slowly. She could see the canister, the long finger-nails splayed across it, its silver case glowing in the low light of the dawn. It would only take him a second to open it and poison the water. Gavvers could come at any minute, but for now, he was alone. She couldn't stop him from here, though. She would have to go on to the walkway. She stood up. She watched as his head pivoted in her direction.

'Letta!' he said sharply, a deep frown furrowing his brow. 'What are you doing here? How did you get in?'

'I wanted to talk to you,' she said.

She moved along the wall, her eyes riveted to the scene before her.

She was at the walkway now. How could she walk out there? There was no handrail. Nothing to hold on to. Nothing to stop her tumbling down ... down ...

'Well, Letta?'

She had to get closer to him.

She stumbled forward, stepping onto the narrow platform. She dared not look down. Even so, she was intensely aware of the sheer drop either side of her. The walkway seemed to swing up towards her, making her head spin. Black dots danced in front of her eyes.

'Go back, Letta! Go back before you fall.'

His voice was gentle and she wanted nothing more than to obey him.

'Look down, Letta!' he said. 'See how high up you are. What if you stumble?'

Don't listen to him. Concentrate. I have to distract him, she thought. *Keep him talking.* She took another step. Every atom in her body was screaming at her to lie down on the ground, to curl up in a ball, eyes closed.

'You don't have to do this,' she said.

Even as the words left her lips she heard a massive roar from outside. Orders were being given. Urgent commands. She couldn't make out what they were saying but there was no mistaking the tone. The gavvers had reached the far boundary. Despite herself, her eyes went to the opening in the wall.

'They will all die,' Noa said, following her gaze. 'Like lambs to slaughter.'

The cold words crawled towards her like cockroaches.

'Please,' Letta said, 'listen to me. You may be powerful enough to destroy language, but even you are not powerful enough to bring it back. "Extinction" is the saddest word of all. Benjamin told me that you told him that, a long time ago.'

Lambs to slaughter. Marlo!

Focus, she told herself. *Focus! Don't let him deflect you.*

'There must be another way,' she said, though her vertigo was attacking her again, leaving her mouth dry and her head light.

'No!' The word had the force of a bullet, making Letta take a step back. Her stomach lurched.

'No. There is no other way. I cut out their tongues. I instigated List. Nothing works, Letta. Language is what makes man ungovernable.'

Letta felt the blood rush to her face.

'But it is also what makes us human and different to all other creatures on the planet.'

She had to be near enough to him to grab the canister should the chance arise.

Noa laughed.

'Different? Do you know that we and the common fruit-fly share the same biological structure? Not so different, Letta. But we are the only ones who can take an idea and plant it in the mind of another. Like the Desecrators did with you.'

His voice trailed off. Letta struggled to line up the words in her head as she imagined the people outside were lining up their soldiers. The room was spinning round and round. She put her hands out to steady herself.

'We *need* words,' she said. 'Why can't you see that? We can think because we have words. Without them, we won't have memory to look at the past or imagination to glimpse the future. Without words we will be imprisoned in the here and now for ever.'

He shook his head.

'Would that be so bad?' he said.

'Yes!' Letta shouted. 'Of course it would. The here and now is only the smallest part of who we are. Each of us is all that we have been, all of our stories, all that we could be. You of all people should know that.'

Her throat constricted. Emotion was hitting her in waves but she struggled against it.

Noa shrugged. 'It doesn't matter,' he said. 'We won't need words –'

'Of course we will,' Letta threw back at him. 'Words have the power to change everything.'

Her voice cracked. She bit her lip, trying to steady herself. Her head was swimming, a cold soup of muddied thoughts.

274

She could feel her body being drawn to the edge of the walkway. She had to keep talking.

'Without words, how can we reach out to others? How can we express our love for one another?' she said.

She was thinking of all the words she and Benjamin had shared. Thinking of the few precious words she could remember from her parents. Thinking of Marlo and all the words she desperately wanted to say to him. Layer upon layer of words. Suddenly, a roar from outside filled the room. The unmistakable sound of a battle commencing.

Noa cocked his head. 'Listen!' he said, as the cries from outside tried to drown out his words.

'See how we express love for one another? No, Letta. The time for words is gone. We can control men's bodies but their minds teem with words and the words are rotten to the core.' He was roaring now, his own words bouncing off the high walls. 'They need to be cauterised, cleansed, eradicated. How do you like those words, Letta?'

'You all right, master?' came Werber's voice from somewhere beneath their feet.

Letta dared not look.

'All well,' said Noa, and Letta could see him breathing rapidly, trying to calm himself. 'Stay. Guard door. I can handle this.'

Noa held up the canister. He could open it in a heartbeat, she thought. A flick of his wrist and it would be done. Letta walked further along the walkway, a pulse throbbing in her throat. Images filled her head of her body falling into the chasm below. She dug her nails into her hands.

'The Green Warriors and I will still have language,' he said. 'To finish what we started, but the next generation and all

275

other generations will be Wordless, because they will never be contaminated by language.'

His words were flying all about her now. Red fireflies, chaotic, out of control. The room was spinning faster, drawing her towards its vortex.

He raised his hand to open the canister.

'You think you have all the answers, Letta. In that, you are very like your mother.'

She managed to take a step, but the dizziness almost overpowered her. *Don't slip*, she told herself. *Don't slip!* She was near enough to grab him, she thought. Throw him off balance. His hand still hovered over the top of the canister. He was talking again. She tried to focus on what he was saying. Outside, the noise of battle was getting louder.

'I knew her, you know, your mother. I knew her very well.'

'I doubt that,' Letta retorted. 'I doubt you really knew her at all. You didn't know Leyla, did you? You didn't think she would stand up to you and try for something better. And you didn't know my mother. She was the bravest of them all. That's what Amelia said. The bravest of them all.'

She saw the confusion on his face and, for a second, she forgot her fear, forgot that she was on a high walkway with a drop on either side, forgot about her mother, forgot everything but what she had to do. Her legs stopped shaking, her heart slowed.

'Put down the canister,' she said.

And suddenly the knife was in her hand.

'It is over for you, Letta, but not for me, and not for Amelia –'

'Amelia?'

The word shot from her mouth sharp and true.

Noa stood up taller.

Letta laughed then, a harsh, forced sound.

'Really?' she said. 'You believe that? After what you did to Leyla? You think Amelia will stand by you? How little you know her!'

'Amelia will forgive me,' he said. 'She will understand that –'

Letta took another step towards him.

'No!' she said. 'She will never forgive you. Have you not wondered how I knew where to find you? And when to find you? How I knew about my mother?'

She saw the confusion on his face again. A flickering light in his eyes, there and then gone. He shrugged.

'What does it matter who told you?'

Please let this work, Letta thought. *Let him love her as much as I think he does.*

'Amelia told me.' Letta's words slipped into the half-light, testing, challenging.

'No!' he said. 'Liar.'

'Yes,' Letta said, taking another shaking step. But it was as if her body had woken up again and realised where it was – poised on the edge of a precipice. She could feel the sweat prickling her skin, her breath coming in laboured gasps, too fast, not enough air. Her brain was screaming at her to go back, her head pounding, her legs weak. His face was splitting into two faces, one overlapping the other, the edges blurred, everything in constant motion.

'Amelia betrayed you.' She forced the words out and was rewarded when she saw the colour drain from him.

She took another step. She felt as if she were walking on a high wire. She looked down, despite herself, and felt an overwhelming urge to jump, to let her body fall down into that abyss. A mist descended before her eyes. The background noises receded. She was going to faint.

No! Talk to him! Talk! She forced herself to look at him.

'You thought she loved you, didn't you?'

His hands began to shake. 'Get back!' The words came out like a whisper.

Letta stopped. Was the walkway swaying? She had to take advantage of his shock. Words would only get her so far. She took another step.

'She doesn't love you, John. You lost that when you broke her heart.'

'No!' he cried. 'You're lying. Amelia would not betray me.'

Outside, Letta heard uproar from the front yard, as what sounded like a herd of wild animals came teeming through the out-of-sight boundaries and hurtled towards the tower.

For a second all was quiet as if the building itself was holding its breath. Then a ferocious crash rent the air, a bang like a cannon-blast. Letta screamed as the old wooden door below splintered, sundered and fell. The noise of battle filled the tower. Men and women shouting, screaming, scuffling, grunts of pain mingled with the smell of fresh blood. Letta glanced down. Creators and gavvers swarmed beneath her feet, locked in battle. The picture swam before her eyes. She saw people hack and stab one another, beat and kick one another and, in the middle of it all, Marlo, locked in hand to hand combat with a gavver twice his size.

'Marlo!'

Distracted, he looked up, and Letta watched in horror, as the gavver raised a finely honed dagger and aimed it at Marlo's throat.

'Marlo!' she screamed again. She saw him turn and grab the other man's arm, forcing the dagger to fall to the floor. Marlo raised his own knife and Letta could almost feel the soft flesh yield beneath the blade, feel the veins slice and rupture. The body sagged. The man fell to the floor.

Noa lunged at her then, throwing his body forward, trying to knock her off balance. She felt the rough cloth of his coat under her hand and clung to it. On either side of her the void loomed. She could feel herself falling, losing balance. She managed to drop to her knees. From there, she grabbed onto his legs. He kicked out, knocking her onto her back.

She looked up to see him fumbling with the top of the canister. She hauled herself onto her feet. She stretched up and grabbed his wrist. The canister was so close she could see her own eyes reflected in it. He jerked his arm, pulling her towards him. She could feel his breath on her face. With his other hand he caught the back of her neck in a vice-like grip.

'Look!' he said. 'Look down!'

She glimpsed the drop beside her and dizziness overcame her. *Don't let go of him!* She raised the knife and bore down with all her strength. She felt it cut through flesh and hit bone. Somewhere, far away she heard him scream. As he did, she lost her balance, stumbling backwards. She fell heavily, narrowly avoiding the edge of the walkway, her elbows and the back of her head smashing into the wooden slats..

Painfully, she hauled herself to her feet. He was still struggling with the top of the canister. Her whole body swayed. *This is it*, she thought. Images of the Wordless flashed before her. She had to try one more time. Her heart thumping, she made a wild lunge at Noa's hand. She felt the cold metal under her fingers for a second, and then it was gone. Noa had yanked his arm backwards to avoid her, but the sudden movement unbalanced him.

As she watched, he lost his footing, stumbled backwards and then, in slow motion, she saw him topple, tumble and dive over the edge of the platform, down, down into the throng of bodies below, a wounded bird, buffeted on a seething wave of humanity, his coat flapping in the stale air. She watched until he came to rest in a crumpled heap on the stone floor.

There was a stunned second of silence, and then commotion broke out, with screams and cheers and roars from the opposing forces. For a moment, Letta was aware of Werber standing slack-jawed, staring down at his master's body. Slowly, he raised his head and looked up at her. Their eyes locked.

The canister rolled along the floor lit by the bright new sun pouring through the windows and then she heard Carver's voice like a roar of thunder:

'Get her!'

It seemed to Letta that the scene below shattered into tiny fragments:

Carver with three of his men advancing on the stairway.

Finn slammed to the floor by a gavver, his hands covering his head.

Another gavver thrown across the room by a ferocious Kirch Tellon.

Marlo on his feet, blood streaming from his head, blocking the stairs supported by a squad of his own people.

Beside him Mrs Pepper swinging a wooden bat at anyone foolish enough to come within her reach. Mrs Pepper a Desecrator!

Carver shrieking at his own men as they spread out in a line in front of the doorway.

And then Finn looked up at her.

'Letta!' he shouted.

She was about to rush to the stairs when she noticed the canvas pipes. Maybe she could use these to create a distraction.

Pulling out her knife she began to hack at the pipe nearest to her. But the thick fabric resisted the blade.

'Letta!' she heard Finn's voice again, more urgent now.

She raised her arm and stabbed the fabric with all her might and was rewarded with a spray of water that hit her in the eyes, blinding her for a second.

Disappointment surged through her as she realised it was nothing like she'd hoped for. In her imagination a huge wave of water would burst from the pipe, creating enough of a distraction to give her friends a chance to escape, but now she saw that her gesture was pointless.

'Letta!' Finn's voice rent the air. 'Now! Jump!'

She stumbled towards the stairs. Beneath her, the hall was still thronged with people, grappling, stabbing, falling. She stopped and looked down the length of the stairs. The Creators were losing ground, being pushed back up the stairs by a pack of resolute gavvers, led by Carver. There was no way she could force her way through. She looked down and to her right. The grey wolf had closed the tunnel but if she could get to it...

Bang! A hook narrowly missed her head and caught in the banisters. Beneath it like a long tail a rope fell into the hall.

'Come on, Letta!' Finn shouted at her. 'Grab the rope!'

She looked down. She couldn't do it. But even as the words formed in her head she was swinging her leg over the banister. Her hands felt the coarse rope. She jumped. All the air was sucked from the room. She wrapped her legs around the rope. Her body swung out over the void, momentarily becalmed above a boiling vat of fury.

Marlo! Where is *he?* Her eyes scanned the room. There he was! At the bottom of the stairs still pushing back the bank of gavvers who assailed it. Beside him, Mrs Pepper battled furiously. And then she saw it. Carver! He was standing, gun in hand, aiming it at Marlo.

'Marlo!' Letta screamed but her warning was drowned in the waves of noise coming from the battle. Then she reached out, and kicked the wall behind her with all of her force, propelling herself forward. With both feet she struck Carver's head with as much power as she could muster, and felt the satisfying heft of his body being pitched forward. He staggered. The gun went off.

'Marlo!' Letta screamed just as Mrs Pepper stumbled and fell from the stairs, her head smashing on to the stone floor. Marlo looked up at Letta, his face white and drawn, eyes wide and staring. What had she done? Had she killed Mrs Pepper?

'Letta!' Finn's voice called urgently from the hall.

Letta slid down the rope, white-hot pain searing her hands as the rope burned her palms. She had to get to the canister.

She stumbled across the hall, dodging bodies as she went, Finn doing his best to shepherd her. She pulled away from him, dropped to the floor and crawled, the prize only strides from her, sparkling in the sunlight. With one huge effort she pushed her way through and grabbed it, its metal casing cold in her hands. And then pain exploded in her lower back as a boot crashed into her. She looked up in time to see Carver staring down at her.

'Give it to me!'

He drew back his boot to kick her again when two men locked in combat fell across his path. Letta looked around desperately, trying to see a way through, but her path was blocked by a phalanx of gavvers, truncheons in their hands, coming straight for her.

It's hopeless, she thought when suddenly, above it all, she heard a loud rip, a groan from the top of the tower, as the canvas pipe burst. Then, the gushing fall of water, inflated by enforced containment, swallowed all other sounds, drowning them in the noise of its own rage. Whoosh! The torrent hit the stone floor, scattering bodies as it fell on the battle, in one giant exclamation. Letta gasped as she was thrown back.

Clutching the canister to her chest, she hesitated for only a second and then, her clothes heavy with water, her feet slipping and sliding, she dashed for the grey wolf stone. She placed her hand on the wolf's head and pushed. The stone moved to reveal the gaping mouth below.

It was too dark to see much, but the air that rushed back at her was fusty and dank. There was a ladder attached to the wall of the tunnel. With her free hand, Letta grabbed it and started to descend. Just as her foot hit the third rung a hand clamped down on her arm, the fingers digging into her painfully. *No!* she thought. *I can't fail now.* She looked up fully expecting Carver's small eyes to look back at her. But it wasn't Carver. Her throat constricted, she could barely force the word out.

'Werber!'

His grip tightened.

'Please, Werber,' she said, staring into his eyes. Deep pools of brown like she had seen in the fields on harsh winter days. Letta held her breath. He looked back over his shoulder, a quick, furtive glance, then turned and faced her again. His mouth opened.

'Go!' he said in a jagged whisper. 'Go!'

Above her head, the stone slid back into place, blocking out the light, enveloping her in darkness.

CHAPTER 25

OUT on the ocean, the night had started to give way to the day. Standing at the edge of the sea, Letta listened to the beat of the waves as they hit the shore and wondered what the future would bring. It had scarcely been a week since the confrontation in the water tower. The canister with its lethal contents was in safe hands. They still had to find a way to destroy it, a way to make sure it could never threaten them again.

She had escaped the clutches of the gavvers, crawled through the secret passage Noa had built from the water tower to the basement of his house. She had survived, but many of the Creators had not. Some had died in the battle at the tower. Others had been arrested later and executed. Amelia had taken power. Her *aunt* Amelia. Even now she struggled with that reality.

Letta herself was on the wanted list, and she knew that if caught, she would be shown no mercy. In the seven days that had passed, Amelia had already proven herself a ruthless enemy. Tonight, Letta would slip into the forest and start again. She was a wordsmith, a colour-catcher, just like Benjamin and Leyla and her parents had been. That knowledge was what she would take with her.

She looked at the parcel in her hands. As Benjamin had promised, Finn had found it in the bottom drawer of the old man's desk. Brown paper tied with hemp string. She pulled at the knots and they fell away before her awkward fingers. She smoothed back the wrapping. Inside she could see folded sheets, which smelt of beetroot. She tore more of the wrapping until she was able to lift the contents clear.

She opened the first document. It was a map. Hand drawn and a little faded but totally legible. She frowned. What did it mean? The other documents were also maps and charts. Finally she saw the note.

These are the maps and charts your parents took with them. I copied them so that one day you might have them. Go safely, little one.

She almost stopped breathing. Nothing moved. She could hear her own heart, feel the blood rushing through her veins. She steadied herself and wrapped the papers up carefully.

She was the wordsmith. That would have to come first: people needed her and she would not let them down. But somewhere, in her future, she knew that the boat with the silver sail had come just a little closer.

'Letta!'

The voice made her jump.

Marlo.

She watched him as he walked towards her, her heart quickening. In her mind, she could see the blue-grey eyes and smell the faint hint of sage. With a light heart, she turned and walked towards him.

Behind her, the sea lapped gently onto the sand, and over her head a chattering of starlings wheeled in the air and headed south.

Letta turned and, raising one finger, she saluted the horizon, as she always did, just in case they were out there and could see her and would know that she had not forgotten them. Out on that far horizon, where they now lingered, if not in body, then at least in spirit.

FIN